Binds and Breath

GODDESS OF THE TREES: BOOK TWO

Binds and Breath

GODDESS OF THE TREES: BOOK TWO

Sorrel D. Richmond

TULIP POPLAR PUBLISHING, LLC

Front cover image by My Lan Khuc.

First printing edition 2025.

Tulip Poplar Publishing, LLC
P.O. Box 392
1612 Jordan Dr.
Saxapahaw, NC, 27340

www.writersdrichmond.com

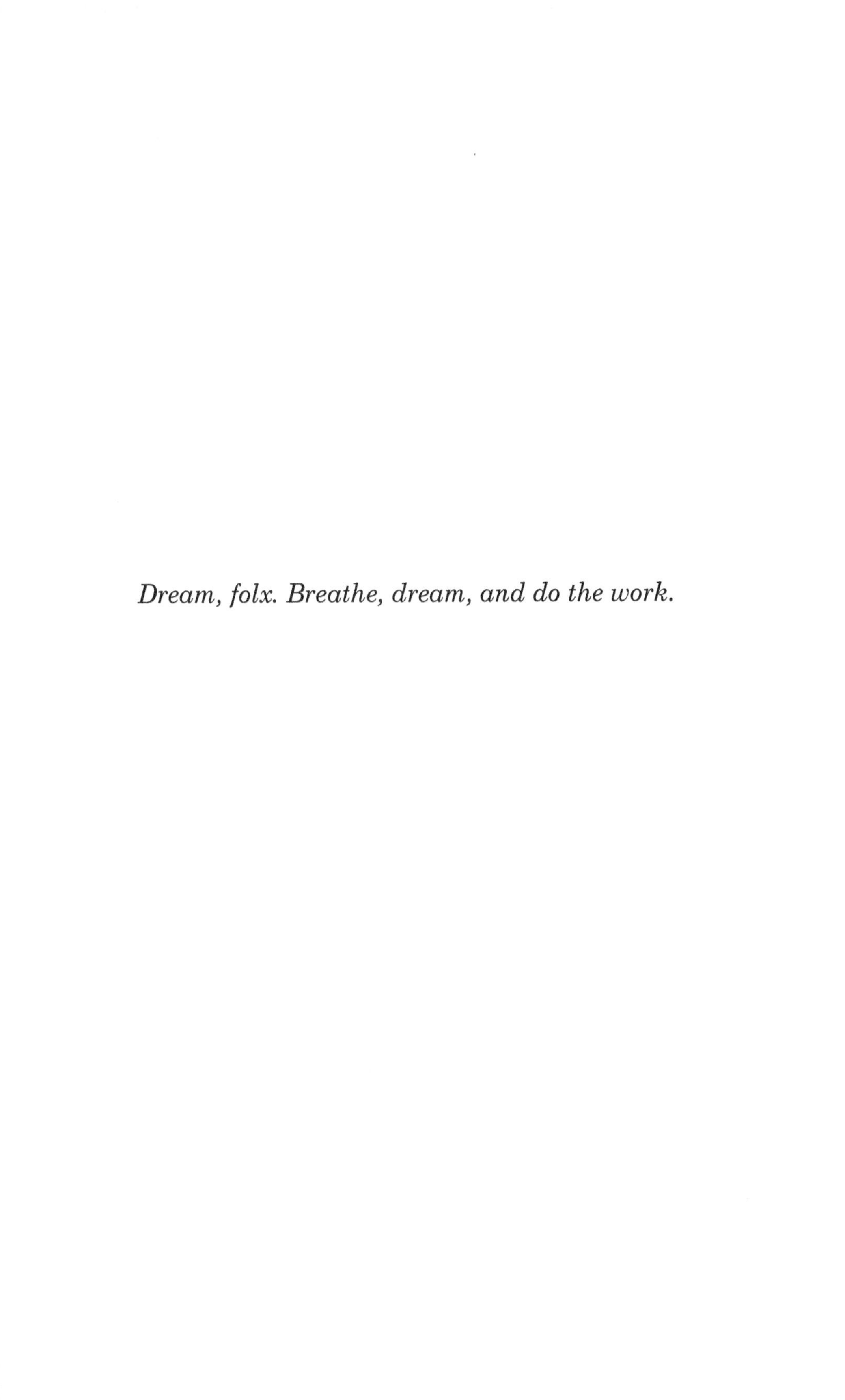

Dream, folx. Breathe, dream, and do the work.

*We are the children of the woods. Born on a slab of lime-
stone under the full, brilliant face of the moon. We are
set high on a hill over looking the world. We are the
pine, the oak, and the pawpaw. Our roots grow deep.*

THE TREES

First Mother
Black Cherry

Imogene
Oak

Ida
Papaw

Martha
Red Maple

Thelma
Cedar

Edith
Sweetgum

Ola
White Ash

Beulah
Birch

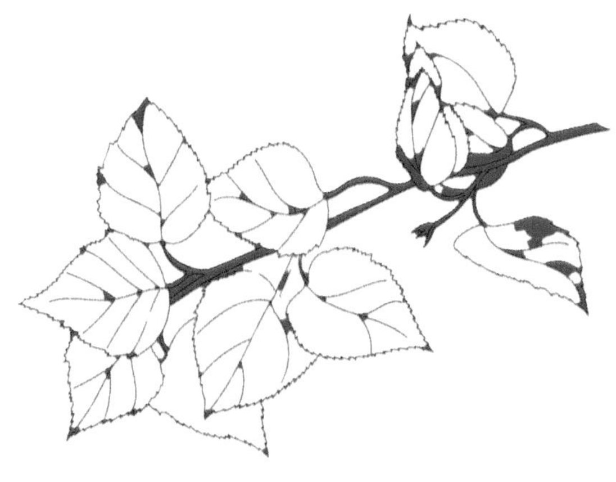

CHAPTER 1

Beulah

The urgent resurrection that bore Beulah up into a tall birch tree had been too quick to be painful the first time. Now, the cold dirt pressed against her from all directions. Downward against her skull. Upward against her feet. Down her throat. Unable to breathe, she questioned if her body was alive or frozen in some frigid hell.

Signs of life provided evidence that the world she left behind still thrummed around her, and somehow, she was still part of it. Some days, Beulah could focus so much attention on the sense of hearing that the voices of her family singing penetrated through, and when she brought awareness to her skin, she could feel earthworms slither across her hands and feet. Gentle drips of rain slipping down. The taste of beets in her mouth. She warred with the desire to thrash against the pressure encasing her, but over time, she understood that stillness, patience, and time were necessary if she wanted to surface.

One day, the rain didn't come as a trickle, but as streams flowing down her sides, icy rivers that brought shivers and achy bones. She knew she was getting closer. Rising somehow. And with that rising, she sensed the earth had lost its tight rigidity, so she squirmed in the looseness. Roots retracted into fingernails, and though she couldn't see them, Beulah imagined them twisted and gnarled. She wiggled her jaw and contracted and extended her knees and elbows with minute movements. Soil plugged her nose and ears.

How am I alive?

After what Beulah estimated were days of the motions, she focused solely on one hand. She pressed it upward, tiny wiggle after tiny wiggle, corkscrewing her long fingernails until a cool breeze met her fingertips. An exultant scream filled her chest, but she didn't dare attempt to open her dirt-clogged throat. Adrenaline encouraged her whole body to wriggle as much as each individual part could.

When she heard her mother's voice, her body stilled.

How am I back at the Rock? And when did my mother start speaking again?

"What is that?" the tree murmured with astonishment in a voice that only Beulah would know as fake.

"It's…" Another voice entered the air. Ida's voice. "I can't tell, Ola. Send down roots! Investigate."

"I don't know that we should." Ola's voice, deep and sorrowful, trembled as she spoke. "We have no idea what's underneath."

Beulah's mother was right to be scared. Ola alone knew of the powers her daughter had hidden from the other trees her entire life.

"What are you afraid of, Ola?" Ida asked. Silence passed, interrupted by a huff. "Fine. I'll do it."

Beulah waited, feeling her heart pumping Stella's blood through her body. Roots investigated her nails and brushed against her barely exposed fingertips.

Ida gasped and retracted her roots. "It's a buried hand!"

Chatter broke out among the trees.

"Quiet!" This time Edith, Beulah's grandmother, spoke. "Let's work together. Martha, pour in water to soften the dirt. I'll warm it. We can't let her stay in the cold ground."

"You think it's…" Ida's voice trailed off.

"We won't know for sure until we get the body out," Edith said. "But who else could it be?"

Beulah tried to summon her gift of illusion from within her. The power had shown up at a time when she was desperate to keep a curious Madeline away from the Rock. One night, she took her daughter to the edge of the path that led to the Rock and conjured the image of an angry, green Goddess with velvety horns and red eyes. Beulah made the figure growl and writhe, sending Madeline into a fit of panic. Once the two were behind the locked doors of the cabin, Beulah told stories of how the Rock itself grew teeth and shredded mothers into fertilizer for the trees. Now, she needed to cloak her mother in silence or else the woman might share her darkest secrets to stop the trees from helping her.

If they find out, they might leave me buried forever. Or has Mother already told him? Do they know? Do Stella and Madeline and Beatrice know the truth?

The trees clamored over one another as warm water flowed around Beulah. The sensation skewed her thoughts away from fear and toward hope. She wanted to open her mouth and laugh. To open her mouth and drink! She hadn't been warm in so long.

A creaking sound alerted Beulah that more roots were coming; they slithered down her arms and sides, all the way to her feet. They pushed the earth away from her aching body and, with a gentle pull, began to extract her.

Beulah was being born again.

Sunlight hit her eyelids with a jolting brightness so harsh she couldn't open them. Once the earthly grave released her head, air hunger took over, but her mouth refused to draw in breaths. Her stomach lurched, and she vomited piles of mucus and soil as the trees continued to excise her from the ground. After what felt like hours, the vomiting ceased. Silence filled the space all around her. She wasn't at the Rock. Instead, the homestead stretched out in front of her, and when she wheeled her head around, she found the trees staring at her.

"How did..." Her words released in a ragged whisper.

"Beulah." Ola's voice wrapped around her like a warm embrace. Beulah could almost feel those strong arms enveloping her. "There you are."

Beulah wanted to give into the comfort. To wrap her arms around her mother and allow the tree to hold her back. Disgusted both by the taste of vomit and earth as well as what she had to do, she closed her eyes tightly and imagined it—a glass encasement walling her mother in, blocking out her voice. She needed time to assess the situation.

"Beulah, you don't have to..." the tree uttered in a voice so low Beulah trusted she was the only one who could hear it.

Beulah opened her eyes and aligned them with her mother's deep, warm brown gaze. "I'm sorry," she whispered. Once the illusion was complete, Ola's eyes closed. Beulah hated this—the necessary secrecy that came with her overwhelming abilities. She couldn't bear the rest knowing, so her mother had to stay quiet. At least for now.

"You are a mess!" Ida said. "Let's get you cleaned up."

"Wait," First Mother, the tree that trumped all others, commanded. "What did she mean—you don't have to do this?"

"I don't know." She weaved innocence into her voice, dropped her chin and looked up at First Mother with wide, confused eyes.

Beulah craved belonging, but she never allowed herself to trust anyone in her family. For a while she trusted Madeline, it was true, until the woman betrayed her, went to the Rock despite Beulah's warnings, and allowed the Goddess in. She suspected that First Mother knew exactly what Ola meant, and she worried the tree intended to trap her, forcing her to confess her sins. Blinking at the thought, she looked down at her body.

Pieces of bark clung to her in patches while soil filled the cracks in her rough, flaming red skin. Her long, gnarled fingernails prevented her from peeling the bark away herself.

I'm at their mercy.

"I need your help."

"I can use fire to burn your nails down, Granddaughter," Edith said. "Hold still."

Beulah shook her head, unable to speak. Roots moved toward her.

"Give me your hand. I'll be gentle."

Beulah swallowed and stretched her hand toward a tiny root that now blazed orange. A thicker one wrapped around her wrist to keep her still, and the heat moved toward her finger. A horrendous smell wafted from the smoke produced, but at least there was no pain. While Edith worked, the trees' voices filled the space with exclamations and questions.

"It worked!"

"How do you feel?"

"Wait till Stella sees you."

"Beatrice will be so happy."

"They'll be home soon!"

The last statement drew Beulah's gaze away from the heat and toward the trees. "Where did they go?" Her voice barely cracked a whisper.

"Madeline and Gwen are getting married in two weeks!" Ida said. "Beatrice, Stella, Forest, and Dani went to New York to be with them."

Forest had shared stories about his friend Dani, but Beulah hadn't heard the name Gwen.

"Who is Gwen?" A deep sense of loneliness and disconnection hollowed Beulah's heart.

"Gwen is Madeline's partner, dear," Ida said.

Married.

Her mind shifted to Stella. The woman had promised to kiss her. Beulah's gaze and shoulders dropped, and she knew if there was enough wetness within her, she would have cried. She glanced at her mother, quieted in her glass tomb, and wished she could talk to her alone.

Do I have enough energy to keep her quiet? I need Stella here.

"I want to go to them," Beulah said.

"We all want to be with them." Edith finished up the last nail. "They promised they would be back on the equinox and have a huge celebration with us, too."

"What day is it?" Beulah glanced around, trying to determine the season. "End of February? First of March?"

"March second," Edith replied. "All done."

I've been buried for over two months.

Beulah regarded her fingernails, which still needed tidying, then shifted her gaze to her toes, still vile with twisted nails.

"Let me make a place for you to sit," Ida said as she twisted vines and roots to form a chair. Beulah rested herself within it.

"Should we tell her all that happened?"

"I want to know everything." Beulah leaned her head back and allowed Edith to work on her toes.

"You must be so cold." First Mother redirected the conversation. "Once we're done here, go soak in the tub. We will tell you everything, Beulah, but let's get your body taken care of first."

"How about some water?" Martha moved a leaf full toward Beulah.

She drank the water in two large gulps, then pleaded for more. The dissipation of initial adrenaline provided space for Beulah to reconnect with her now very human body. Gooseflesh pebbled her chilled, itchy skin from her scalp to the bottoms of her feet. Once she drank until her stomach ached, she cleared her throat. "How are they?"

"They're alright, more or less," First Mother said. "Stella is the worst off, I'd say."

Beulah pressed her body forward and looked into the tree's eyes. Now, her skin itched with an irritation that came not from the bark still clinging to her, but from the need to get to Stella.

Those wide green eyes and freckled round face. An ache that was more than longing burned in her lower belly. Being near the woman whose blood ran through her veins seemed vital.

"What's wrong with Stella?"

"It's her heart, dear." Ida wove a few vines around Beulah in a hug that only brought claustrophobia. "She misses you. She comes here every day whether it's freezing, snowing, or raining. She's been with you always."

A flush passed over Beulah, the need to move quivering inside her. "Hurry!" she demanded.

"Beulah, I don't want to hurt you."

The trees worked together to remove the rest of the bark off Beulah's flesh, leaving stripped, raw patches of flesh. Embarrassment threatened to overwhelm her body and heart as she became aware of her naked filth, the smell of the burned nails, and the rot of her skin. And the trees sensed it.

"Don't worry." Thelma's voice was warm and encouraging.

"We're here," Imogene added. "We're your family, too."

"I need to take some of your hair as well," Edith said.

Beulah tugged at the clumped strands. Edith's concerns were valid. Thick with mats and caked dirt, her hair wriggled with crawling grubs and beetles. She gasped and vomit rose to her lips. "Take it all!"

Not inches, but feet of hair fell to the ground. With each burning slice, Beulah felt pounds removed from her head. She choked on a sob. She loved her hair. She had kept it long, clean and brushed until it shone bright and golden. Beulah glanced at her mother, whose hair had been dark like Beatrice's, but more textured, and her skin dark and warm. She loved her mother and her gift of strength, the gift that shielded Beulah from her most destructive power: the breath.

"Please! Not too short!" Beulah begged, contradicting her earlier plea.

More hair fell.

"Done."

Edith and Martha sprayed cascades of warm water onto Beulah's scalp and down her body, asking often if the temperature was right; each time, Beulah answered with "hotter." Ida created a comb of branches and attempted to work through the mats. Thelma tutted. "Here, let's try something different." The tree produced a metal brush and handed it to her.

"That's all we can do," Thelma said. "Go take a bath now."

Beulah scanned the different eyes and face shapes watching her, and for a moment, she belonged.

"Thank you," she said, then scurried to the bathhouse.

***

The structure of the bathhouse had changed since the last time she'd been inside of it. Shelves lined the wall and held shampoos, soaps, soaks, and lotions, and three robes hung on the back side of the door. Beulah smiled. Beatrice. Forest. Stella.

My Stella. How could two months feel like an eternity?

Beulah dipped her fingers into the tub into steaming water that came just short of being too hot. She climbed in and allowed herself to sink into the deep water. She considered how her family held her with such care. How could she be anything but grateful?

"Thank you, Edith. Thank you, Martha."

Beulah inspected herself. The red splotches that covered her skin were set ablaze by the hot water, and her finger and toenails still needed work. She examined the quality of her skin. The firmness answered the question she'd asked Stella months ago: *What if I come back old?* Rubbing her fingertips along the ridged scars, she tried to determine if the marks were new ones from being ripped from the earth or old reminders of the battles that she had fought against herself her whole life. She focused her energy on the disfigurements, smoothing them inside her mind, but she was too tired to create the illusion.

If I can't use my gift to hide them, I'll just have to lie to them.

Stella's crimson blood came to mind. Both the liquid running through her veins and her very heart belonged to the woman who seemed an impossible distance away.

I have to get to her.

She wasted no more time enjoying the silky water. She grabbed a cloth and a bar of soap, finding comfort in the herbal combinations Beatrice had used. Beulah washed with tenderness around the rawest areas of her flesh, but the rest of her skin she scrubbed. She picked at the dirt underneath her fingernails until it was gone. Finally, she approached her hair, which now hung just below her chin. Tears threatened to rise, but Beulah chastised herself.

No crying over hair.

The shampoo smelled of lemon balm, rosemary, and lavender, and it soothed her scalp as she worked the lather from roots to the tips. After four washes, all dirt and twigs and insects were gone. Then she combed the conditioner through it. Finally, Beulah lifted herself out and looked back at the water, which was once again clean and steaming. A new sensation overtook her as she wrapped the largest of the three robes around her. Hunger. She became acutely aware of her rumbling stomach and hurried to the house but slowed as she reached her hand toward the door. Emotions battered one another as if competing for dominance. Sadness. Regret. Love. Longing. Fear.

Beulah closed her eyes, chose love, and walked through the door. Beatrice had grown vining plants that twirled themselves around the rack that held pots and pans and nestled themselves on the tops of the cabinets. The kitchen table was as large as Stella and Beatrice had described before their trip to New York, and Beulah trembled as she ran her fingers across it.

Maybe things will work out.

In the living room, a couch now sat in front of the hearth with the ancestral rocking chairs on either side. Within the hearth, a small fire burned. Beulah perused each bedroom, including the one that was once hers. She smiled at the basket of wood that sat on the floor next to a desk in Forest's room, a whittling knife resting on top. Forest had shown her so many of his carvings, but Beulah's eyesight was much keener now, and she picked up piece by piece to admire. She surveyed her own whittling work within the scars on her skin, silvery and stretched. Stella would know they were old. Beulah would have to use the gift of illusion, or Stella would ask questions about where they came from.

Her heart beat harder and faster as she approached the last room. Stella's room. She opened it slowly. She found the bed neatly made. A rocking chair sat in the corner and a cardigan lay across it. Beulah couldn't help but pick it up and bring it to her nose. So many interactions passed between the two of them, but the only smell and taste of Stella that Beulah ever experienced metallic blood. She pulled open a drawer and drew out a sweater she recognized, one that was large on Stella. She tugged it over her, then found a pair of pajama pants that she slipped on without underwear.

Her stomach smarted again. She hurried to the kitchen to scrounge for food. Her family must have left a while ago; no bread or fresh vegetables were in the home. Beulah slipped on an extra coat left hanging near the door and made her way to the dairy shed. The frigid stream still ran through it. She pulled a heavy wheel of cheese off a shelf, the odor of which was both pungent and delicious. She sniffed the milk that rested in the cold stream until she found the buttermilk. Despite the countless amount of burned bread she'd baked over the years, she would try her hand at biscuits.

And try she did. After following the directions Madeline had shown her time and time again, Beulah placed perfectly cut dough in the stove, then sliced thick slices of cheese for herself. She made herself a cup of chamomile tea and sipped it while she waited on the biscuits. Tea gone and stomach furious, she pulled the biscuits from the oven. They were as small and hard as Beulah remembered. Still, she ate her fill of the biscuits and cheese, then made her way back to the trees.

"Tell me everything," she said, sitting down at the feet of

First Mother.

The trees told all the stories they could tell. About Arcas bleeding all his blood into the blanket of snow, and about how close to death both Beatrice and Forest came. They told of Ola finally joining the rest of the family and how she saved Beatrice.

"She came for her?" Beulah asked the rest of the trees.

But the hold on her mother's tongue loosened just long enough for the woman to breathe, "Yes. I came for her. And you cleaned up for them."

"What do you mean?" Beulah released the hold on Ola just enough to hear the answer.

"You fell on the men. All of them. And Madeline set you on fire."

"I told her to." Her guts twisted. She had wanted to be warm. Yes, the men had been a threat to her family, but did they all deserve to die? And like that? A shiver ran through her, and she swallowed, using her power to quiet her mother again. "Keep going."

Beulah listened to stories of Madeline and Gwen and Ben, and when they were through sharing narratives, a tense silence stretched between them.

"What about me?" Beulah asked, her voice quivering. "Did any of you try to help me?"

"None of us could help you," Ida explained. "I surveyed your roots. Nothing but blood and rot."

"You burned until nothing was left but ash."

"Listen, I need to get to Stella. I don't want to wait."

I can't wait.

"We certainly don't know how to help you get to New York, Beulah," Edith said. "Go rest. See how you feel tomorrow."

Beulah stood. She glanced over her shoulder at the cabin behind her, then turned her head to peer through the trees.

"Could you at least point me in the right direction?"

The trees exchanged glances. Imogene stretched out a branch pointing in the exact opposite direction of the cabin. Beulah bobbed her head and ran. The forest floor was cold under her feet which, unlike Beatrice, she used to keep in shoes during all the seasons. Eventually, Beulah could see down the mountain. Her eyes moved across the road and took in the expansive river, and the town nestled alongside it. The thudding of her heart echoed in her ears as she peered down the mountain's side. It seemed so impossibly high. Exhaustion and disappointment had taken over. She turned and trudged back past the trees, through the cabin, and into Stella's bedroom where Sasha met her with a fierce rattle of her tail and a menacing hiss.

"Sasha." Beulah took a step toward the snake. "Easy, there. It's me," she said, bringing her fingertips to her chest, "Beulah." Without a moment's hesitation, the snake ceased its hostile behavior and moved to the other side of the bed. "May I?" Beulah asked. The snake simply curled up at the foot of the bed and made no fuss when Beulah slipped between the sheets.

CHAPTER 2

Stella

Stella's skin burned. Sizzled as if it could rip away from her muscles and leave her raw, undone, exposed. It had done so since the moment the plane left the tarmac in Charleston. Her soul needed her corporal form to lie back down on the ground where Beulah fell and stay there. Two and a half months had passed since that night with no ease in Stella's grief. It settled in her like pounds of granite, locking her into herself. Spring in New York entered with a lion's roar, and a coldness Stella couldn't shake lodged deep in her bones.

The chill started when Madeline set fire to Beulah, and now nothing could warm her. Not cup after cup of hot tea nor a bath that Edith heated to almost scalding just for her. Stella's lack of appetite certainly didn't help. She cared less and less about eating, and as she withered, so did any warm blanket her body itself could provide.

But she ate a little so Beatrice wouldn't worry and slept

inside instead of on the ground when Forest begged her to. She'd even left the holy ground where she spent her days to come to New York to watch a woman she despised bask in the happiness of love. And today she agreed to meet Beatrice, Gwen, and Madeline at a yoga class after the brides-to-be had gone for their final fitting of their wedding attire.

The white tiles blurred as the subway car swept Stella to her stop, and she thought of Beulah. Lovers surrounded her. Gwen and Madeline flaunted the most obnoxious displays of affection, but even Beatrice and Ben's surreptitious hand holding vexed her. At least Forest and Dani had the propriety to keep their physical attraction to themselves when they were around her.

She stepped from the subway train onto the platform and followed the river of people up the escalator, numb to the bodies shoving past her. Her yoga pants, loose from weight loss, swished as she walked onto the New York street. The March wind whipped around her, and though she shivered, Stella didn't bother tightening her coat.

Gwen's studio was lovely. Floor to ceiling windows allowed ample light to provide energy for the multitude of plants that filled the space. Lavender floated in the air but did nothing to relax Stella. Perhaps she should be grateful for Beatrice and Forest for encouraging her to take another step, eat another bite, and share space with others when she could tolerate it.

The instructor standing at the front desk took Stella's name and gestured to the cubbies where she stored her things. The chill of the hardwood floor reminded her of the cold ground where Beulah fell.

I shouldn't be here.

She followed the woman into the studio space where Beatrice, Madeline, and Gwen waited. Beatrice grinned at Stella's arrival and patted the mat beside her, giving her the distinct impression that her friend was surprised she made it. "I saved you a spot."

"Thanks." Stella settled on the mat and crossed her legs.

"Hey, Stella," Gwen said with a small wave. Madeline glanced at Stella, gave a nod, then looked away. After several tries at connecting with her, Madeline had finally given up.

Thank goodness.

The instructor guided the practitioners through sun salutations to warm up, then moved them through a series of standard standing poses. Occasionally, Stella caught Beatrice watching her, unsure of the postures. Then she'd follow Stella's movement, grunt when things were uncomfortable, and roll her eyes when the instructor offered a toxically positive statement like "the universe doesn't give you what you want, it gives you what you need."

Stella needed Beulah. Nothing in this class would ease the itch, the burn that came with the woman's absence.

"Let's practice balancing now," the instructor said.

"Are you alright?" Beatrice whispered, drawing close.

Stella shrugged.

"Thank you for coming," Beatrice added, giving Stella's arm a gentle squeeze.

"Vrksasana. Tree pose."

Stella's heart stumbled at the words. Her mouth parted, and she glanced toward Beatrice, who smirked, waggled her eyebrows, and said, "I bet I'm good at this one."

Turning her attention back to the front of the room, Stella worked to slow and deepen her breath. She brought her foot to her calf and pressed her hands together in front of her heart, steadying her gaze on the center of the teal mandala painted on the burnt orange wall at front of the room.

"Once you find yourself grounded, grow your tree."

Stella knew the cue and, without glancing at the woman, she pulled her palms apart and stretched her hands to the sky.

"Now, do something to challenge yourself. Close your eyes or take your gaze up the wall toward the ceiling. Good!"

Around her, other practitioners giggled as they lost their balance, but Stella held steady.

"Timber!" a man in the front row said as he stumbled.

And that was all it took. Stella was no longer in the light-filled, lavender infused space. Her body flooded with heat while her skin goose-bubbled at the remembrance of snow. The devastating sound of Beulah's roots ripping from the ground filled her ears, and a birch tree reduced to cinders overtook her vision.

"Let's get out of here." Beatrice's hand wrapped around Stella's upper arm and pulled her through the room, bumping her against people until she stood barefoot on a New York sidewalk. Stella closed her eyes tightly and allowed the scream that had built up inside of her to tear up her spine and out of her throat.

"I shouldn't be here," she spat, then opened her eyes to find Beatrice's.

Tears dripped from the woman's chin. "Me either." Beatrice opened her arms and Stella shuffled closer. "I didn't see it happen like you did, Stella. I was..."

"Bleeding in the snow." Stella sniffled against Beatrice's shoulder. "I don't blame you." A sob shuddered through her body again and Beatrice tightened her embrace. "I blame your mother."

"I know, Stella." Beatrice rocked side to side, as if the movement would comfort her. "Perhaps we shouldn't have expected you to come to the wedding, but we couldn't..."

Take care of me if I stayed on the mountain. Make sure that I ate and slept.

Beatrice released Stella and used her thumbs to wipe her tears as she had done so many times. "Do you want to wait on them, or should we go on?"

Before Stella could answer the question, the studio door swung open, and Gwen and Madeline, who carried Stella's coat and shoes, joined them on the sidewalk.

"You okay?" Gwen asked. She pulled a tissue from a leather crossbody bag and handed it to Stella.

Stella took the tissue, wiped her eyes, and blew her nose. Teeth clenched, she shook her head, then after a beat answered, "No. I'm not okay."

"Yoga can crack us open." Gwen took a step closer and placed her hand on Stella's shoulder, rubbing against the skin she'd left exposed to the March chill. "Let's get you warm." She helped Stella slip into the jacket she'd left in her rush to leave while Madeline sat her shoes down. "Hungry?"

"I am," Beatrice replied. She, too, had cleaned the wetness from her face, but her countenance remained sad. "That was more work than I expected." She attempted a smile. "Is there anything you'd like to eat, Stella?"

Stella inhaled deeply and exhaled through parted lips. She glanced at Madeline. As much as she hated the woman, those biscuits she made were the only things she could consistently stomach.

"We can eat at home," Madeline said to Beatrice, since she and Stella never spoke directly to one another anymore. "I'll make a pan of biscuits." Then she turned her back to the group and started walking toward the subway, her long white braid swinging at the backs of her knees.

Gwen and Beatrice locked arms with Stella as they followed. "Stella!"

Stella froze at the voice.

Dear god, no.

***

Though Gwen, Beatrice, and even Madeline, who had walked ten paces ahead, had turned to face the stranger, Stella kept her back to her mother until the clickety-clack of her heels on concrete stopped.

"Stella."

Unable to do so much as twitch her fingers, Stella closed her eyes. Her mother's body moved around her, and cool hands planted on her face. The shock of the gentle touch opened Stella's eyes wide. Her mother's shorter hair revealed the gray she'd always tried to hide, and her skin sans makeup stirred feelings of concern within Stella. Helen wrapped her arms tightly around her and pressed her close.

"Hi," she whispered. Then her mother unraveled her arms, pulled back, and scanned her daughter from head to toe.

Tension muddled the tenderness Stella felt for Helen as she braced herself for what was coming—a litany of shortcomings, comments on her appearance, and interrogations on where she'd been and why she hadn't answered her calls. Mother and daughter stared at one another in awkward silence.

"Hi. I'm Beatrice." Stella watched as Beatrice stretched out a hand for her mother to shake and introduced her to Madeline and Gwen. "We were on our way to lunch. Would you like to join us?"

"Well, we were going to eat at home. I—" Madeline said, and Stella felt a surprising flicker of gratitude toward the woman.

"I won't be in New York much longer," Beatrice interrupted. "Surely there's something we can grab quickly." Beatrice shot Stella an apologetic look. "I'm starving."

A whip of March air whistled around them. Gwen wrapped her arms around herself and gestured down the road with a nod. "There's a ramen restaurant that way."

Stella's shoulders released.

Thank god for soy allergies.

"Sounds fine," Helen said.

"What about your allergies?" Stella asked, the first words she'd said to her mother.

"I'm sure they have soy-free options." Helen smiled, and it seemed genuine and warm. "Are you alright to walk?"

"Why wouldn't I be?" Stella's voice sliced out of her, more defensive than she intended.

"Let's go." Beatrice took Stella's arm once more, and this time, Helen took the other.

No one spoke as they walked. A chafing pressure scratched up and down the skin of her upper arms as she prepared to defend each one of her choices, prompting her to jerk from Beatrice and Helen's binds. Beatrice ran a warm hand up and down her back; Stella shrugged it off.

The savory smells of warm, spicy broth and roasted meats used to make Stella's mouth water, but today, they turned her stomach. The host sat them at a circular table. Gwen and Beatrice sandwiched Stella, leaving her to face her mother and Madeline.

"Stella," Helen said. "What's happened? You look so..." Stella's belly contracted, and her jaw tightened again as she waited for her mother to finish the sentence. "Sad."

Stella readjusted herself in her seat. Somehow, it never occurred to her she would see her mother again, so she hadn't words for the woman. The thought pierced her with guilt. After silence lingered too long for Helen's comfort, she pulled back, served everyone else at the table scathing looks, and presented the question again.

"What happened to my daughter?"

Stella locked eyes with each woman, daring them to speak on her behalf. Drawing in a deep breath and straightening her spine to regain a shred of her strength, she locked eyes with her mother.

"I lost someone I love." A frog's croak was smoother than Stella's voice.

"My sister," Beatrice said, pressing a hand to her chest.

"My daughter," Madeline added.

Stella lifted her eyes to Madeline's as rage filled her body, and she wanted nothing more than to slam the table with both hands and shout "You killed her!" in the tiny restaurant. She closed her eyes briefly before redirecting her attention to her mother. Helen's eyes were soft under the hood of furrowed eyebrows. Even though her countenance revealed compassion, when the woman opened her mouth to speak, Stella steeled herself again.

"I'm sorry, Stella." Her mother reached across the table and gave her hand a squeeze. "My condolences to all of you." Helen's eyes moved to Madeline, and Stella knew she was thinking about her brother, the little baby she lost. "Things make more sense now. Roger and I waited a couple of weeks, but then we filed a police report." Helen's eyes scanned the table. "I'm sorry. I don't enjoy discussing things like this in mixed company, but here we are." Stella noticed her mother's nails were bare of shiny lacquer as the woman flipped her palms and shrugged. "They closed the case after a week."

"Cell service isn't great where we live," Stella said. *Not entirely a lie.* "But I guess I should have made more of an effort."

"He thinks you're in a cult being held against your will. Are you?"

Stella felt Beatrice stiffen beside her. "No." The statement held a firm but warm kindness. "Stella asked us to stay. And we are not a cult."

The table was silent until the server came to take their orders.

"Look," Helen said after the server left, "I know you don't owe me anything. But I'd love to know everything. I miss you."

Stella caught the glance and brief smile between Madeline and Beatrice.

I bet they think that if they can work their differences out, my mother and I can, too. But they don't know Helen.

Even as a part of her scoffed at the idea that Helen cared, another part, a deeper part, insisted this moment was different.

"Alright," Stella said with a nod.

She told her mother about Forest's wand and the need she felt to interview him. To her surprise, Helen didn't roll her eyes or sneer at Stella's explanations of magic. Lunch came, and Stella stirred and poked the ramen around as she spoke, stopping occasionally to eat a spoonful. She shared stories about Beatrice, the climb to the peak, and how they jumped off a twenty-foot cliff into a swimming hole, all while avoiding references to talking trees that healed with glowing roots.

"And what was *she* like? The woman you left New York for?" Helen asked.

"Beulah."

It was time for Stella to practice her fiction skills. She wove a tale about meeting Beulah for the first time on top of the mountain, taking her on walks through the forest, and staying up all night counting the stars. She and Beulah had done the last one once, before the tree insisted that she get herself home and into bed. The more she built the narrative, the more she ached for it. Perhaps one day she would be well enough to write it down, as Imogene had asked. And in the story, she would imagine that Beulah loved her back.

"What brings you back to New York?"

"We live here," Gwen said, speaking for the first time since they sat down. "And we're getting married." She and Madeline gave one another beatific smiles, and Stella's mouth grew sour.

"Lovely," Helen replied and gave Stella a sympathetic look. "When's the wedding?"

"Two weeks away."

"Oh." Helen took a drink of water, then peered at the brides-to-be. "You've heard there's supposed to be a snowstorm."

"They can't predict that this early," Madeline said, waving the comment off.

"People are already gearing up for it. Canceling events left and right. Snowstorm of the century, I hear." Helen scooped a spoonful of ramen into her mouth with annoying grace.

Let it come. It would serve Madeline right. Then again, I'd be snowed in with them.

The conversation tilted away from Stella and her stories and toward snowstorms and Helen's insistence that Gwen and Madeline research other options.

Typical...prying into everyone's business.

Once bellies were full and brains talked out, Helen paid for lunch and asked for a few moments alone with her daughter. Madeline, Gwen, and Beatrice left the table, and Helen scooted next to Stella.

"I'm in therapy." Her voice had turned sharp again, and she sniffed as if the action of getting help was beneath her. "He says I have...narcissistic traits." Helen cut her eyes toward Stella's whose own were wide and her mouth agape. The woman smirked and pressed a finger underneath Stella's chin to close her lips.

"And you're still seeing him? After he called you a narcissist?"

"No." Helen lifted her finger and took her gaze to the table. "He said I have narcissistic traits. Tendencies." Then she looked at Stella with eyes so apologetic her breath caught. "And they'll always be there. I'm learning to catch myself, but I won't always see it." Stella opened her mouth to speak, but her mother stopped her. "I'm sorry for always centering myself."

"You didn't today."

Helen shook her head. "No. I didn't. But it took a lot of work." Her lips broadened into a smile, and she released a laugh. Stella, despite herself, joined her. Helen grew serious again. "I know what it feels like when the people in your life are happily in love while you're barely finding the strength to get out of bed each day. I'm just now coming out of that cynical, bitter and, dare I say, selfish place. Our relationship suffered because of it. Get the help you need."

"There's no help for this," Stella confessed, tears stinging her face. "What Beulah and I had wasn't normal."

"There's no such thing as normal when it comes to love. Will you be alright with them?"

Stella thought about Beatrice and Forest. "We take good care of each other."

Helen stood, opened her arms, and gave Stella a long, tight squeeze. "Could you call me at least once a month?"

Stella offered a half smile. "I'll do my best, Mom."

"Do you think I could come visit over the summer?"

Stella glanced outside and took in Beatrice, who stood with her chin raised and eyes narrowed like an angel with talons ready to rip Helen's throat out if she dared hurt her friend.

"Only if Beatrice allows it."

"She seems protective."

"She's my best friend."

"Go on then," Helen said, waved her hand toward the door, then sat back down. "I think I'm going to have some tea."

"Bye, Mom," Stella said and left the restaurant.

Standing on the sidewalk, Stella peered through the glass at her mother, whose gaze pointed softly in front of her.

"You okay?" Beatrice asked and placed her hand on Stella's arm.

With the touch, all the warmth from the previous moments chilled.

"I just want to go home."

CHAPTER 3

Madeline

Madeline went to work on a pan of biscuits the moment the group arrived home. She didn't stop to say hello to Forest and Dani, who rocked on the balcony, his fingers whittling a piece of wood into something stunning while theirs strummed a guitar. Beatrice, with a resigned look on her face, followed a stolid Stella back to the guest bedroom. Gwen entered the kitchen and watched Madeline retrieve flour from the pantry along with butter and buttermilk from the fridge.

"Still hungry?" she asked, though her expression suggested she understood Madeline's actions.

"Stella didn't eat much." Madeline kept her eyes on the task before her. "It's all I can give her, you know?"

In truth, the meditative act of creating the peace offerings was all Madeline could give herself. Months of Stella's cold rage had sewn doubt into Madeline's mind, and she wondered if it had been a mistake to follow her mother's command that she burn the tree. Reduce her to ashes. The intensity of Stella's anger put Beatrice in a tough spot, but it gave Madeline moments to witness her daughter's character: compassionate, forgiving, patient, and fair.

"Meet me in the living room once you've popped them in," Gwen said.

She cut the dough into circles and tried to pray—tried to connect to the Goddess she had faith in once.

Please open Stella's heart to forgiveness.

Sliding the biscuits into the oven, Madeline conjured a new prayer. An unbidden plea she hadn't dared ask the Goddess.

Please bring my mother back.

Madeline clasped a hand over her mouth to stifle a sob. That cold day she managed to make it past the Hedge and all the way to the cabin, only to receive her mother's final words. All her energy had been so centered on Beatrice and Gwen that she hadn't processed that her mother was gone.

Please. Please.

Standing straight again, Madeline swallowed deeply and dabbed the corners of her eyes with the sleeve of her shirt before entering the living room. She sat next to Gwen on the couch, who hovered over examples of bouquets pictured on glossy pages. Smatterings of bridal magazines lay scattered around the table, and Gwen had her laptop open, her attention moving from the magazines to the screen, searching all sorts of March wedding recommendations. A bouquet of lavender and baby's breath caught Madeline's attention, while Gwen favored fresh peonies.

"If my mother were alive, she'd insist we have matching bouquets," Gwen said.

"Well, I think we can do whatever we want, Gwen," she said, and she wondered what her own mother would say.

"I'm not so sure." Gwen released a breathy laugh through her nose. "Based on Helen's snowstorm of the century prediction."

Madeline waved a hand to shew the suggestion away. "Do you think Stella will come to the wedding?"

"Of course she will," Gwen responded with a smirk on her face. "She still likes me."

"Gwen!" Madeline swatted at her love with a magazine.

"Hey! I'm just trying to lighten the mood." Gwen placed her palm on Madeline's face, who leaned into the touch. "Remember, you almost burned the forest down when you thought Beatrice was hurting me. And I lived," Gwen continued. "Your mother didn't. Stella's anger makes sense."

Madeline rubbed her forehead with her fingertips. For a moment, she allowed her eyelids to flutter, forgetting the newest round of visions that tormented her each time she closed her eyes. The moment they touched, the thunderous roar of a violent waterfall crashed through her ears. She swallowed quickly, widening her eyes. "I'm having visions again," she whispered, drawing Gwen closer.

"Oh?" Gwen stroked her hair. "Wanna talk about it?"

Madeline shook her head quickly.

"You know you can always come to me, Maddie."

"I know." Madeline swallowed. "I keep hoping they'll go away."

She pressed her forehead against Gwen's and breathed with her for a moment, then the door of the guest room opened, and she pulled away. Beatrice entered and settled down in the armchair across from her and her bride.

"So..." Beatrice managed a grin, but Madeline knew taking care of Stella and having little time with Ben weighed on her. "Have you decided on bouquets yet?"

Gwen leaned forward, grabbed her laptop, and turned it toward Beatrice. A furrow had returned to her brow, and Madeline could read between the frown lines.

"I want fresh peonies, and Madeline wants lavender and baby's breath."

"I can do that." Beatrice narrowed her eyes and tilted her head, assessing the situation. Madeline gave a small smile at her daughter's ability to tell when she was sad. "Is everything alright?"

"Stella's still so angry. A snowstorm may white out our wedding..." Madeline's eyes moved from Beatrice to Gwen and back, surveying the two women she loved the most. "And I'm seeing things again."

She wished she had chosen different words. Words with substance that didn't imply flakiness.

"Well, we've learned that sometimes your…impressions don't paint the full picture," Beatrice said.

"Yes, that happened. Once." Madeline swallowed. "But most of the time, my visions are spot-on. I need to be honest with you, Bea." She had never told her daughter about seeing Forest bleeding in the snow. "I had premonitions before the solstice that I didn't share with you."

For a moment, the only sound came from light conversation and giggles from the balcony.

"Well, are you going to tell me?" Beatrice demanded, her jaw tight, her eyes glowering at Madeline through her thick lashes.

"I saw Forest before I ever met him. In the snow with blood all around him." Beatrice's throat bobbed as Madeline continued to speak. "And it felt like losing Gertrude all over again, and I can't talk about this new thing yet, but…" Madeline looked down at her daughter's bare feet. "It feels exactly the same."

"Stop," Beatrice said as she pressed her hands on her legs and stood. She looked down at her mother, then began to pace. "Why didn't you tell me about Forest sooner? We could have prevented so many things."

Madeline hung her head and gave it a shake.

"Maybe we should go home." Beatrice expanded her arms wide. "Before the snow."

"Is this punishment for not telling you?" Madeline asked, annoyed at her own defensiveness.

"No, but if something is coming, I'd much rather be home."

This was Madeline's second visit with her daughter in twenty years; the thought of Beatrice leaving now scraped her heart. She closed her eyes. A mistake.

This time, she felt her lungs fill with sticky, wet heat. By the time she felt Beatrice shaking her and heard Gwen calling her name, Madeline was coughing and sputtering. "Someone's drowning," she choked, "in hot water."

The strength of the vision had brought Madeline to the floor, and every part of her trembled.

"Here, let's get you back up on the couch," Gwen whispered.

Madeline felt her daughter's strong hands help Gwen in hoisting her back up.

"Let me make you some tea." Beatrice attempted to deliver the words with compassion, but Madeline could hear the feelings of betrayal and anger in them. "Want some, Gwen?"

"Yes, please," Gwen said, her hand gripped tightly around Madeline's arm.

"Maybe she's right," Madeline whispered, then leveled her eyes with Gwen. "And maybe we should go with them. I don't want any of us to be alone right now."

"We'll talk about it."

Beatrice sat two cups of tea on the coffee table and took one with her to the armchair, swirling the bag around with the string. Then she looked up and leaned forward. "I love you, Mother. I wish our time together was easier."

That familiar pang of guilt and shame sliced into Madeline's aging womb. They each sat sipping their tea, and Madeline kept her eyes open, blinking only when absolutely necessary and without letting her eyelids close all the way. Forest and Dani came in wearing big smiles, smiles that slid into frowns as they read the surrounding room.

"We smelled biscuits," Forest said. He jerked his thumb toward the kitchen.

"I'll make you some tea to go with them." Beatrice pressed herself from her chair and headed to the kitchen. "Save one or two for Stella. We ran into her mother."

"Oh god," Dani murmured. "How did that go?"

"Come on. I'll tell you about it."

Interactions between Forest's friend and Beatrice intrigued Madeline. She had had little opportunity to speak with Beatrice privately about them, but certain things were clear: Dani had no intention of taking shit from Beatrice, and Beatrice liked them all the more for it.

"Hey," Gwen said, pulling on Madeline's sleeve. "What if we…" She jerked her head toward their bedroom.

Madeline's muscles grew rigid. It took effort to tug her lips into a smile. She stood, reached for her lover, and urged her toward the bedroom, then encouraged her onto the bed. Making love to Gwen was easy, but receiving was far more difficult. Instead of straddling Gwen, Madeline plopped herself by her side.

"We could move the wedding up. See if there are venues open this weekend. Then we could go with them and get snowed in on the mountain again."

"Maddie, tomorrow is Friday."

"Or we could get married under the trees. Have a party when we come back."

"There are legal processes, Madeline."

"Yes, I know that, Gwen. I bet Wanda could officiate," Madeline responded. Gwen just shook her head and looked away. "Look, I'm not trying to back out of it. I don't have cold feet. If anything, I'm trying to make sure it happens sooner."

Madeline's behavior over the past month compelled her to reassure Gwen of her commitment to the relationship. Something had shifted in the quiet times between the dramas, and while Madeline knew it had nothing to do with diminished love, convincing Gwen was a different matter.

"You have changed, Madeline," Gwen said. "You're distant."

"I don't want to invalidate your feelings, Gwen, but that's just not true."

And it wasn't true, at least not in the ways that mattered most. She and Gwen had grown more emotionally intimate with one another since the solstice, even going so far as working through their trauma bond in couples' therapy. But Gwen wasn't referring to vulnerability. Madeline sighed. She struggled to admit, even to herself, the truth she was about to share.

"Is this about sex?" she asked.

After a few silent moments, Gwen's shoulders slumped, and she looked away. "We used to make love so often, Maddie." She picked at a piece of thread that had pulled away from the quilt on the bed. "And I don't know if it's that you don't want me anymore or if I really messed things up in December when I..."

Images from the night Gwen left her flashed through Madeline's brain. The feelings of Gwen stretching her past her comfort zone and doing so out of anger brought a moment of confusion. Could that be it? She scanned the somber face that peered up at her. Madeline hadn't tried to stop her lover that night and she had, despite her anguish, felt pleasure. How could she lay all the blame at Gwen's feet?

"Well, I never want to do that again," Madeline admitted.

Gwen's face flushed. Madeline put a finger to her lips when she started to speak.

"But that's not it. It's not you. It's my body." Madeline's eyes moved toward the floor. "I'm struggling to..." She paused, searching for the words. "I'm not aroused as easily as I used to be. I'm not..." Her voice quieted to a whisper. "...taking care of myself either."

An understanding passed over Gwen's face, and she gave a little nod. "Maddie, maybe you're starting menopause."

Of course Madeline knew about the process, about women on the other side of motherhood ceasing to bleed and going through all sorts of changes. Perhaps she thought the divinity of the Goddess would protect her, or perhaps it was her own vanity that made her feel immune.

"I know it's not who we are," Madeline said, allowing herself to grieve for those moments. "We were like rabbits for a while."

"Bodies change," Gwen said. "Relationships grow."

"I can still love on you, Gwen."

"How about now?" Gwen asked with a cocked eyebrow and a smirk on her face.

"Yes, my love," Madeline said, and she kissed Gwen on the

temple. "But just one more question before we start. We're going to move up the wedding, right? We'll lose deposits and guests, but I don't want to postpone it."

Gwen's lips formed a line and Madeline worried she would resist, but then Gwen closed her eyes and gave a nod. "The most important people are with us. It's the best thing."

Madeline spent the next thirty minutes coaxing two orgasms from Gwen's receptive body, after which a warm thrum tingled in her own center.

"Touch me." She panted the words. "But no expectations, okay?"

Gwen rolled Madeline over and trailed her fingers down her body, holding her gaze as she offered gentle strokes. Madeline's body relaxed fully to the touch in a way it hadn't in so long. The climax shivered through her, small and light but present, nonetheless. Gwen grinned, satisfied with her work, then sat up and pulled her clothes on.

"Alright. Let's see if we can make this happen."

***

While Gwen went to the bridal shop, Madeline made phone calls to wedding venues. Beatrice and Dani sat on the balcony and called the caterer, DJ, and officiant to see if they were available for a schedule change. Forest moved to the bedroom to focus on carving the wedding present he'd been working on. Madeline cracked her neck, interlaced her hands, and pressed them away from her. Stella entered the room with pillow indentations on her face.

"I made a pan of biscuits."

Stella moved to the kitchen. Madeline listened to the scrape of a plate, the opening of the toaster oven door, and the pouring of a beverage into a cup.

Moving up the wedding will get you home earlier.

"The caterer and DJ both declined, but the officiant offered backup options." Dani combed their fingers through their hair as they laid a notebook and pen on the table facing Madeline.

"I'm going to check on Forest. See how much progress he's made."

"Thank you," Madeline said.

"Any luck?" Beatrice sat down on the chair across from Madeline.

"Not yet. If the caterer's out, we should book a restaurant if possible."

Stella carried two piping hot biscuits covered in butter and sat next to Madeline, tucking her legs underneath her. "Thank you."

Though stiff and perhaps forced, the words of gratitude brought a smile to Madeline's lips.

"You're welcome, Stella. Not sure if you've heard, but we're working to move up the wedding to avoid the snowstorm of the century."

Green eyes widened, and Stella's entire demeanor changed. "Really?"

"Yup."

Stella smiled, the first Madeline had seen since the solstice.

"I should get back to it." Madeline continued with her venue search, her hope dwindling when a scheduler at a rooftop bar and restaurant said, "We could accommodate a group up to fifty tonight."

"Tonight?" Madeline's heart rate sped up with excitement and terror. She looked at her daughter who mouthed "We can do this," then blurted, "We'll take it."

***

Madeline stood at the door leading to the rooftop, admiring the floral decorations. Beatrice had draped wisteria along each railing and around the doors, and centerpieces of green hydrangea, pale pink ranunculus, and coral peonies adorned each table where guests sat.

Beatrice and Ben stood under a wooden archway waiting for Madeline and Gwen to make their way onto the rooftop. Her daughter wore a moss green chiffon dress with flowy sleeves, and Ben's tuxedo vest and bow tie matched. Madeline's presence grabbed their attention. Ben looked toward the door where his sister stood while Beatrice locked eyes with Madeline, smiled, and gave a nod. Madeline pushed open the door and found Gwen, a bouquet of fresh peonies at her chest, resplendent in her ivory boho jumpsuit with fitted V-neck top and wide-leg trousers.

There had been a brief rehearsal. The two were supposed to walk around the tables of guests and meet at the arbor, but their bodies drew them to one another. Madeline cupped her lover's face and kissed her deeply. To hell with traditions. To hell with what the surrounding guests thought. Both of their faces were wet when they pulled away from one another and faced the sunset.

"It's beautiful, Maddie."

"Mm."

Madeline wrapped one arm around Gwen's waist and walked her to the arbor. The crowd, which was larger than Madeline expected with the date change, cheered, silencing only when the officiant settled them. Madeline and Gwen handed their bouquets over to Beatrice and Ben and reached for each other's hands. Gwen gave her vows first, ending them with, "And in the end, we'll walk one another home." Behind her, Madeline heard Beatrice sniffle. Ben pulled a handkerchief from his pocket, reached in front of Madeline, and handed it to her.

Madeline's voice trembled as she spoke her promises to Gwen.

"So many things in life worry and confuse me. But not this. Not us. You are my peace."

The two kissed again, and celebrations erupted when the officiant announced them as wife and wife.

"Grandmother. Gwen. Can I show you the gift I made?" Forest's eyes shone the same way Beatrice's did when she was little and couldn't want to tell Madeline a story. "It's this way."

Forest led them to the corner where a table sat stacked with cards and a few packages. Reaching under the table, he pulled out a trunk from underneath. A tree with branches full of expertly carved leaves and roots that spread the width embellished the top of the trunk. Madeline kneeled on her haunches to survey the carvings along the sides. Eight faces were etched into eight trees of different varieties. She matched the tree types with the names of her ancestors as she took in each one. Beatrice had helped her memorize them. The eyes of each tree were open, except for the last. Her mother. Madeline pulled her hand back and rubbed it against her chest. Her eyes burned.

"Forest, this is…" She tried to swallow, but the constriction of her throat prevented it. "I'm overwhelmed. Thank you."

Forest reached down and offered her an arm, and she stood. His lips pressed together, and his red eyes brimmed. When she wrapped him in a hug, he released a sob.

"I miss her, too."

Forest pulled back and wiped his eyes. "Now I know I cry at weddings." He smiled now. Perhaps the smile should have relaxed Madeline, but she remembered how close she was to losing him, how close she was to losing someone again. Nausea brought bile to her throat, but she smiled back and gave his arm a squeeze.

"First dance time!" Dani called, guitar in their lap.

Madeline found Gwen, wrapped her arms around her waist, pulled her close, and swayed with her to her favorite Elton John ballad.

CHAPTER 4

Beatrice

Beatrice trusted Ben's graceful steps to keep her steady as they moved around the dance floor. After several songs that ranged from thumping beats, which overstimulated Beatrice, to romantic ballads, the two tucked themselves into a secluded corner away from the crowd that had avoided the unheated space. In Ben's arms, her face pressed to his chest, Beatrice felt no chill.

"I wish they hadn't moved up the wedding," Ben said, ending the comfortable silence.

Beatrice looked up at him and furrowed her brow at the disappointment on his face. "Oh?"

"I can't go to West Virginia for another week. I have a meeting next Friday."

Beatrice's eyes moved to her shoes, and she pressed her forehead into his chest once more. She'd been in New York for three days, and during that time, she and Ben had one lunch together, after which he'd planted a gentle kiss on her lips when he dropped her off at her mother's apartment.

"I'll come to you when the snow clears," Ben continued. "But

I don't know when that will be. It shortens our time together quite a bit."

The wind nipped at Beatrice's exposed neck, and this time she felt it. She shivered, and Ben pulled her closer.

"Could you reschedule?"

"Believe me, love, I've tried."

Love.

Until this moment, the prospect of a giant snow cloistering the family in where they could eat and laugh and share stories had thrilled Beatrice. She'd envisioned tucking Ben into her room where she could demonstrate the feelings she couldn't find the words to explain.

This won't do.

She took a step away from Ben and her eyes swept over the crowd that had gathered to celebrate love. Forest and Dani held hands as they ate. Stella stood at the corner of the balcony, staring out at the New York skyline. Her mother and Gwen, each holding a glass of bubbling champagne, danced and laughed. She'd chosen to stay at their apartment instead of Ben's so Stella wouldn't be alone with Madeline, but tonight, the women were staying at a hotel.

"Give me a minute." Beatrice kissed Ben's cheek before making her way to Stella. "You alright?" she asked her friend.

Stella drew in a deep breath and turned toward her. "Jealous, heartbroken, and bitter, but other than that, I'm fine."

Beatrice clicked her tongue and turned to face the glittering city, choosing silence.

"I've lost people before," Stella continued. "I lost my dad when I was nineteen, but it didn't hurt like this. It's not just my heart. My body can't take it. Being here is excruciating. I'm not sure exactly what she did to me, Bea."

"Well, we'll be home in two days."

Stella squared her body to Beatrice. "My mother reminded me today how grief destroyed her. Made her cynical and angry. It poisoned her relationships." Her throat bobbed. "You're my best friend, and you've taken good care of me, but it's not your job to pull me out of this. I suppose it's not Madeline's either." After an eye roll and a heavy sigh, Stella added, "Don't tell her I said that. I'm milking these pity biscuits for as long as I can." She offered a small, rueful smile. "So, go dance with him. I can make it through the night without you."

Beatrice embraced Stella. She spied her sister on the edge of a rooftop across the street. Gertrude had come along for the journey, which brought feelings of home but also feelings of guilt. Beatrice caught Forest watching her and the eagle talking from time to time. Whenever he realized she was looking, he pulled his sad eyes away. He lost his best friend when Arcas died. But tonight, he danced, capturing the attention of many who urged him on.

I can't do their healing for them.

"Go," Stella said again, and Beatrice hurried away.

"Let's get out of here." She took Ben's hand and pulled him toward the door.

"You want to leave now?"

"They've said their vows. We've celebrated. We've danced. I want time with you, Ben."

Ben's lip twitched. "Shouldn't we at least let them know?"

Beatrice huffed, searched the crowd for her mother and Gwen, gave a big wave and called, "We'll see you in the morning." Tugging Ben's hand again, she chuckled. "There. We let them know."

Once on the sidewalk, Beatrice waved for a cab instead of waiting for Ben to do so. When a yellow taxi pulled up, she grinned, delighted that she conquered a city feat. Ben laughed and opened the door for her. Tendrils of disappointment at how little time they had threatened to creep around her mood, but Beatrice took Ben's hand, kissed it, and looked into his face. What she found etched on it tightened her chest. Pensive eyes locked on hers, bringing a wave of embarrassment that forced her to look away.

"I just realized I invited myself to your apartment. It was

forward of me. I'm sorry."

Ben took Beatrice's chin and tilted her face back toward him. "I've wanted time alone with you for the past three days." His lips curled into a crooked grin. "But I want us to be on the same page about what we want to happen tonight."

Beatrice flushed. In the time between the solstice and traveling to New York, she found herself more curious than ever about sex. Stella's grief prevented her from asking the woman questions, so she ended up broaching the subject with Wanda, of all people. The amount of trust she'd shown Wanda left the older woman stunned. But she recommended books on sexuality that were helpful and accessible.

She met Ben's eyes, cleared her throat, and said, "I want to be as physically close to you as possible."

"I want that, too, Beatrice." He leaned forward to kiss her when the cab driver slammed their brakes hard, leaned on the horn, and screamed "asshole!" out the window. "Hey, it's okay." Ben pressed a hand against Beatrice's cheek to calm her shallow breathing and quickened pulse. "That's just New York for you."

Beatrice's nervous system didn't find stasis until the two entered Ben's home. The event terrified her, but more than that, it crystallized how different her world was from his. Ben and New York couldn't offer her forever. Glancing around at the apartment confirmed the chasmic differences between her and the man she wouldn't let herself love, or at least not out loud. Clean lines, all white and bare, save a few monochrome paintings on the walls, brought a coldness that made Beatrice even more eager to crawl in bed and curl up next to him.

Ben scratched the back of his head. "It could use some plants and warming up a bit."

Beatrice walked toward him and wasted no time unbuttoning his vest, depositing it neatly on the back of a kitchen chair. She loosened his tie, then his shirt, revealing pale skin and a lean but strong torso. Before moving to his pants, Beatrice ran fingers through the hair on his chest and leaned in to breathe in his scent.

"I've missed you." Gooseflesh erupted, spreading out from the spot where she breathed the words.

"I've missed you, too."

He trembled as Beatrice undid his pants, responding to the closeness of her hand against him. Her own center quivered, remembering the way his tongue felt months ago. Ben slipped off his shoes before Beatrice slid the pants and his boxers down his legs, then pulled off his socks. She loved the effect she had on him. She loved the strength of his vulnerable softness as her gaze took in his naked body before she came closer, bringing her hands to his waist, and kissed him. She wanted to be that soft and open for him, but her body insisted on protection, so she reached behind her and slid the zipper of her dress down as far as she could before turning and allowing him to finish.

"Let's go to bedroom," Ben breathed against her ear, and she shivered, feeling the tension increase. Once in his room, she slid the dress down her body and faced him. During their time on the mountain, Beatrice kept most of her clothes on; now, every inch of her was on display, save the places her underwear covered.

Ben made his way to the bed and sat cross-legged on it. "Come here."

Without removing her underwear, Beatrice climbed onto the bed and scooted toward the middle, sitting on her ankles and leaning in toward him.

"I want to try. But if I can't, we will still be okay?" Beatrice asked.

His kind eyes crinkled, and his lips spread into a warm smile.

"Beatrice, there are a million ways to make love. To be as close to one another as possible." He kept his voice low as he repeated the words she used in the cab. He laced his fingers through hers and raised the joined hands up for her to see. "This is making love." He pulled her closer and brushed his lips against hers with the most chaste kiss. "This is lovemaking." He distanced his body from hers but maintained eye contact. "You're safe with me, Beatrice."

Ben's tongue and fingers gave Beatrice their undivided attention, and she lost control twice before he lay beside her, trailing a finger down the scars on her belly, through her damp patch of hair and to her center. This time, he raised himself on one arm and explored her eyes as his finger moved past the place he'd worked over toward her entrance. Beatrice swallowed as he circled the opening.

"You're so warm. May I?"

Despite the fear that pressed against her chest, Beatrice nodded. She wanted him inside of her, even if only for a second. Ben kissed her as he entered, venturing deeper with each return. Beatrice gasped as she felt more pressure.

"Too much?" he asked.

She shook her head quickly, savoring the gentle burn.

Moments later, Ben withdrew completely and repositioned himself between her legs. "I love you, Beatrice." He pressed himself up, reached into his bedside table, and pulled out a plastic wrapped package. A condom. She had educated herself and knew the purpose.

Before he opened it, Beatrice stopped him.

"I don't want anything between us, Ben."

Ben gazed down at her through narrow eyes, his head tilted.

"I brought a tea with me. I won't get pregnant."

"But what if it doesn't work?"

"Then there are other teas I can use to take care of it. I want you as close as possible."

Ben drew in a breath and returned the condom to the table. He moved between her legs once more, guided himself to her opening, but before pressing into her, he whispered, "May I?"

"Yes."

Beatrice wrapped both legs around him and drew him into her. His movements massaged her core, and she wept at the satiation of her need for closeness.

Ben shuddered and collapsed, breathless, beside her. He

smiled and swept aside her hair, which was wet with sweat and tears. "Are you alright?"

Beatrice could only bob her head. As she lay with her head on his chest, her mind and heart came to an agreement.

"It's unacceptable that we've had so little time together." She ran her fingers through the hair on his chest. Her eyes fluttered, lids heavy with sleepiness. "I don't blame you, but I can't accept it when there's another option for us to be together." Ben's body grew still and rigid. "I'll stay with you until the snow clears."

"It might be a while."

"We'll make do."

***

The next morning, after sharing breakfast with Ben, Beatrice took a cab to her mother's home. The newlyweds were already home from their one-night honeymoon and preparing for their trip to West Virginia. Ben had given Beatrice running pants, a sweatshirt, and a Mets cap to wear, which made Gwen giggle. She threw Beatrice a knowing smirk.

"Where's your dress?" Dani asked with their right eyebrow cocked and arms crossed. The question landed in the nebulous space between accusatory, playful, and concerned.

"I'd assume on the floor of my brother's bedroom," Gwen said.

Heat waved across Beatrice's skin at her comment. It stung that the time she and Ben had spent together was being reduced to a joke.

"Don't tease her," Madeline said.

Gwen's mouth parted and her eyebrows jerked at the seriousness in Madeline's voice, but then she grinned and turned to Beatrice. "But I'm the wicked stepmother now."

Beatrice's eyes flicked to her mother again, who said nothing this time, but gave a small shake of her head and an apologetic glance before taking a sip of coffee.

"Hey." Gwen reached across the table now for Beatrice's hand. It took everything inside of her not to pull away. "Did I hurt you?"

"No. Of course not." Beatrice attempted to soften the edge in her voice, and Gwen pulled away in reaction.

"I'm sorry," she said, sighed, and took a bite of a bagel.

Forest cleared his throat, drawing his mother's attention toward him. He lost his battle to hide a smile and released a small chuckle.

"Stop." Dani, a scowl on their face, bumped their shoulder into Forest and locked eyes on Beatrice. "I did not mean to start this."

"What did you mean to do?" Stella asked.

Quibbling between Stella and Dani happened frequently when the conversations circled Beatrice. Most often, Stella perceived Dani's quips as insulting Beatrice and Dani defended themselves. Perhaps the intentions of each party were pure, but it always left Beatrice tasked with the job of making things right between the two of them.

"I just wanted to make sure you were okay." Dani's eyes were on Beatrice. "Jesus Christ."

"Sorry, Mother," Forest said before spreading a load of cream cheese onto a bagel.

"Anyway." Beatrice put her palms on the table and focused her gaze on the bowl of fruit in the center. "I've decided to stay with Ben until his business is settled, and we'll travel home together."

Dani snorted. "You are going to stay here..." They poked the table to emphasize their point. "In this cold, gray hellhole just to be with a man you've known for less than three months."

It's not a hellhole...

Beatrice had warmed a bit to the city. Still, the defensiveness she felt surprised her. Having enough, she stood and answered with a clear, "Yes. I'm going to go gather my things."

***

Beatrice didn't know why a lump formed in her throat and her eyes stung. She knew that no one at the table meant her harm, especially Dani, who had about the same amount of social prowess as Beatrice herself. After minutes of folding and fighting the inevitable, she sat on the cane chair in the corner and allowed tears to fall. A light knock at the door brought her fingers to her face, and after a beat, she said, "Come in."

Gwen took a step in. "Can we talk?" Beatrice nodded, and Gwen closed the door behind her. She took light footsteps across the room and sat on the edge of the bed facing her. "I really am sorry. We are all happy for you, Beatrice." The woman's gaze bore into her, but Beatrice refused to look away, even at the discomfort of feeling thoroughly dissected. "Well..." Gwen tilted her head from side to side. "...I think Dani is genuinely worried about you and doesn't want you to do something stupid. And Stella is jealous, but we all want you to be happy."

"I'm not like my mother." Beatrice glowered at Gwen as she spoke. "I don't romanticize being in love." Gwen's eyebrows twitched, and a twinkle brightened her eyes, but Beatrice continued. "It's painful to have something that feels so sacred be the source of my family's entertainment."

"Oh, honey." Gwen edged closer to Beatrice and took both of her hands. "I'm sorry that's the impact we had. I would never hurt you on purpose."

Beatrice swallowed. "Okay. I believe you." More words swarmed through her mind, but she refused to let them escape her mouth.

I don't know how to tell him I love him.

I don't know how we're going to make this work.

Why did it have to be him?

"Was the wedding everything you hoped for?" Beatrice asked.

Gwen grinned. "I loved every minute of it."

Beatrice's gaze fell to the floor as she replayed moments from the ceremony when she and Ben should have focused on the brides but couldn't take their eyes off each other. "You were so angry when Mother said no that you left her." She brought her eyes back to Gwen who winced at the reminder. "If she hadn't proposed to you on the Solstice, would have stayed with her?"

"Yes, I would have," Gwen said with no hesitation. "But we're not talking about me anymore, are we?"

Silence lingered between them. Beatrice stood and peered out the window. The towering buildings stood so gray and cold and imposing.

"What if I can't give him that?"

"Has he mentioned marriage?"

"No."

"Beatrice, the two of you have all the time in the world. Just enjoy each other."

All the many ways she and Ben had enjoyed one another flashed through Beatrice's mind and she smiled.

"I'll leave you to it." Gwen pressed herself up from the bed and left the room."

***

Later, Dani came in with their arms crossed ready to make their amends.

Beatrice peered up into the young face and smiled. She knew how she could be—how her quick, simple questions could become interrogations, and after the experience she'd just had at the kitchen table, she didn't want that for Dani. "Are you going to get snowed in on the mountain again?"

"I'm headed back to Asheville. I start a new job soon." Dani cleared their throat. The sardonic snark that usually laced her words was gone, leaving only a weary sadness. "I don't think I have a choice."

"Did Forest ask you to go with him?"

"He did." They released the bind around their chest, sighed, and sat next to Beatrice. "He said he'd ask you about it. I told him not to bother."

Beatrice tilted her head so she could meet Dani's eyes. "Listen..." She paused. She wanted to give them a reassuring touch of some kind—a hand on the shoulder or the knee—but didn't think Dani would appreciate it. "I've told Forest many times now that he doesn't need my permission to do anything. You've stayed there before, and—"

"But it's your house, too." Dani's voice grew pointed. "And it doesn't matter. I can't quit this job or break my lease."

"Break your lease?"

"I'll lose my security deposit and have to pay an extra month's rent if I leave before the rental agreement is up."

"I see," Beatrice said. "What would you do if you had a choice?"

Dani turned their gaze to the floor. "I'd go with Forest."

Beatrice smiled. "I'm sure between Forest and myself, Mother, Stella, and Gwen, we can pull together your rent. And, unless you really, really love it, you can quit your job. We've got what we need on the mountain."

Beatrice and Dani searched one another's eyes for several breaths, then they broke eye contact and Dani shifted.

"Dani." This time, Beatrice reached out and gave their arm a squeeze. Dani couldn't lift their eyes from the floor despite Beatrice's efforts to force a connection. "I really like you."

Dani's hand covered their mouth and chin for a moment. "You sure don't act like it."

"I'm sorry," Beatrice said, giving the shoulder she'd been holding a rub. "That's just kind of how I am when I'm first getting to know someone."

"I know I'm not a nice person," Dani said, and Beatrice cocked an eyebrow.

"Neither am I. I don't understand how to play the games they play out here any more than you do." Dani released a laugh. "But we are kind." Dani nodded. "Call your job. Call your landlord. And let us know what you need." They stood to leave, but Beatrice stopped them. "Have you noticed how bad off Stella is?"

Dani scoffed. "It's impossible not to."

"I remember Henry talking about binds at the equinox gathering." Beatrice shifted her weight on the bed and hoped they could read the question in her eyes.

"You think your grandmother put a binding spell on her?"

"I don't know enough of about spell work, but I can imagine blood could be a dangerous and powerful ingredient. Maybe that wasn't Grandmother's intention. But Stella's a mess."

"She is. Grief manifests itself in different ways. We'll keep an eye on her. I promise."

This feels bigger than grief.

"Thank you," Beatrice said. Dani nodded and left the room.

Beatrice tucked in the last of her things and zipped the suitcase. Her family was so big now. She tutted to herself. She would miss them just as she missed the trees and their constant chatter. Squeezing her eyes against the burning tears that threatened, she thought about her grandmother. The timber and cadence of her voice and the way the bark of her face rippled into a grin came to her mind easily. A deep, childlike part of her waited for a miracle, but each day that past tugged at the threads of her faith.

"All this wanting," she mumbled as she stood and eased the suitcase to the floor.

Who am I to ask for love and miracles?

Beatrice dragged the suitcase behind her to the living room, and her gaze moved straight to her mother's alter and the red-haired Goddess. She could feel eyes on her as she kneeled and lit incense at the Goddess's feet.

I want him, Goddess. If I cannot have him, take the desire away. And I want my grandmother back. Forgive her. Please.

"You can take her with you if you want."

Beatrice felt the gentle touch of her mother's hand on her shoulder.

"I would appreciate that. Thank you."

"Visit with us until the incense is finished."

Beatrice stood, but her eyes lingered on the Goddess.

"Do you think She answers prayers?"

"I've had wishes come true. Did She grant them? I don't know."

"Do you think She's angry with us?"

"Why would She be?"

"Never mind," Beatrice said, shaking her head. "Let's have a cup of tea."

CHAPTER 5

Beulah

Beulah rested longer than she intended, existing between states of sleeping and eating bowls of jarred soup she'd found in the cupboard. Between dozing in and out of consciousness, she grappled with the fact that she wouldn't see Stella or the rest of her family for weeks. For an entire day, fatigue and brain fog kept her confined to the bedroom she had no authority to consider her own. There were many things she needed to understand about her new existence, things that could only come by leaving the cabin, but her body wouldn't allow it.

By the second day, energy swirled more smoothly through Beulah's veins. She even took the time to make the bed before soaking in a hot bath. On her way from the bathhouse to the cabin, her eyes scanned the trees, who called their greetings. She surveyed her mother from the tallest branch to her sprawling roots to ensure the illusion she'd draped around the tree was holding. Then she smiled and waved but did not go visit. There was too much to take care of. Her mother's book, for starters, which Beulah feared contained the secrets of her gift.

The wooden floor under Beulah's feet creaked as she made her way through the living room and toward the old bookcase crafted from warm oak wood. Beatrice had not only unlocked the case, but removed the doors from it completely, leaving exposed, weathered spines that Beulah ran her fingertips over. The volumes were arranged in chronological order, starting with First Mother's and ending with Ola's.

Stella must have mine.

The thought of Stella reading her journal over and over again, perhaps tracing her fingertips over the curled writing, warmed Beulah's heart. She thanked herself for curating only the stories she wanted future generations to know about her and leaving out the ugly parts. Her eyes flitted toward Beatrice's room briefly as she thought about the hidden pages of her journal she hadn't shared with Stella.

The rest of the spell.

Beulah shook her head, then pulled Ola's book toward her. If she couldn't change the words on the pages, she would have to burn it and tell the others it was out of rage. She knew Beatrice had kept her promise never to read it, or she would have come to her with questions. Her granddaughter still held the unfortunate belief that Beulah was honest. With a sigh, she flipped over the front cover.

I owe it to Mother to read it, though.

The first several pages of crudely scrawled letters strung together in misspelled words and awkward sentences made Beulah smile. She had caused Ola so much trouble from her very first breath that the woman never had a chance to share stories from her own childhood. The first two hundred pages were full of stories of Ola exploring her gifts, like the first time she lifted a boulder the size of a bear out of her mother's way so that she could plant a little garden, or when her healing power showed up just in time for her to save her mother's leg from copperhead venom.

Reading the diary gave Beulah the opportunity to get to know her grandmother, Edith, a little more as well. Memories flooded her. She remembered Ola taking her to the Rock to visit Edith every day until Beulah's gifts came in. The two women loved one another deeply; Ola would cry, and sap would weep down Edith's bark when their visits were over. Beulah's fingers scanned the lines as she read about her own conception, about how her mother had gone to the Rock, lay down on it, and watched, amazed, as a green glow surrounded her belly.

Reliving her own early years when she ate wild blackberries straight from the vine and made friends with a little white rabbit brought a lightness to her heart. There was a time, Beulah considered, when she was innocent.

The top of the next page started with *I think Beulah got her gift today.*

Beulah gently folded the corner of the page, closed the book, and made her way to the kitchen. Anticipating the onslaught of sorrow and anxiety the next pages would bring, she made a cup of Beatrice's calm blend. If she had faith that the deity cared anything at all about her, she'd cry out to the Goddess for help, but decades of pleading for shifts in her spirit with no relief left her cynical at best. Tea in hand, Beulah sat back down on the couch and took a sip of steaming liquid. Sasha lay coiled on the hearth with her yellow eyes surveying Beulah.

Beulah's stomach tensed, and her throat grew dry. The sinking feeling that she would forever live in fear of herself took over.

Beulah came to me today holding a dead mouse she found at the bottom of the front porch steps. Her body was trembling, and her eyes were wide and watery. I've never seen her so afraid. She's seen plenty of death before, so I asked what on earth had her so frightened. She didn't say anything. She just drew in a breath, pursed her lips, and blew on the mouse. The mouse twitched at first, then wiggled to its feet and scampered from her hand. We stared at one another for a long time, then she said to me, "I can do it the other way, too."

"Why did the Goddess do it, Sasha? Why would she give me a gift like that? My mother begged her over and over again to take it away. She was so scared of me. Of what I could do. I was a terror."

At those words, Sasha grew to her full height, shook her rattle, hissed, and bared her fangs. Then she brought that hissing, triangular head within an inch of Beulah's face. Just when she considered testing to see if the power still lived inside her, Sasha's anger relented, and she rubbed her head against her cheek. The snake slithered into a spiral on her lap. Beulah took a gulp of her tea, then set to work, changing the narrative, erasing all moments when she breathed life into and out of creatures and plants alike. She warped her mother's stories of holding a raging Beulah, who threatened to kill everything, including her mother, into stories of abuse, painting Ola as a parent who bound her child to a chair as punishment. She used her power of illusion to remove phrases like *Goddess, please don't let her kill me,* and *Please, take this gift from her before her child comes!* completely from the book. The reference to Madeline sent a shiver along Beulah's spine, and she quivered as she looked at the scars along her body. Though her methods had been self-masochistic, those cuts had kept her daughter safe from her rage. Safe from her breath.

Her tears splashed onto the paper as she worked. Her mother didn't deserve this, but neither did she.

By the time she finished, the muscles behind her eyes ached, and she trembled from the exertion. She pressed herself off the couch and moved to the kitchen to peer out the window at the trees. Her mother's eyes were still closed, the mouth shut, and she could see the glimmer of her deception around the bark of the white ash. Parched, she grabbed a jar from the cabinet, filled it, and gulped the contents without taking a breath. She flipped once more through the book. The changes were still there, but Beulah felt no more at ease as she closed the cover and placed the book back on the shelf.

"I'm sorry, Mother."

Her right eyelid twitched. Even though she knew the next task would be even more physically and mentally taxing, Beulah couldn't bring herself to eat dinner or even climb into bed. Instead, she sat by the fire, gathered her knees in her arms, and stared at the spine of her mother's book.

*****

Sasha's rattle woke Beulah out of the awkward fetal position she'd fallen asleep in on the wooden rocking chair. She groaned as she unwrapped her arms from her legs and placed both feet on the cool floor.

"What's wrong, Sasha?"

The snake stopped rattling and glided to the kitchen. Beulah followed, wincing at the aches in her joints and the creak in her neck. She opened the door, surveyed the sun's station, and determined it was almost noon. Glancing back down at the snake now curled beside her feet, she murmured, "You wanted me awake, didn't you?"

An affirmative shake of her rattle served as Sasha's answer.

"Well, you don't know what I have to do today. Perhaps if you did, you would have let me sleep."

Or pumped me full of your venom...

It took Beulah fifteen minutes just to dress and move through the kitchen without stopping for a morsel of breakfast. She walked away from the trees and toward the Rock without responding to their morning greetings. Shivering in the frosty air, breath swirling in steam around her face, Beulah tightened her coat around her neck. Like turtles driven to the same beach year after year to lay eggs, Beulah knew her way to this spot. The rain had worn away the footprints of the trees, including the space she inhabited when she had bark for skin. A part of her wondered where it all went, all that bark and roots.

Awe filled her as she stepped to the middle of the flat limestone slab and turned in a circle, taking in the trees that stretched overhead. The spell had worked. Beulah's deepest cells knew she wasn't powerful enough on her own to change back to human; the Goddess sanctioned it. Why, she could only guess.

Sliding her gaze to the forest floor, Beulah searched for small lifeforms on which to test her most loathsome power. A plump black ant scurrying along the bark of a tree would suffice. Bending over, she picked up a fallen leaf, placed it in front of the ant, and pitied its submission to her will. A tingling heat spread from the center of Beulah's chest, across her clavicle, and down to her hipbones. She swallowed, cupped the leaf in her palms, and brought it to her lips.

Please let it be gone.

Thinking death thoughts, she apologized to the ant, then blew over the tiny little body. Though Beulah couldn't see the minute movements, she imagined knees buckling and antennas drooping before the ant collapsed in her hand. Beulah crumpled, too, sinking to the ground, the ant still delicate and dead in her upturned palm. Disbelief blurred her eyes as she disassociated from the world around her. This thing—this power she'd wanted rid of since the day she'd discovered it—still swirled within her, and that realization was a boulder pressed so hard against her chest she couldn't catch a breath. The movement of a squirrel scampering up a tree returned Beulah to the present, and she forced air into her lungs and looked down at the black segmented body. Imagining life returning, she exhaled, and once again, the ant was alive.

"There you go," she whispered, bringing the back of her hand to the cold ground and urging the insect to leave the leaf. "You're alright now."

Beulah drew her knees into her chest and watched branches sway in the breeze. Time passed, and the afternoon sun warmed the air. The full extent of Beulah's power was unknown. Ola had always wrapped those bear arms around her and tethered her to the closest immovable structure she could find before Beulah could wield it against her or any other creature.

I need to know what I can do.

Beulah pressed up to stand and shook out her legs, which now tingled from sitting so long.

"I guess I'll start with you," she said to an ash tree that didn't answer back.

Beulah's breath blackened the bark of the tree and branches clattered to the ground. Then, she exhaled a breath of life. New buds formed at the ends of new branches, and the bark returned to gray. She closed her eyes with a sigh, then walked through the forest seeking different creatures. Sneaking up on a redbird and then a chipmunk allowed her to test two different families of animals. More trees and plants shriveled under her expirations, only to return to life when she readjusted her thoughts.

The most curious moment of discovery came when she approached a deer carcass. Dried strips of unconsumed tendon and muscle clung to the bone, and if it had been a hot day the smell would have made Beulah's next effort impossible for her to stomach. She squatted, blew, then watched with horrified amazement. Bones gathered themselves, joints locked back in place, and from the very dust of the ground grew tendons and ligaments until the deer with velvety horns dipped its chin and pranced away.

Beulah walked through the forest with methodical steps, experimenting as she moved toward home. When she came to the cabin, she stopped, her eyes darting between the door and the grove of trees—her family—the only ones who could help her. She turned toward the trees, and with each step she took toward her mother, her anxious fears returned.

"Hi, Beulah," Ida said, and as she did, all the trees except her mother opened their eyes. "Are you alright?"

Beulah's mouth couldn't form words, and she shook her head.

"What's wrong?" First Mother asked.

Beulah's eyes traveled to Ola, who stood shackled by the power she had wielded against the tree. Her mouth parted and stayed that way for a while before she voiced, "I have a gift."

The expected, "Oh, that's wonderful!" and "Show us!" and "We're so happy for you" never came.

"Did you know?" Beulah asked the trees while keeping her eyes on her mother.

"No, dear," Imogene said. "We never learn of a daughter's gift before she does."

Beulah swallowed, wishing she could feel relief and wishing she could trust these women.

"I don't want it." The words scratched her throat. "I want to give it back."

"I don't think you can," First Mother said.

"Ask Her," Beulah said, tilting her chin up and bringing her hands on her hips. "Ask Her to take it away from me. Please. She's answered so many prayers for the rest of you..." She widened her arms in an encompassing gesture. "And for Beatrice." Beulah gritted her teeth and added, "Perhaps, just this once, She could take care of *me*."

Beulah balled her fists at her side, turned on her heels, and walked away without sharing the details of her gift, but First Mother stopped her. "Is your power allowing you to keep your mother quiet?"

Beulah sucked in her lips and bit them to stop her chin from quivering. So many choices presented themselves before her. She could ignore the question or release the illusion she held over her mother and tell the truth.

I can only keep First Mother in the dark for so long.

She turned back, her eyes homing in on the one tree she knew could protect her. Whether she would, Beulah was uncertain. Blood pulsed through her body with so much force that she could only hear the sound of her heart throbbing in her ears. Without closing her eyes, she drew the illusion back into herself, and Ola's brown eyes slid open.

"Beulah has done nothing to me," the tree said, and Beulah allowed a gasp to escape from her chest. "I've been quiet because of my own guilt and shame. The fact that she didn't have a gift embarrassed me. I'm ashamed of it. Beulah…" Ola's eyes locked on hers as she crafted lies about the real reason she stopped bringing Beulah to the trees. "Can you forgive me?"

Beulah ran toward the tree and threw her arms around it, releasing a sob up from her bowels and into the bark. Ola's roots wrapped around her.

"I do love you, Beulah. I know I didn't show it."

Beulah's emotions spurred new floods of tears.

You loved me the only way you could.

"Now…" Ola's roots receded, and Beulah pulled away. "Tell us about this gift."

Beulah stared into her mother's eyes with the absolute conviction that no mother in this line had ever protected their daughter the way Ola had just done. After a hard swallow, Beulah opened her mouth.

"I can breathe on dead things and bring them back to life." The trees gasped and began to whisper, but First Mother shushed them quickly. "And I can breathe on living things and kill them."

The last statement was met with silence.

"Have you practiced it?" First Mother's voice held a grim fear.

"Yes. Plants and animals and fungi. All living things."

"I need proof," First Mother said, and Beulah glared at her as she imagined a woman with eyes like Ola's crossing her arms with the challenge.

She was exhausted. Even though she had released the silence she'd placed around her mother, she was hungry and dehydrated. If First Mother needed her to use any more energy, it had to be worth it. Her mind wandered to Forest and that sweet, black bear. Lifting her gaze, Beulah demanded, "Show me where Arcas is buried."

Ola released a long root and weaved it out to the edge of the forest where a rectangular spot of earth lay barren of grass. Beulah trudged to the porch to retrieve a shovel that leaned against a stack of firewood. As she walked toward Arcas's grave, she heard the trees rustling in the background, questioning her every movement. After an hour of digging, the shovel met bones.

Drawing her face close, Beulah breathed. Just as with the deer in the forest, layers wrapped upon layers until the bear stood on his hind legs, expressing a triumphant bellow.

"Arcas," Beulah whispered.

The bear brought his front legs down, moved his head toward Beulah, and nuzzled her neck.

"Forest will be very excited to see you."

Beulah strode back to the trees, lay her shovel down, then sunk to the ground at the base of her mother. Arcas plopped down beside her.

After a long stretch of silence, First Mother said, "Try it on me."

Beulah's breath hitched and her skin prickled with anxiety at what she suspected to be a trap. If she used this power on the Goddess's closest companion, would the deity ever help her?

"Why?" she asked.

"I want to know how it feels."

"Mother, please..." Imogene's voice was thick with worry. "What if she can't bring you back?"

"Then, I guess that's it for me."

Beulah's mouth parted at the stoicism.

"Why?" Imogene cried.

"Imogene!" First Mother's voice brought unease to the entire forest. All sounds, even bird twittering, ceased. Beulah felt heat rise to her face, an embarrassment on behalf of Imogene. "I said I want to know how it feels."

The thought of saying no, of turning and running back to the house, scurried along each of Beulah's raw nerves. Arcas rose to his feet and nudged her shoulder with his nose. She glanced at her mother, who somehow shrugged her limbs as she would her shoulders. Then she padded to First Mother, placed a hand on the bark, and blew.

The trees whispered and gasped. All the tender almost-buds forming on First Mother's branches fell, and darkness took over the bark. Beulah and the trees knew she had the power to destroy the whole forest.

"Bring her back!" Martha urged in a terrified voice.

Beulah brought life breath through her lungs and onto the tree's roots.

"It worked!" Elation filled First Mother's words.

"What did it feel like?" Ida asked.

"Do you remember that moment when you weren't human but weren't a tree yet, either?" The trees offered a variety of affirmations. "It's like that. A moment of nothing."

Wide-eyed, Beulah turned to her mother. She didn't hesitate and didn't explain herself as she scurried around, casting the spell on each of them quickly before they could use their roots to stop her. Then she fell at her mother's feet, pressed her forehead to the bark, and allowed her tear ducts to open.

"I know, my sweet daughter. I know." The voice, rich and soulful, wrapped around Beulah, as did the tree's roots. "They have no idea what you've been through."

"What we've been through," Beulah corrected. She pulled away and studied Ola's eyes. "You lied for me."

"Of course I did. I've never told them about your gift."

"What about Beatrice or Stella?" Beulah's chest tightened at the idea. *I won't be able to stand it if they're afraid of me.*

"Well," her mother started, "I did mention to Beatrice that you're the most powerful of us all. I wanted to give her hope." Beulah let out an exasperated sigh, prompting Ola to add, "I don't *think* the rest of the trees heard."

Beulah thought she saw a blush on her mother's barked cheeks. She rolled her eyes and scratched Arcas behind the ears. "I don't know if I can trust myself with it." She kept her eyes on the gentle bear that slumbered under her touch. "I want it gone."

"You're much older now. And you're surrounded by love. Beatrice and Stella will be back soon. Madeline, too. You can trust us to help you."

Beulah had carried the burden since she was so young, but

she was never alone. Her mother had done so much of the heavy lifting.

"I changed your book," Beulah confessed. "I couldn't risk them reading your story. Our story."

"You did what you felt you needed to, just like I did." Ola released a sigh. "But now, I think it was wrong to hold you down."

"I was dangerous."

"Fear has given this thing too much power, Beulah. If I had guided you, you could have practiced and—"

A wave of nausea passed over Beulah. She closed her eyes and waved away her mother's words. "I can't talk about this right now."

"I'm sure you're exhausted."

Beulah scanned her body. "And hungry."

"You should wake them back up before you go."

"Think I'll be in trouble?"

Another shrug of branches.

Beulah started with First Mother, whose lips spread into a smile when she opened her eyes.

"I needed time with my mother."

"It's alright, Beulah."

Beulah moved from tree to tree, each of which vocalized their feelings.

"Don't ever do that to me again, Beulah."

"I thought it was lovely."

"What happened?"

"Daughters," First Mother said, and the trees looked at her. "I'd like you to call me Alice from now on."

Beulah's brows lifted, and she glanced at Ola, who stared wide-eyed.

"Go eat and rest, Beulah. We will talk more tomorrow," Ola whispered, and Beulah did as she was told.

***

The next morning, Arcas and Beulah made their way to a pond to fish. Beulah allowed Arcas to do the fishing and gathered his catch in her basket to be cleaned. She laughed, watching the bear. How often had he and Forest played at her roots when they were younger? Beulah couldn't wait to see them all. Beatrice and Forest. Madeline. Beulah had almost faded completely when she whispered her few words to Madeline. And what would her bride be like?

But most of all, Beulah couldn't wait to see Stella. Now back in her body, Beulah could imagine Stella kissing her like she promised. She closed her eyes and pictured her round, freckled face, green eyes and brown hair.

"Stella," she whispered, full of hope.

Chapter 6

Stella

Preparing Beatrice for life in New York, even if it were only for an extra week or two, had distracted Stella from her increasingly itchy, burning skin. Beatrice and Dani flanked her as the three of them, swaddled in winter coats, scarves, hats, and gloves, walked down the crowded sidewalks to the cell phone store on Fifth Avenue.

"I hate March," Stella said, her words steaming in wisps around her face.

"I love it," Beatrice said. "It's unpredictable, and everything starts coming back to life."

The woman's good mood made Stella even more grumpy. As much as she hated herself for it, she had allowed resentment toward Beatrice to fester.

How are you so goddamn happy?

She dreaded the trip home. Madeline had insisted on renting a minivan so they could all ride together instead of taking two separate cars.

Dani swung open the door of the brightly lit store, and their eyes widened. "Jesus. This may take a minute," they said. Dani, it seemed, had as little experience with large cities as Beatrice, and this was perhaps the only thing Stella found charming about them.

Stella directed them toward the brand of phones she was used to, waved her hand along the most recent models, and said, "Pick."

"You *are* going to show me how to use it, right?" Beatrice asked.

"We both will," Dani said, and Stella gritted her teeth.

It took twenty-five minutes for Beatrice to choose between a purple case and a green one. Stella could hear her own irritation spill into every word she spoke and every move she made. It pained her that she couldn't join in her friend's joy, and Beatrice's atypical indecisiveness grated on her nerves. Once Beatrice made the purchase, the three loaded into the subway, and Dani wasted no time in opening the box and setting up the phone, chatting the whole time about all the things it could do.

"Will you call?" Stella asked, interrupting Dani's instructions.

"Of course, I will. And you..." The woman tied Stella down with her eyes. "Don't waste away while I'm gone. Remember that I'm a call away. I know you can't have a friendship with my mother right now, but you have Gwen, and Forest is the next best thing to me."

"I'd like to think I'm not so bad myself," Dani chimed in. "Here." They handed Beatrice the phone, which was now screen protected and tucked in its green case.

"Thank you," Beatrice said and smiled.

Stella and Dani took turns showing Beatrice special features on the phone and downloaded a few games, including solitaire. By the time they reached the apartment, Ben was waiting.

I'm not ready...

A selfish, jealous part of her wished Beatrice would change

her mind so that she wouldn't be left with Madeline without a buffer. Pressure built behind her eyes as she watched Beatrice show off her new phone and fill her bag with the few things she'd left in Madeline's apartment.

"Well," Beatrice said, turning to the others. "I guess it's time."

Stella's eyes went straight to Forest, whose chin quivered despite how fiercely he pressed his lips together.

"I will come home as soon as I can." Beatrice put her hands on Forest's shoulders. "You're in charge now. Take care of everyone."

Internally, Stella thanked the Goddess that Beatrice proclaimed Forest the leader instead of Madeline. Forest held his mother for a long time, tears streaming down his face. Dani gave her a quick hug. Gwen's goodbye felt easy, while Madeline took several minutes to review what she felt were the most important safety measures. Tears streamed down Beatrice's face as she held her mother.

"Try not to worry too much about the vision, Mother."

What vision?

"I'll try."

Stella narrowed her eyes at Beatrice but glanced at Dani who gave a shrug and a shake of their head.

When Beatrice came to her, Stella wrapped her arms tightly around her friend, squeezing her and breathing in the smell of rosemary, sage, and lavender. Beatrice sniffled and pulled away.

"You're going to be okay, Stella."

Stella nodded, not because she agreed, but to reassure the woman in front of her. Watching Beatrice turn, take Ben's hand, and walk out the door gutted her. After a few breaths of silence, the five remaining glanced around at each other, not sure about the next steps.

***

"Okay, I've got to ask." Dani lathered their hands at the sink, eyes focused on Stella's reflection in the bathroom mirror. "How did you fall in love with a tree, anyway?"

Forest, I am going to kill you.

Stella opened her mouth, hoping some quick retort would find its way to her tongue, but then closed it and shook her head. What was there to say?

Shaking their hands off, then wiping the remnants of water on their jeans, Dani continued, "I do my best to avoid those trees when I visit. Do they really have faces? Don't get me wrong, I believe Forest, but I'm getting a little..." A panicked look—one look Stella had never seen on Dani's face before—passed over their features. "Freaked out. He's insisting that I get to know them. What if they don't like me?"

"The trees?" Stella asked, suddenly unable to recall anything about any individual grandmother other than Beulah.

Dani's eyes widened, and she tilted her head and gave it a nod with an obvious "what else would I be talking about" gesture. Stella shrugged. "Or the Goddess...or..." Dani continued.

The urge to grab Dani by their shoulders, shake them, and growl "I don't care if they like you or not" roared through Stella, but she closed her eyes and swallowed it down.

"Listen. They love Forest, so you're safe."

"Thanks." Dani lifted her hands, then let them fall to her knees with a slap. "That's all I needed to hear."

The rest of the group loaded up on snacks while Stella filled the car with gas and washed the windows with a squeegee and dirty water. She offered to drive the rest of the trip since there was only an hour left until they made it to the rental place. Stella tuned the radio to a public station and listened to a storytelling podcast while the couples behind her chatted quietly.

After they returned the rental car, an Uber drove them the rest of the way, dropping them off at the diner across the street from their climbing place. Forest gave his mother a call, and they all gathered around so that they could see Beatrice's face. Unpracticed at using video chat, Beatrice shared several shots of the inside of her nostrils before positioning it so that her whole face was in view.

"Guess what?" she said as a huge smile stretched across her

face. "Ben is trying to push up the meeting so we can get home soon and stay on the mountain longer."

Stay longer? Is she planning on staying in New York forever?

"Yes!" Gwen shouted. "Where is he?"

"He's lying down. Fighting a headache."

A wave of jealousy cascaded over Stella. Everything was going to work out for Beatrice and Ben. For Dani and Forest. Gwen and Madeline. She stared up at the mountaintop and for a moment wondered if it made any sense for her to go up it.

"Stella?"

The sound of her name coming from Beatrice's mouth grabbed her attention.

"Hi," she said, looking back down at the phone.

"You okay?" Beatrice asked.

"Mmhmm. I am."

"Take a nice, long bath this evening. Eat one of Mother's biscuits."

Stella smiled because she knew it would make Beatrice feel better.

"Well, I guess we should get climbing," Madeline said, and everyone said their I-love-yous and crossed the street.

"What vision was Beatrice talking about before we left?" Stella asked, eyeing Madeline, whose face dropped at the question.

"Someone drowning under a waterfall. A hot waterfall." Madeline made eye contact, and Stella saw that same agitation the woman had when she faced Beatrice in the forest after twenty years of separation. "I really wish you had your visions still."

I wouldn't help you if I did...

"Okay," Gwen said as the group crossed the street. "I especially wish Beatrice was here now. She would give us a hand. Or a vine," she added with a chuckle.

"You'll be able to do it easily this time," Madeline reassured.

The crew hoisted their camping packs onto their backs and began the climb. Stella started followed by Madeline, Gwen, and Forest. Weeks of undernourishment left Stella lightheaded and weak. Madeline moved up to Stella's side.

"We're almost there. I promise. You can do this."

Stella closed her eyes and continued the climb. By the time they reached the top, Stella was shaky, and her palms were slick with sweat.

"Have some water," Gwen said and handed her a bottle. "Can I offer you something to eat?" She held out a banana, and Stella took it.

"Thank you." She managed four bites before she had to throw the fruit to the side. "I'm sorry I can't go any faster."

"Hey, it's okay," Gwen said. "We're all doing the best we can."

"How long did it take you?" Stella asked.

Gwen stared out into the woods. Her salt and pepper hair was pulled back in a low ponytail. She took her time, searching the branches on the trees for the words.

"I didn't shower or get out of bed except to use the bathroom for three or four weeks. Eating was hard for me those first weeks, too. When I finally made it out of my bedroom, the first thing I did was buy a yoga mat. I started practicing when I was eighteen, but I moved away from it. Landing on my mat for the first time after all those years—" Gwen looked down.

"I wish I had a coping mechanism like yoga."

"Ha," Gwen said, "it looked healthy from the outside, but it became all that I did. I isolated myself from Ben and dove into training program after training program. I opened the studio and dumped all my energy into my students." She shook her head as if to clear her thoughts. "Anyway," she said, "I didn't open my heart for ten years, but I'm so glad I did."

Stella stood. "I think I can make it the rest of the way." She wanted to get home. Nothing remained of Beulah but a small ring of rocks where Stella brought flowers and poured coffee and broke off pieces of chocolate, and though she couldn't even feel the woman's spirit, that spot meant the world to her, and she needed to tend to it again.

The group strolled through the woods. Madeline offered

Stella a piece of chocolate, and Stella ate the whole thing. Her heart felt more settled on top of the mountain, and she felt roots digging back in the closer they drew to home. Eventually, the company came to the Hedge.

"I hate this thing," Madeline said.

"It will move for us now," Forest reminded her, then walked to the wall greenery and pressed his hand against the foliage. An opening formed, and they all walked through. Just on the other side of the Hedge stood the circle of ancestral trees.

"Something's wrong," Madeline said as she looked up toward the branches.

Stella took in the sight of the darkened bark and the sap weeping from holes in the trunks. The silence confirmed unspoken fears.

"They're dead," Forest said, his hands touching tree after tree.

"How could they be dead?" Madeline asked, circling around, investigating roots and bark and branches. She turned quickly toward Gwen. "Do you see any of their spirits?"

"No, Maddie."

"Let's get to the house," Forest said and walked ahead. Everyone breathed a sigh of relief to see the homestead standing, but a rustling in the woods quickly gained their attention. The trees seemed to move aside for the black bear that came bounding toward them. Forest dropped his pack to the ground immediately.

"Arcas," he whispered under his breath, and then shouted the name loudly, running toward the bear.

"That can't be him," Madeline said and ran toward the scene.

The bear knocked Forest to the ground and nuzzled his nose into his neck. Madeline and Gwen slowed as they moved closer, and Stella followed behind, unable to keep up. The bear was indeed Arcas. Forest stood and scratched him behind both ears; Arcas grunted and gnashed his teeth.

"I can't imagine the story you would tell, buddy," Forest said. Then he directed his gaze toward his grandmother. "How?"

"I don't know." Madeline shook her head and drew her hand to her mouth for a moment. "But the trees are dead, and a bear buried three months ago is alive." Madeline scanned the sky, the landscape, the ground. "Someone's here," she said. "Someone did this. And we need to find who it is. Gwen, come with me. We'll handle the perimeter to the east and search the greenhouse."

"We'll search the rest of the perimeter and the Rock," Forest said, eyes darting to Dani, then back to Stella. "Stella, can you look through the buildings?"

"I don't know that any of us should be alone," Gwen said.

"I'll be okay," Stella replied and moved toward the house.

Nothing was out of place in the kitchen, and the living room seemed left exactly as they had left it. Beatrice's bedroom, as well as Forest's and Madeline's, showed no display of disruption. Stella's heart pounded as she approached her own room. She could sense a presence on the other side. She opened the door to find nothing but a small stack of papers clearly torn from a journal resting on the left side pillow of her bed, and Sasha, who rattled her tail and zipped toward Stella.

"I've missed you, too, Sasha." In the same way Madeline had surveyed the homestead, Sasha took in Stella, sniffing and rubbing, wrapping her body around an arm, then a leg, then her waist as if to make sure Stella had been eating.

"Did I pass the test?" Stella asked as Sasha finished and wrapped herself around her neck.

Stella leaned down for the papers on the bed, brought them toward her, and surveyed the handwriting. Her breath stopped. Beulah. Stella didn't stop to read the words, nor did she try to find the others to tell them what she found.

She scurried out of the house and went from building to building, praying she would find Beulah first. The dairy shed and the smokehouse were both empty. Then she turned her attention toward the bathhouse. A pulling stemmed from a place in Stella deeper than her bones and it urged her toward the door, which she knocked on gently.

She heard someone slipping out of the bathtub, followed by the patter of feet on the floor. The door opened slightly, and she stepped through.

CHAPTER 7

Beulah

It was a foolish decision to breathe on the trees and leave them dead for an extended period, but Beulah and Ola needed privacy for another long, exhausting conversation. By the time she finished sharing all her worries with her mother, she had no energy to revive her family. Their stillness peeled the charms from the house, leaving the bathwater water tepid and oil lamps dimmed.

At least now I know what happens to the house when they're all gone.

Beulah dunked her head back into the water one last time before stepping out of the tub. She stood naked and shivering, her eyes wet and puffy from the time she had spent crying with her mother, when the door cracked and Stella entered. Terror that Stella had seen the dead trees gripped Beulah and prevented her from taking a step forward or even thinking about the kiss the woman had promised.

Stella didn't seem afraid, though; instead, her eyebrows furrowed with concern. She closed and locked the door behind her, then moved closer and closer to Beulah until her jacket pressed against her breasts. Time stretched as Stella's breath mingled with her own, and an intense craving for touch—one she'd never felt before—created an ache in Beulah's womb.

"Beulah," Stella whispered, bringing a warm hand to Beulah's face. "It worked." The woman's fingers trembled with excitement. "Why are you so cold?"

"I—I," Beulah stammered, her body shaking.

"Here." Stella turned, searched for Beulah's clothes and, seeing none, grabbed a robe and slid it onto her, one arm at a time. "It's too cold in here. Let's get you into the house."

"Wait." Beulah, hoping the woman remembered her promise, slid her hands around Stella's waist.

"Do you still want me to kiss you?" Stella lifted Beulah's chin and tilted her own head down.

Beulah nodded, her chest warming while other parts tingled, but her mind wandered back to the trees and what Stella would think of her. The worries dissolved and her skin turned to gooseflesh as Stella pressed gentle lips against her own. She didn't stop at one, thank the Goddess, but continued to massage Beulah's mouth, ending with a lick of her upper lip.

Stella's mouth slid into a smile. "Did that warm you up a bit?"

"Yes," Beulah replied. Her body buzzed. The bind she'd woven around the one she beckoned to the mountain with the incantation she'd written years ago locked more firmly into place. She released a sigh. *I have to tell you eventually, but not yet.* "Is everyone here?" she asked.

Stella's gaze dropped to the floor as she shook her head. "No," she said. "Beatrice stayed in New York to be with Ben, Gwen's brother. Gwen is Madeline's wife."

"The trees told me about Gwen and Ben." Beulah's eyebrows scrunched, and nausea sloshed in her belly. *I need Beatrice here.* "Why did she stay?"

"The same reason I gave you liters of my blood." Stella kissed Beulah's cheek. "She loves him."

Oh Stella, you may think you love me, but you don't.

Stella stepped back and her eyes roamed over Beulah's robed body. "It worked. I can't believe it worked." Her eyes brimmed with tears, and she sniffled, wiping the saline fluid away. Now the woman appeared exhausted in a way that only comes after an adrenaline crash. She pulled Beulah into a tight embrace and released a sob.

"I'm here, Stella. It's okay. I'm here."

Stella moved to open the door, and cold panic flashed down Beulah's body. She wanted to cry out "wait!" and somehow convince Stella to stay in the bathhouse while she breathed the trees back to life, but her mouth couldn't form the words.

"Come on." Stella tugged Beulah's hand. "Let's get you warm."

As they exited, Beulah heard several voices call Stella's name, but the woman didn't respond. Instead, she led Beulah back into her bedroom and helped her into pajamas.

"Beulah," Stella said, sitting on the edge of the bed, "what happened to the trees? And how is Arcas alive?"

Beulah swallowed.

How do I explain?

"I have a gift." Beulah chose not to qualify it as new or old. She lowered herself to her knees and peered up into Stella's face. It seemed right to make herself small before delivering the truth about her power to breathe life and death. Closing her eyes, she prayed Stella wouldn't be too frightened. "Powerful and terrible."

Stella narrowed her eyes. "What is it?"

"I—"

The two started at the sound of the front door opening and voices calling for Stella.

"Do you want to tell me before they bang the door down?"

"I can breathe life and death into things." Stella's eyes widened, so Beulah continued, "I'll show you. I'll show everyone."

"Want me to go out first?" Stella offered. "Prepare them a bit?"

Inhaling her shoulders in a shrug, then releasing a sigh, Beulah shook her head. "I don't know the best thing to do."

An urgent knock on the door followed by Madeline's voice decided for them. Beulah's daughter twisted frantically at the locked door. "Are you in there?"

"Coming." Stella turned toward Beulah. "She and I aren't in a great place."

"Why?"

"Because she burned you to the ground." The bitter words ground through Stella's tight jaw, and in the woman's eyes, Beulah caught the flash of fierce protectiveness.

"I told her to do that. I needed to be warm. And I thought perhaps it would help the process."

Beulah couldn't bring herself to use the word spell. Though she had no personal biases toward the idea of witchcraft practiced by the folks off the mountain, she knew Beatrice did, so she tucked the word inside. Stella's jaw tensed and released before she opened the door.

"Where have you been, Stella?" Madeline gave Stella's shoulders a gentle shake. "We've been looking all over for you."

Stella dipped her chin toward Beulah. Madeline's eyes tracked the motion, and when they came to her mother, her hands fell to her sides and her eyes expanded. Emotions too many to list flooded Beulah's system and weighed her legs to a heavy stillness despite her desire to propel herself toward her daughter. Neither woman spoke. In the background, voices still shouted for Stella, who turned and told Madeline, "It worked. I'm going to give you two a minute. Coming!" she called as she scooted out the door.

A sense of abandonment threatened to overwhelm Beulah, but she closed her eyes and drew her strength back from the talons anxiety.

Walk, Beulah. You're the mother. Walk to your daughter.

Opening her eyes and forcing her lips into a smile, Beulah strode to her daughter and gathered her trembling hands into her own. She studied every line around Madeline's eyes. Tears welled but didn't spill over. Then she ran her hand over the thick white braid that draped over Madeline's shoulder, and her smile became easier.

"At seventy," Madeline finally croaked, "you should have more wrinkles than me."

Beulah laughed, and her shoulders released from her ears. She lifted to her tiptoes and opened her arms for a hug. Madeline obliged, but Beulah could feel the tension in her daughter's body.

"How did you do this?"

"Blood and sheer will, I suppose."

"Your hair." Staying in the hug, Madeline touched the ends. "It's so short."

"I was in the ground for six months. All sorts of things were…" Beulah shuddered. "It had to go. The trees helped me."

"What happened to the trees? Are they gone?" Madeline released the wrap around Beulah's shoulders but kept her hands around her biceps. The question didn't seem an accusation. Beulah responded with a smile and a shake of her head. "And Arcas. How?" Madeline continued. "Did the Goddess come?"

Beulah held in the scoff that rose to her throat. Her mind whirred with the illusions she could spin, the lies she could tell to keep from revealing her gift to Madeline.

They'll be so scared of me if they know.

The power Beulah wielded tethered her to silence, frozen to a spot in the bedroom, the terror closing her throat. She cursed herself for telling Stella so quickly. She hadn't known the woman for long, after all. She recalled the words of her incantation. Words she hadn't yet shared with Stella. Words that bound the woman to her but didn't ensure trust. She thought of Ola, who had lied on her behalf for years.

Is Mother right? Am I wiser now? My temper subdued?

Staring into her daughter's face, which grew more impatient the longer Beulah took to answer, she thought of all the times she kept from hurting the baby who grew into a child, then into the woman who stood in front of her. Scars along Beulah's arms and legs told the story.

Even if I can't trust myself, I can trust Mother to help me. Damn it Beulah, you are the mother!

"It'll be easier to show you than to tell you."

Madeline pulled from Beulah's arms. "Show me now."

"Can't you introduce me to everyone else first?"

Beulah thought she saw Madeline's eyes travel to her forearms and scrutinize for a moment. She had the urge to rub them or tuck them across her body, but knowing that would only draw more attention, she focused all her energy to the surface of her skin to smooth the raised ridges of flesh and smiled. Madeline's silence held the quality of distrust, and Beulah couldn't take it.

"Come on. Introduce me! I'll show everyone at the same time."

Madeline hesitated before turning and leading Beulah down the hall to the kitchen. Forest was the first to greet her. He stood still initially, his eyes wide and his mouth parted in an open grin. Then, with two quick, large steps, he scooped Beulah up in his arms and spun her around.

"Great-grandmother!"

"Hi, Grandson. Call me Beulah. Great-grandmother is a mouthful." When Forest eased her back to the ground, his face grew serious, and his brows knitted together. "You look so much like your mother when you make that face," Beulah said, placing her hand on his cheek.

He scanned her through squinted eyes. "How are you so young? You look Mother's age."

"I suppose it's magic, Forest."

Forest laughed, then grew somber again. "Do you know how Arcas—?"

"Yes. I'll show you. Now, introduce me." Beulah gestured to Dani, who swallowed and took a step forward.

"I'm Dani," they said. "I'm Forest's…" Dani glanced at Forest, then back toward Beulah. "Partner."

Beulah's eyes traveled to Forest, whose cheeks flushed.

"It's nice to meet you."

Until today, the opportunity to say those words had only presented itself when Stella arrived on the mountain, and the thrill of meeting new people made her heart beat wildly in her chest—from excitement or panic, Beulah wasn't sure.

"And I'm Gwen." A woman significantly shorter than Madeline stepped forward with open arms. "I'm a hugger."

Gwen embraced her tightly, and Beulah wondered what the first meeting between her and Beatrice must have been like. Beulah released herself, took a step back, and surveyed the group before her.

"I wish Beatrice were here," she said, and the whole group nodded and voiced agreements. A stinging behind Beulah's eyes prompted her to squeeze them tight. She couldn't waste energy on tears. "Alright, let me show you."

***

Beulah donned her coat and led the others across the clearing to the trees, where Ola's eyes opened.

"Ola," Madeline grumbled and crossed her arms. "Your eyes weren't open when we first got here."

"Madeline." Ola gave a smirk. "It's good to see you again."

The interaction made Beulah's insides squirm. What happened between the two of them while she was underground?

Madeline seems to have made enemies with both Stella and Mother.

"And who is this?" Ola's roots ripped from the ground and moved toward Dani, who stiffened.

"Don't you dare." Madeline stepped between the tree and Dani.

"Oh, now, Madeline," Ola chided. "She'll be just fine."

"They'll be fine," Forest corrected.

"Forest, I'm more worried about those..." Dani jutted her finger at Ola's roots. "...than what pronouns she's using at the moment."

For a second time, Beulah watched her mother shrug her branches. The act the tree was playing tickled her a little, but she suppressed the giggle that threatened to bubble up. Ola pressed Madeline aside and reached Dani, wrapping their legs, waist, and arms in vines.

"Don't turn them upside down, Ola," Forest said.

The tree did the opposite of Forest's request, tipping Dani's head toward the ground and bringing her eyes to meet their own. Dani released a squeak. "I promise I won't shake you like I did Madeline."

"What?" Beulah whipped her head toward her daughter.

"Oh, yes," Madeline grunted as she pressed against the root that pinned her against another tree. "I got a good shaking and a good mouthful the last time I was here."

"Tell me one interesting thing about yourself, Dani." Sincerity warmed Ola's voice, but Dani hung speechless in the air. "Or maybe I will shake you!"

"I'm a witch!" Dani shouted.

"Very good," Ola said and returned Dani upright.

Once on the ground, they scurried to Forest, who wrapped a protective arm around them. "I'm sorry," he whispered to them. "Are you okay?"

"Yes."

"Go on, then, Beulah. Show them your new gift."

The way Ola sneered the word *gift* almost convinced Beulah that the resentment her mother displayed was real. She swallowed and moved to Alice first, breathing gently on the bark. Deep brown eyes opened lazily, and Alice smiled.

"Did you have a good talk with your mother, Beulah? Is she being kind to you?" Alice's eyes traveled from Beulah and scanned the rest of the faces. "Oh! You're all home!"

"Well, Beatrice stayed in New York with my brother Ben," Gwen answered.

"New York?" The tone of Alice's voice bordered on disdain. "Why?"

"Because she loves him."

"Oh my," Alice said. "Beatrice in love."

"She hasn't talked about him?" Gwen asked.

"Of course, but I didn't realize she was this far gone."

Beulah glanced at Stella, whose lips quirked.

"Wake them up now, Beulah," Alice encouraged.

She moved from tree to tree, rousing them again. Some voiced continued frustrations while others did their best to yawn off the sleep, wooden faces creaking with the effort.

"I don't understand," Forest said, his jaw tight and expression pinched.

"I can breathe life into things," Beulah explained. "And death."

"Arcas." Forest whispered the name into the chilly afternoon air.

Gwen, Madeline, and Dani exchanged glances. For a few moments, only the sounds of a crow's caw and Arcas's snorts echoed through the forest.

The unease that flowed from everyone except Stella caused Beulah to shiver. "Are you upset with me?"

Forest took a while to answer, but a shake of his head relieved the tension in Beulah's chest. "No. Of course not."

"I'm tuckered out." Beulah glanced from face to face. "I could use a rest. Madeline…" Madeline didn't turn toward Beulah, rather, she her eyes panned up and down the trees, scrutinizing them. "Will you make a pan of biscuits?"

Madeline stepped backward from the trees and settled her gaze on her mother's. "Of course, Mama."

***

Taking Beulah's hand, Stella led her into the house and back to her bedroom, then she turned, locked the door, and moved closer.

"How tired are you, Beulah?"

Something in the timbre of Stella's voice caused Beulah's center to clench, and a shiver ran down her spine. Saying nothing, Stella kissed Beulah on the lips, then brought the soft, warm pillows down one side of her neck and then the other. Muscles tensed even more as Stella slid her hands underneath the bottom of Beulah's shirt and her breath released in a shudder.

"Oh," Stella said, pulling back. "I'm sorry. I shouldn't have done that. This is too fast." Her face revealed both guilt and embarrassment.

Adorable.

"No, I…" Beulah swallowed. "It felt nice. I'll tell you if I want you to stop."

She pulled Stella's hands back to her shirttail, then lifted her arms overhead. As soon as the garment was off her body Beulah, working to keep her eyes soft, surveyed her own skin. A few of the scars were visible, but Beulah could explain them away as part of mountain life.

Stella bent down and made circles around Beulah's perked nipples with her hot tongue one at a time. A feeling Beulah could only assume was pleasure rolled in waves down her body as Stella moved to a flicking motion.

"Oh," she whispered, and her head tilted back. More moans came as Stella suckled, circling her hands around Beulah's bottom, and pressing her closer. Her tongue and teeth moved up Beulah's collarbone and to her neck again.

No. Go back. Please don't stop.

Beulah couldn't speak. Stella encouraged her pants off as well as her panties. Beulah took a moment to scan her legs and found only one scar visible on her right shin. This one came from a fall, not her own doing. Stella encouraged Beulah to sit on the edge of the bed, then cradled her calf in her hands, placing soft kisses along the scar. The action brought a burning to Beulah's eyes, and she put a hand over her mouth to stifle a sob.

"I want to make love to you, Beulah," Stella said, looking up. "Do you know what that means?"

Beatrice had come to her once with a book she'd acquired from the farmer's market. It was a biology textbook, complete with graphics and diagrams. "I know how they did it!" she had said, holding a squirming eighteen-month-old Forest in her arms. She pointed out all the reproductive organs and described the process of sex. "That's how they made Gertrude!" But was that lovemaking?

"I don't know," Beulah replied with her most honest answer.

"Ahh." Stella hung her head, and Beulah could feel her disappointment.

"I didn't say no, Stella."

"I know," Stella said, nodding. "But I want you to be comfortable and enthusiastic." Her lips stretched into a grin.

"What you were doing felt very good." Something about this admission brought a wetness in between Beulah's thighs. "What else are you wanting to do?"

"Do you want me to explain it or start and you just tell me when to stop?"

"Explain it, I think."

Stella smiled again and started detailing her intentions for Beulah's body. Listening to the plan only made Beulah more confused until finally she pressed a finger to Stella's lips.

"Maybe you should just...do it."

Stella laughed aloud, a mature, ancient sound of someone who knew loss. Her soul had aged while Beulah was tucked in the earth, and now, they seemed equals. The sharing of blood had mixed the essence of each woman into a powerful concoction that flowed through each of them.

Stella pressed her hands against the insides of Beulah's knees, encouraging her legs to open wide. Then she kissed the inside of her thighs, working her way up.

"That feels so good."

Beulah tilted her head, furrowed her brow, and watched curiously as Stella moved the fleshy sides of her center away, then pressed her tongue firmly in between. The hot wetness returned, and Beulah's tremble grew into an uncontrollable shaking as she rocked her hips against Stella's tongue. Just as she had with Beulah's nipples, Stella changed the pattern from circling to flicks and Beulah cried out. She grasped Stella's head with both hands and pushed her hard against her flesh, hips grinding, until an intense clenching brought her legs tightly against the woman's temples and a wail to her own lips. She released her hold and flopped back on the bed as the quaking aftershocks continued to pulsate.

"Beulah." Stella's voice had changed. Something solemn had replaced the warm seduction. Something was wrong.

Beulah jerked up and found Stella eyeing scars on her legs. She searched every corner of her body —every cell—but she couldn't muster the energy to blur the scars. The pain of each time she took a knife to her skin to keep from hurting others flooded her eyes with tears. She covered her face with her hands, leaned forward, and sobbed. Stella stayed kneeling, pressing her forehead against Beulah's, and rubbing the tops of her thighs with her warm hands, but she didn't interrupt Beulah's expulsion of woe. Eventually, the tears stopped, Stella pulled back, and Beulah straightened. Every disfigurement lay bare on her skin.

"Do you want to tell me about it?" Stella asked. "You don't have to."

"No, Stella. I don't want you to know. I don't want any of you to know."

Stella pressed herself up, walked around to the other side of the bed, and crawled in.

"Come here," she whispered, and Beulah scooted close. "I have no idea what all you've been through, Beulah." Stella stroked strands of Beulah's hair, and as she spoke, her voice returned to the old, knowing warmth. "I'm looking forward to getting to know all sides of you."

Beulah tucked her head underneath Stella's chin. "I want to make you feel those things soon."

A throaty laugh made Beulah smile. "Soon," Stella said, then pressed a kiss to Beulah's head. "For now, let's rest."

CHAPTER 8

Madeline

Madeline sat down on the couch in front of the fire Edith had restarted once Beulah had woken her up again. The energetic flames danced within the fireplace, working desperately to warm the chilly house.

"Are you alright?" Gwen asked, sitting next to her and taking her hand.

Madeline managed to smile. "I'm not sure."

It was becoming easier to keep her voice calm and measured even when anxious. She attributed her newfound skill of presenting a calm demeanor in the face of chaos to the time she'd spent with her daughter, who was much better at regulating her emotions. Madeline wished Beatrice was here more than she could express.

"It worked," Gwen said, a grin spreading across her face. "What do you make of it?"

Madeline's smile fell. Conflicting emotions of guilt and regret, fear and unease, excitement and gratitude all twisted inside her like old spaghetti noodles that clung together in a sticky ball. More than fear pressed upon her. Dread. Mistrust. How? How had it worked? What kind of power revived the dead and breathed death into the living?

She closed her eyes, momentarily forgetting that the visions would come; when she felt the pounding of water atop her head, Madeline's eyes flew back open.

"Goddamn it." She balled her hands into fists and stood, pacing in front of the fire. She glanced down into Gwen's apologetic eyes. "I'm sorry. I just keep forgetting that every time I close my eyes for longer than a second, I see and feel drowning." Sitting back down and taking Gwen's hand once more, she attempted to sort through the feelings. "It's surreal." Her voice transitioned to a whisper, and she glanced around from face to face. "I feel like I should be happy—and I am—but—"

"It's terrifying." Dani entered the room, leaned against the wall, and crossed their arms. "It's too much power."

Forest followed and sat down at the hearth, gesturing for Dani to sit, but they refused.

Madeline had to agree with Dani. When she was a small child, her greatest fear was disappointing her mother, whose sad disposition Madeline felt it was her responsibility to remedy. Now, the power that returned Beulah back to her body and restored Arcas's bones and brought the trees to ruin—that was her greatest fear.

"Listen," Forest said, opening his hands to the rest of the room, "I know Great-grandmother. If there is anyone who can handle this gift, it's her."

Madeline nodded as though she agreed, then stood again and placed a hand on her belly. "Well, I'll make us something to eat."

"Want help?" Gwen asked.

"I need to think," Madeline said. "But thank you."

As she left the room, she heard Dani ask, "Ever heard the phrase 'absolute power corrupts absolutely?'"

She took a few deep breaths before starting the process of biscuit making, focusing on keeping her eyes open. Once her heartbeat regulated to a consistent rhythm, Madeline pulled flour, baking powder, baking soda and salt from the baker's cabinet and sat them on the counter. Then she tucked herself in her coat and made her way outside to the dairy shed, where the stream flowed so cold that slivers of ice clung to the edges. She pulled a container of buttermilk toward her, swirled it around to check the consistency, gave it a whiff, and grabbed the covered bowl of butter. She left the shed and stepped once more into the bright day, her gaze moved toward the trees, zeroing in on her grandmother.

What a piece of work...

The urge to stomp toward the tree and demand answers to her questions was overwhelming, but the rest of the trees would overhear. And she refused to risk her own mother waking to hear her share a conversation with Ola, the woman who had brought so much suffering.

Madeline wondered if anyone else had noticed the scars along her mother's forearm. Where had they come from? How long had they been there? She stared at the tree—who now stared right back at her—and tried to remember if she'd ever seen them before.

No. Never.

A slap of cold wind refocused Madeline's attention, and she turned back to the kitchen and the mission at hand: dinner. Once she had cut dough into discs and placed the raw biscuits into the oven, Madeline went about piecing together a vegetable soup. It was never her favorite, but it was Beatrice's, and she knew that if her daughter was here, that's exactly what she would cook for the family.

As she pulled a quart of home canned beans from the pantry, a memory came to her. She was three, and Beulah had given her chores to do around the kitchen, such as taking a bowl of beans from the counter to the table. Once, she dropped a bowl of new potatoes onto the kitchen floor where they mingled with scattered ceramic shards. Madeline, horrified at her accident, slunk back into her room and listened to her mother cry from the kitchen as she cleaned up the mess. It wasn't until Madeline was older that she understood why her mother had cried: Beulah struggled with both hunting and maintaining a garden. Food was never abundant. That night, when Beulah had come to retrieve her from her room, she whispered, "It's alright, Madeline. It was an accident. I cleaned them up and popped them back in the oven. I love you, and I'll always love you."

Then there was the time Madeline strayed farther into the woods than Beulah allowed, all the way to the edge of the Rock. When she found her, she had grabbed Madeline's wrist, ran her through the woods, and growled threats as their feet pounded the forest floor. Madeline remembered slamming the door to her room and crying into her pillow. But once again, her mother came to her and said, "I love you, and I will always love you."

Madeline hadn't noticed that she had frozen in place with a jar of beans in hand, eyes blurring.

"Grandmother," Forest said. "Are you sure I can't help you?"

"Oh," Madeline said, giving her head a shake. "Sure. Is vegetable soup okay?"

Forest's lips curled. "It's just what mother would make. Besides, we have two vegetarians to take care of now. How can I help?"

"Here," Madeline said, handing her grandson the jar. "You can be the official jar opener." Then she turned and pulled jars of carrots, pearl onions, tomatoes, and peas, along with fresh onions and potatoes from the cupboard.

"You know," Forest said, removing lids as Madeline handed him jars, "my biggest question is why the Goddess gave her such a powerful gift. And why now?"

Madeline filled her belly with air, held it for a moment, then released it through her mouth as she dumped tomatoes into the pot. "You think it's new?" she asked as she focused on stirring the vegetables together.

"Ola said 'show them your new gift.' You think she's lying?" Forest asked, his hands paused on the lid of a jar of peas.

Madeline lifted her eyes to meet his, and for a moment, it wasn't her grandson, but her daughter standing before her. She searched his eyes as if she could measure his trustworthiness within them. After glancing behind each of her shoulders, Madeline lowered her voice.

"I saw something that..." She swallowed. "She had scars on her arms that I've never seen before. Did you notice?"

"No," Forest said, handing her the last jar. "I didn't. You know, we're family, but each one of us, individually, has their own thing...their own..." Forest ran his fingers through his hair. "I hate to call it a burden, but we all have one... heavy, lonely thing we carry with us, and—"

"It's not just your family." Gwen's voice entered the room, and Madeline turned to see her love stepping toward the stove. "That's the way we all move through our lives. Of course, we can help each another, but only if we're willing to share."

Forest's throat bobbed and he nodded. "Ask her about them," he said to Madeline. "Let her share it with you."

"Ask who about what?" Gwen asked.

Madeline looked down at her and shook her head. "I need time with it, okay?"

Gwen pressed her lips together and nodded, then moved to the cabinets and began quietly setting the table.

"I can take it from here," Madeline told Forest and went about making Beatrice's favorite meal.

***

Madeline's breath caught in her throat when Beulah entered the kitchen. Even though her frontal lobe understood that her mother was back, and even though her arms had hugged the woman an hour ago, watching those bright blue eyes crinkle as she smiled stilled every one of Madeline's systems.

"Smells wonderful," Beulah said, standing behind a kitchen

chair.

"Vegetable soup. Bea's favorite." Madeline wiped her hands on her apron, then removed it.

Forest took position at the head of the table, and Dani stood next to him. Once the group circled, Beulah drew in a breath and sighed it out. "Well then, Madeline, are you going to—"

"I'll do it," Forest interjected. Then he smirked. "I'm not sure either of you knows how to do it correctly."

"Hey! I've heard Beatrice do it," Madeline replied, and Gwen added, "Me too!"

Madeline's shoulders slumped, and she dipped her chin. She watched Forest close his eyes and everyone else follow his lead. Keeping her own eyes open served two purposes: she could witness her grandson's devotion and keep the visions at bay.

"Great Goddess of the Woods, thank you for creating this family. You have blessed us from one generation to the next."

Noticing a shift in her mother's posture, Madeline's eyes moved in her direction. Beulah frowned and shook her head.

She doesn't feel blessed by the Goddess?

"Thank you, Imogene, the weaver, for creating fabric from thread and stories from words," Forest continued. "Thank you, Ida, for showing us how to heal with plants."

Madeline kept her eyes on her mother as Forest continued the prayer. A tear slipped down the woman's cheek when he mentioned Ola, and flew open when he said, "Thank you, Great-grandmother, for breathing life back into Arcas. Thank you, Grandmother, for your healing and saving us with your fire."

She and her mother locked eyes, each of them bewildered. Choking on his words, Forest offered the last bit of gratitude for his mother. "And thank you, Mother, for feeding us." Forest opened his eyes, the rims of them glistening with tears, and gave the instruction to eat.

"You added that last part," Madeline said, waiting for her grandson to sit before sitting herself.

"Is it alright?" Forest asked, but the grin, the same that

appeared on Beatrice's face so often, contradicted his need for approval.

"Of course it is," Beulah answered, dabbing at her eyes with a cloth napkin. "I wish she was here to hear it." She reached for a biscuit with a ravenous gleam in her eye. "I haven't had one of these in thirty-five years."

Madeline blushed despite herself as she watched her mother peel open the biscuit, slather it with butter, and take a large bite, humming as she chewed. She glanced at a visible sliver of her mother's forearm to find that no scars were present.

"We can call her tomorrow, Mama. Cell service in town is much stronger."

Beulah swallowed her biscuit and took a long drink of water. "I would like that."

"Great-grandmother—"

"Forest, call me Beulah."

"Beulah...You were in the ground so long. What did it feel like?"

Beulah's face fell and clouded over with the ghost of a painful memory. "Claustrophobic and cold for a long time."

Madeline recalled the night she went into labor with Beatrice, and the look of panic on her mother's face as the baby came.

Forest took in Beulah's answer and nodded slowly, his eyes drifting down to the table.

"How long have you been...back?" Dani asked before taking a spoonful of soup.

"Not long," Beulah answered, dipping a bite of biscuit into the steaming bowl. "A few days."

"When did you realize you had your gift?" Gwen asked, and everyone stopped eating and turned their attention toward Beulah.

"Well, I spent the whole first day talking with the trees and the second one resting. The next day, I woke up with a little more energy. I was tidying up a bit, and I blew a spider out of the corner right over there by the window."

All eyes followed the direction of Beulah's pointed finger, except for Madeline's. She watched the woman bite her lower lip the way she always did when she was nervous.

"Then I started practicing on other things. It is exhausting."

Dani's face had lost its color, and they sat staring at Beulah, stirring their soup mindlessly.

"Are you alright?" Madeline asked them, and they took a deep breath.

They nodded, but their eyes focused on some distant place, and their hand made absentminded swirls around her bowl.

"Well, you get to see all sorts of things on top of this mountain," Madeline said, doing her best to lighten her own mood. "Mama, what all did you practice on?"

"Every category of living thing I could find." Beulah took a bite of biscuit.

Madeline's mind went to her grandmothers. "Did the trees give you permission to—?"

"You heard Alice, Madeline." Beulah's gaze grew hard, and Madeline felt the chill of the reprimand slice through her. "It's the only way I can speak with my mother privately."

"So they gave you permission?" Gwen asked Madeline's question again with a reassuring squeeze to her thigh.

"Some of them don't like the way it feels, but yes, this morning they gave me permission."

"What did you and Ola talk about?" Madeline asked.

Beulah's chest heaved as her breathing intensified. "That is between me and my mother."

"I'm sorry." Madeline took a drink of water, then cleared her throat. "Have you seen Beatrice's greenhouse?"

Beulah shook her head. "No. You know me, Madeline. I stay close to the cabins."

Beulah spoke the truth. Fear kept her in place, and she guarded Madeline like a bear with her cub.

"I'll take you after dinner." Madeline smiled at her mother, then glanced over to Stella, who was eating more than she had in weeks. "Your appetite is back," she said.

Stella wiped her mouth, then smiled. "One hundred percent back." After taking a drink of water, she looked back up at Madeline. "I owe you an apology." She paused, her gaze traveling to the table. "The grief was greater than I'd ever experienced. I'm sorry I thought the worst about you."

Beatrice's words echoed in Madeline's mind: *you believed the worst possible thing about me.* Perhaps if she'd known Stella longer, the woman's lack of faith in her would have cut Madeline deeper.

"Thank you." Madeline fought the urge to reach across the table and take the woman's hand. "We don't know each other well, but I promise you, I would never intentionally hurt my family."

"Somehow," Beulah chimed in, beaming, "I knew I needed fire." *You told me you wanted to be warm.*

"So, was it the spell or was it your power that brought you back?" Dani asked.

Madeline noticed Dani had eaten little of their meal. They were anxious, yes, but there was something more in Dani's distrustful gaze. All eyes turned once more to Beulah, whose face flushed pink.

"I wish I knew," she said, her spoon hovering over her soup.

The six of them finished their lunch in a silent room. Occasionally, Gwen reached down to give Madeline's thigh a pat or a rub, a reminder that she had a constant in her life. When all the plates were empty, Madeline amazed a pale-faced Dani with her skill of telepathy by encouraging the dishes to clean themselves. Forest and Dani made their way back to their now-shared bedroom, but Beulah lagged.

"Shall we go?" Beulah drew Madeline's hands close, the skin of them warm and so very alive.

"Alright."

And the two of them slipped into their coats and began their walk through the woods.

"I want to know everything," Beulah said, taking Madeline's hand once more. Perhaps the gesture should have felt comforting, but Madeline's palm only grew clammier as the two of them walked.

"So do I," Madeline responded, looking down into those blue eyes.

"Well," Beulah said, turning her gaze forward and lifting her chin, "which one of us should go first?"

The situation reminded Madeline so much of the time she and Beatrice took that first walk in the woods, reunited after so many years.

"You are the mother."

Releasing her bind around her daughter, Beulah sighed. "I hated being a tree, Madeline. The stillness." Her eyes roved the trees around them as they passed. "The quiet. Being so close to my mother. And I never—"

"What did she do to you?" Madeline's voice came out louder than intended.

Her mother's jaw tensed, and her gaze moved toward the ground. "I was a rambunctious child." She swallowed deeply. "Mother was very firm with me." That seemed to be all she wanted to share, but Madeline needed to know more.

"I saw scars on your arms," she said. "Did she do that to you?"

At this, Beulah looked up, her eyebrows drawn together, then she pulled the arms of her sweater up, rotating her forearms.

"I only have this one," she said, pointing to a raised scar along the top of her hand. "An accident while I was butchering a rabbit."

Madeline questioned what she saw with her own eyes. She could smell fear and deceit, metallic, sulfuric, like blood. Was she seeing things? Or were the scars perhaps a vision, something coming for her mother in the future?

"No," Beulah said. "My mother never cut me. When I was having what she would call a 'fit,' she would use her strength and bind me to a chair until I calmed down. No food. No water.

No bathroom.”

Madeline stopped walking, her eyes welling up with tears. There were no words she could give her mother, so instead, she opened her arms and tucked the shorter woman within them.

“I’m alright, now,” Beulah said, patting Madeline on the back. “And she and I have talked. She knows she was wrong.”

“How could you possibly forgive her for that?”

Beulah wiggled out of the hug. “I choose to believe that we all do the best that we can.”

Empathy replaced some of the unease Madeline felt toward her mother, so she took her hand again, squeezed it tightly, then led them to Beatrice’s greenhouse.

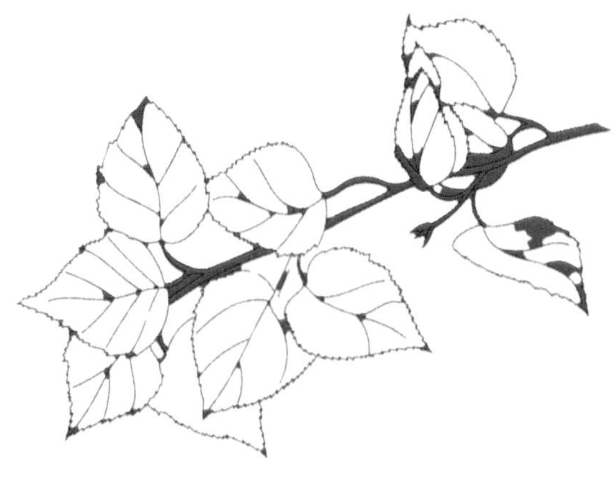

CHAPTER 9

Beulah

Each step away from the cabin—away from Stella—nibbled at Beulah's comfort. She worried that the strength of the tether she'd tied between them was too strong, even for her. Bea's greenhouse was more impressive than she could ever have imagined, but she struggled to focus on the abundance of it all instead of the gnawing suspicion that Madeline knew there was much more to her story.

We all do the best we can...

Beulah did believe that her mother and daughter and the rest of her family all strove to do the next right thing.

But what about me?

A grove of fruit trees offered perfect pears, apples, and cherries. Rows of corn and root vegetables, trellises of green beans, cabbage, lettuces, tomatoes, and peppers filled the space from end-to-end. Beulah understood why Beatrice rarely felt the need to can. She followed Madeline, who pulled a fresh sugar snap

98

pea from the vine, popped it in her mouth, then offered her one.

"Thank you." The crisp pea hull crunched under Beulah's bite, offering sweet, round fruit within. "Delicious."

"We should do some harvesting," Madeline said and led them to a stack of baskets nestled in the corner. "Maybe you could make an apple pie?"

"I'd love that," Beulah answered her daughter and strode back to the granny smith apple trees, pulling the fruit from the limbs and dropping them into the basket. The energy it took to keep her skin unblemished exhausted her, and she suspected that if she wanted to have enough left to make the pie, she'd have to locate a tighter shirt with longer sleeves. "Your turn," she said to her daughter. "The trees told me what happened between you and Beatrice, but I'd like to hear it from you."

Madeline grew still, and regret filling her eyes. Beulah stopped picking and squared her body with her daughter's. "I used fire against her."

Beulah's eyes grew wide at the mental image of Madeline attacking Beatrice with flames. "What? Why?"

"Can we sit?" Madeline asked, then positioned herself under the tree. "I'm surprised Stella didn't tell you right away. She's been so angry with me."

"Well, she didn't."

"I think it's best if I start at the beginning."

Madeline told Beulah stories about Eric and how Beatrice helped her give birth to Gertrude. She gave her account of the baby's illness and the night she left Beatrice on the mountain. Beulah's face flushed with the reminder of how Madeline had betrayed her, too, choosing the Goddess and a daughter over their plan to flee the mountain. Still, her heart seized as Madeline cried while she talked about Gertrude's body failing and finding Eric dead. Out of all the stories, his ending was one she understood.

Madeline listed the multiple trips she took to the mountain trying to get home. The letters she wrote to Beatrice. The violent Hedge.

A thread of guilt wove its way around Beulah's belly and through her chest, tightening her throat. She knew Madeline had made it up the mountain. One day, while sipping on Stella's blood, she saw Madeline struggling at the Hedge. She couldn't help her daughter through the barrier at that moment or tell Beatrice what she saw. Not when she was so close to finishing the spell.

It would have ruined everything.

Madeline didn't notice the flush of guilt on her mother's face, and she continued. The visions. The vines snaking down Gwen's throat. Fire sent to destroy Beatrice's green life. Beulah felt a desperate need to go back in time and prevent the moment from happening. *How could any relationship bounce back from that?* She sat and listened, her jaw slack.

"She's so strong," were Madeline's final, summarizing words.

"And she forgave you?" Beulah didn't intend for her words to come out so incredulous. She chastised herself for the thought. Of course Beatrice forgave.

"She has, I think. Or is in the process." Madeline smiled. "Like I said, she's so strong." She pressed herself up to stand and continued gathering fruit. "Can I tell you some good stories?"

"Yes, please," Beulah said.

Madeline recounted how she fell in love with Gwen, which only took Beulah's mind to Stella. Chill bumps erupted on her skin when Madeline spoke about holding Gertrude's eagle body for the first time, and she found herself missing the bird.

"Gertrude is in New York with Beatrice?" Beulah asked, trying to imagine the majestic creature flying among skyscrapers.

"Wouldn't leave her side," Madeline replied. "She even made the news a few times. She's so huge, and everyone loves an eagle. Anyway, we'll go to town tomorrow and call her. She needs to know it worked."

Beulah grinned at the idea of hearing her granddaughter's voice and seeing that beautiful, wise face. "I wish we could go today."

"It'll get dark on us. I've done it before but going up and down the mountain in the dark is not my favorite."

Beulah nodded, disappointed.

"What does the gift feel like when you use it?" Madeline asked.

Telling the truth here, in this moment, felt safe enough, but Beulah still hesitated. She opened her mouth to speak, then closed it, took a deep breath, and sighed it out. Finally, she cleared her throat.

"I hate it, and I wish it would go away," she confessed.

Madeline blew a laugh through her nose. "I understand that feeling," she said.

"You do?" The surprise of the statement stopped her mid-stride.

"I suppose the telekinesis and healing aren't so bad, and if I could get control of my temper, the fire could be useful." Madeline tilted her face toward Beulah. "I guess I got the anger from Ola."

No, definitely not. You got it from me.

Beulah had to pull her eyes away from Madeline's to keep herself from telling the truth—the truth that her mother was the most loving, fiercely protective person she knew.

"What about seeing the future?" she asked.

"It's the worst part," Madeline confessed. "I have a premonition haunting me right now. It's exhausting."

"Do you want to talk about it?"

"It's so confusing, Mama. Every time I close my eyes, I choke."

Beulah listened intently, unable to make sense of Madeline's vision as she described a viscous, hot waterfall and the feelings of drowning.

"There's nothing that gives you a sense of who is drowning?" she asked.

Madeline's eyes drifted downward. "I haven't told anyone this part. The victim's hair is brown."

Beulah considered who it could be. Beatrice. Dani. Forest. Gwen. Stella. Beulah shivered at the thought.

"What color hair does Ben have?" Beulah asked.

"Also brown," Madeline answered, then sighed and got back to work. "I have to keep my eyes open as I can. Trying to sleep is the worst."

"Have you ever asked the Goddess to take it away?"

Madeline paused and considered, eyeing the apple in her hand as if it held the answer. "No," she said, turning to Beulah. "It's how I've earned a living. I wouldn't have survived without it. Have you asked Her?"

"Yes. Over and over again." Beulah watched Madeline narrow her eyes and realized her mistake. "The moment I realized I had it," she added quickly.

Relief relaxed her shoulders as a look of understanding passed over Madeline's face.

"You didn't answer my earlier question. What does the breath feel like?"

Like cold water sloshing in my stomach. Like no power a human should ever hold.

"Too big. I don't really know how to describe it, Madeline."

"That's okay. I'm sorry to push."

Something in Madeline's tone betrayed her. She wasn't sorry for asking, and Beulah's half answer frustrated her.

"Let's change the subject," Beulah said.

The two harvested vegetables, fruits, and nuts, each filling their baskets to the brim, taking turns sharing stories as they made their way back through the forest. Before the cabins came into view, Madeline slowed, and Beulah followed pace.

"May I ask about Stella? What's happening between the two of you?"

Beulah's exterior hardened while her insides bristled just as they had done when Madeline asked about her relationship with Ola. She had had enough questioning. She wanted to tell her daughter to mind her own business, but she smiled and fluttered her gaze toward the ground.

"We're figuring it out. Her blood runs through my veins. We're bonded now."

"Please don't hurt her."

Beulah's expression grew flat and her gaze returned to Madeline.

"Please don't think the worst of me the way you did of Beatrice." Madeline winced at Beulah's words. "I will never hurt Stella."

CHAPTER 10

Stella

Stella watched Beulah take small bites of apple pie and sips of tea, and her face grew hot as she remembered the sounds the woman made when she came. Just as quickly, Stella recalled the ridges of scar tissue that appeared out of nowhere when Beulah lost control to orgasm, and her desire fled. She didn't know what to make of the scars, or of Beulah's immediate reluctance to discuss who or what slashed her skin open so many times. Of course, Stella's thoughts went straight to Ola, and she had half a mind to chop the tree down.

Stella knew that Beulah had been ready to take her that moment in the bathhouse, but a myriad of hesitations had prevented her from allowing it. The scars had certainly made her pause, but it wasn't the disfigurements that troubled Stella as much as the fear that Beulah wouldn't find her body beautiful.

Once everyone finished their pie and left Madeline to do the dishes, Beulah led Stella to the bedroom. She tugged at Stella's clothes with silent determination. Stella swallowed and looked away as Beulah pulled the sweater over her head. Tears fell from her eyes. Beulah turned her face to force contact, and Stella watched as the look in her eyes changed from compassionate to vanquishing.

"I see you, Stella."

"I want to see you, too, Beulah. Don't hide them."

Stella lifted the bottom of Beulah's shirt, but the woman stopped her, choosing to remove her clothing herself. All the scars Stella had seen before were present, and the desire to kiss each one brought her lips to Beulah's shoulder.

Beulah's fingers grazed down Stella's neck and arms, then down the center of her chest and abdomen, avoiding her breasts. Her fingertips brushed both of Stella's legs simultaneously, and she shivered. She laid Stella down on the bed then her inquisitive hands traced her frame once more, as if searching for the places on her body that brought her the most pleasure. Her collarbones. Her ribs. The inner part of her elbow. Her wrists and fingers. Her ankles and toes.

Beulah brought Stella's right foot toward her and rubbed the center. Then she drew Stella's big toe into her mouth. Without warning, she clinched the big toe hard between her teeth and Stella gave a yelp. Beulah passed over each toe, and though Stella stopped her whimpering, each bite brought a bit of a jolt to her body.

The woman took lips and then her tongue to Stella's ankles. Nibbles to the back of the knee brought less of a reaction, but the attention she gave to Stella's hip points brought moans, and she stayed for a long time. Stella released a grunt when Beulah bit the flesh over the ribs harder than she had any other point. Her teeth clinched so hard on the inside of Stella's elbows she brought blood to the surface. Like a shark attracted to the smell and taste of blood, Beulah sucked in the metallic liquid that had brought her to life again. She looked up at Stella with eyes that displayed desperation and determination all at once.

She opened Stella's legs and licked her groin, then moved her tongue to the fleshy parts of her center. Stella rocked her hips at the feeling, but Beulah pressed on them and gave Stella a firm look and a shake of the head.

"Be still," Beulah whispered.

"Have you ever done this before, Beulah?"

"No."

"How do you know what to do?"

"I'm following my desires. I can feel your heartbeat." Beulah paused to survey Stella's wrists. "The thrumming of your blood."

Stella swelled under Beulah's tongue, but she did not break the sacred stillness even though her body pleaded.

"You taste so good," Beulah breathed.

Stella's hips moved again, and Beulah pressed them forcefully, drawing another soft whimper. Stella rested her head against the headboard and allowed her legs to widen further. Beulah drew two fingers together and slid them into Stella's opening. She pressed more forcefully, and though Stella groaned over and over again, she followed orders to be still. Beulah kept up the motion but brought her thumb back to Stella's pleasure point. Faster. Faster with her fingers and faster with her thumb. Stella's body convulsed wildly, her thighs squeezing together and then releasing. Her chest heaved with deep breaths as she came down from the apex of their intimacy. Beulah lay her on Stella's chest and wrapped a scarred arm across her belly.

"Is it the breath? Is that how you make the scars go away?"

Beulah pressed herself up and glared with a hardness that took Stella aback.

Why did I ask that?

"You told me not to hide." Beulah's gaze turned empty. "Do they bother you now?"

"Of course not. They worry me." Stella took stock of her own courage and determined she trusted Beulah enough to ask this next question. "What are you hiding?" Beulah's body tensed and her nostrils flared. Stella smirked and added, "I mean, are you actually a seventy-year-old hiding under a cloak?" Beulah didn't smile back, and Stella's face fell. Her attempt at lightening the mood hadn't worked.

Beulah worked her way out of the bed, then stood, arms wide, for Stella to view. "This," she said, the corners of her eyes growing wet, "is me." The woman climbed upon Stella, straddling her, grasping her shoulders, and bringing her face close. "And you will tell no one what you saw." A choking sound creaked through Stella's throat as her eyes searched Beulah's. Her whole body trembled. "You know what I can do," Beulah breathed into Stella's ear.

And everything went black. At first, iciness enveloped Stella. Then, she was lost. Then, she was nothing. No color, no sound, no temperature existed because she wasn't there to perceive them. She thought nothing. This was a place beyond death, and for how long Beulah kept her there, Stella would never know.

Sucking in a deep breath, eyes squinting at the brightness of the candlelit room, Stella used all her strength to push Beulah off.

"I-I can't...I can't believe you did that to me," she stammered, hurrying to the other side of the room. "Wh-why would you do that to me?"

"I don't know if I can trust you not to tell them. It's important that you know what I'm capable of."

Stella's lip quivered as rejection and sadness replaced her fear. "Beulah, I care about you. You know that. I would never hurt you on purpose."

"I can't let you hurt me at all." Beulah's face changed, softened by exhaustion and regret. "I've asked the Goddess to take it away, Stella. She won't." She held her arms out, palms open and exposed by her side. "I need rest now."

"I don't feel safe with you." Stella shifted from one foot to the other, hands fisted by her side. Her clenched jaw ached, and she had to force her feet not to run to Madeline, the only person she thought could help her.

"There's no other bed, Stella." Beulah slipped herself between the sheets and rolled to her side. "Now, get in and let's go to sleep."

Stella stood for several minutes before crawling into bed, keeping to the edge to avoid touching Beulah.

She could kill me. She would kill me. She will kill me.

The words were an unwanted, violent mantra that took root in Stella's brain and blossomed into a headache. Sleep, a farce of an idea, refused to come. Hours had passed, by Stella's assumption, when a shudder came from the body beside her, followed by another. Beulah's choked breathing came in and out with stifled sounds. She was crying.

Stella turned toward her, and, in the moonlight, she could see Beulah covering her mouth with her hand, doing her best to silence her sobs. Though her body resisted, Stella's mind, heart, and soul forced it to move, nudging her closer and closer until she pressed against Beulah's back. The body stilled.

Stella wrapped her arm around Beulah's middle. No words passed between the two of them, and as Beulah's breathing regulated, so did Stella's, and the two found sleep.

***

Morning came. Stella woke to find Beulah sitting on the edge of the bed, so stone still that her breath didn't expand her ribs or cause her shoulders to rise and fall.

"I owe you an apology," she said finally. "I shouldn't have done that."

"Beulah, what made you so angry with me?"

Keeping her back to Stella, Beulah responded, "I was so tired, Stella. My nerves were raw. I couldn't handle your questioning me. Doubting me. I had to make you stop."

Words would have worked.

"I trusted you until that moment. But now..."

"I'm sorry." Beulah's voice rose with the repetition of the words.

"How do I know you won't do it again?"

Beulah turned and glanced over her shoulder. "You won't know. Only hope."

"Hope?" Stella's voice rose.

Turning to face the window again, Beulah replied, "I can't even trust myself."

Stella stood and fixed her eyes on the woman's back, remembering the time she spent with her. The times she lay within a nest of Beulah's roots, allowing the tree to drink her blood. The stories they shared. All the wisdom Beulah's tree-inhabited form possessed now seemed untethered from this human reincarnation, as if she had regressed from an elder to a teenager, unable to regulate her emotions. Then Stella's mind conjured the image of Madeline throwing flames toward Beatrice, vengeance in her eyes. Anger lived in these two women. Anger and fear. But so much more.

Circling the bed, Stella kneeled at Beulah's feet, looking up into the stolid face. "Do better than that, Beulah," she said through a tight jaw.

Beulah's eyebrows shot upward. "I don't know how."

"You and I both know that's bullshit." Beulah's face hardened at Stella's words, but she continued. "You have greater gifts than any member of your family, and you have to figure out how to use them." She held tightly to Beulah's legs and ran her thumb over one of the many scars on her calf. "And you don't need to hide your scars from us."

This time, Beulah's response was quick. "I don't think I could survive explaining them."

Stella shrugged, frustrated by Beulah's stubbornness. "Then don't." She used Beulah's legs to help her press up to stand, then turned to make her way out of the room. Before leaving, she told Beulah, "On the way down the mountain, you'll have to figure out what version of the story you want to tell your granddaughter." She knew the words weren't fair, but the woman had killed—no, erased—her from existence, for how long, she didn't know. A sharp tongue was the least she deserved.

The confident prick in Stella's voice was all a show, though. Fear still dominated most of her feelings about the woman she'd brought to life. The woman she'd taken to bed.

***

Breakfast lacked fresh biscuits, but no one complained. Stella found Madeline sitting at the table, her eyes rimmed with darkness brought by sleep deprivation.

"Sorry," Madeline whispered, rubbing her temples with her fingertips. "I just can't make them today."

"Makes for a quicker breakfast," Gwen said, giving Madeline a kiss on the top of the head. "Which means we can talk to Beatrice sooner."

"Do we have time for coffee?" Stella asked, though she moved to start water boiling and heaped coffee grinds into the French press without responses, glancing at Beulah, who sat across from Madeline now, squeezing her hands.

"Coffee is necessary," Dani said as they crossed the room, plopping down beside Madeline. Forest stood behind them and rubbed their shoulders.

"The visions are getting worse?" Beulah asked, and Madeline nodded. "I'm sorry."

Silence pervaded the space while the coffee steeped. Stella poured full mugs and passed them around, then sat in the only available seat next to Beulah.

"I'm nervous about going to town," Beulah confessed, any sign of earlier regret or anger gone.

"If Beatrice were here, it would be easier, that's for sure," Gwen said, taking a bite of an apple.

"We'll keep you safe," Stella said, because those were the words she was supposed to say, especially in front of the people who assumed she still worshiped Beulah.

Who am I kidding? I do still worship you.

Staring out the window at the brilliant sun, she took a sip of her coffee, then turned to Beulah, who hadn't touched her steaming cup. "Take a sip."

Beulah brought the coffee to her lips and took in the brew. A rosy warmth spread across her cheeks and her smile slipped into a grin. Stella knew that grin. Even when her cheeks were bark, Beulah's wide smile always took up her whole face.

"It's fantastic, Stella." When Beulah turned and met her gaze, Stella could see the woman's vulnerability, fear, and remorse, and if they could speak, she imagined those blue pools would say, *It's still me.* But nothing in Stella could believe it.

Once everyone finished eating and plans were solidified, Stella and Beulah returned to their room to change clothes for the trip down the mountain. They dressed in silence. Beulah put on a tight long-sleeved shirt.

"To cover the scars?" Stella asked

"Yes."

"How did you keep them from Madeline? Wear long sleeves all the time?"

"Mostly. I also made up stories about them."

Before joining the others, Beulah took Stella's hands.

"I *am* sorry, Stella." A wash of tears swelled in Beulah's eyes and trickled down her face. "I am..." She swallowed deeply. "...so scared."

"Learn to control the—"

"Yes, of course, but right now..." Beulah swiped her fingertips over her wet cheeks. "I'm terrified of going to town!"

Stella knew the innocent vulnerability in Beulah's voice was real. Amusement crept onto her face and into her throat, which released a small laugh.

"Don't laugh at me," Beulah grunted, but her lips curled up as well, her eyes glistening with tears and something else. Hope, perhaps? "Can you forgive me?"

"I don't know," Stella said. She wrapped her arms around Beulah's waist, pulled her close, and kissed her, confused by the physical manifestations of her mistrust and affection. "Did you knit us together with the spell?"

Beulah's eyes sparked with fear. Or was it anger?

"Yes." Beulah paused, then reached her hand up to touch Stella's cheek. "You are bound to me now."

Stella's skin crawled at Beulah's admission. "What does that mean? Does that mean you own me? That you control me?"

Beulah furrowed her brow. "I don't want to talk anymore. Not about the spell. Not about my scars. Don't ask me about them every again."

"That's not fair to me."

"Life isn't fair, Stella."

Stella pulled away and examined Beulah's face through narrowed eyes, trying to piece the puzzle together. In her gut, she knew that if Ola had been the one who scarred Beulah, she would share the information willingly. Not wanting to test Beulah's boundaries further, she wouldn't ask for the woman's story again nor about the invisible force that tangled their souls together. Instead, she would use the strengths that made her a good journalist, certain that the truth always made its way out.

Maybe Beatrice has a tea that could help me get my sight back. Then I can figure all of this out.

"I won't ask again," Stella whispered. "Just know this—I blew my entire life up for you."

CHAPTER 11

Beulah

Stella's sweaty, tentative hand confirmed Beulah's suspicions: she was still angry with her. Distrust had laced the kisses the woman gave her only a few minutes prior. But the invisible rope bound Stella to walk alongside her, and to hold her hand. Beulah did her best to hide her fear of leaving the mountain from the others and stirred up her powers of illusion, cloaking herself with confidence. When they reached the Hedge, sharp holly leaves and vines, gnarly as ever, she gave Stella's hand a squeeze.

"This is the farthest I've ever been," she whispered. "What if I don't want to go?"

Stella turned to face her, and what Beulah saw on her sweet face made her own hands clammy and sped up her heart. A fierceness eddied around something like compassion, and the strange combination of heat and kindness made Beulah want to take Stella to bed and bring her to the brink again.

"Beatrice deserves to know you're okay." Stella brought a hand to Beulah's face, and she leaned into the palm of the woman who fed her blood to bring her back to flesh. "And I think it will do you good to see her, too."

"Thank you, Stella." The words tiptoed out of Beulah's lips, and the confusion on Stella's face suggested she did not hear. She cleared her throat. "Will you hold me?"

Stella offered a hesitant smile, then tucked Beulah into a hug, pressing her cheek into her chest. Beulah breathed in the smell of her, and for a moment, felt free. She considered finding a way to release the bind just to see if the woman would stay, but she needed the assurance that these arms would always hold her.

"Hey! Come on, y'all," Dani called.

Beulah stiffened. For just a little longer, she wanted to stay enveloped within Stella's comforting embrace. As if she could read her mind, she tightened her arms around Beulah a little more.

"I believe in you, Beulah."

I hope you mean that.

Stella unwrapped her arms and gave Beulah a kiss, and though it was tender and sweet and gentle, the action sent electricity down Beulah's body to that place between her legs. "Will you make love to me again?" Beulah asked when Stella pulled away.

The response wasn't immediate, and when Stella finally spoke, a heavy solemness draped over her voice. "I need to know I can trust you with my body. Can I?"

Squeezing her eyes shut, Beulah allowed all the catastrophic thoughts she'd attempted to ward off to float to the top of her brain. She remembered all the ways she'd hurt her mother. She imagined how terrified and angry her family would be if they learned how long she's had the gifts. She envisioned killing everyone in a bout of anger.

They'll hate me. Then what?

"I think you're right," Beulah said, her eyes opening. "I need to see my granddaughter's face."

Beulah didn't expect Stella to take her hand again, but she did, and brought it to her lips one last time before they hurried to catch up with the other.

Chatter rose and fell amongst the group until they reached the rocky, flat face of the mountain. Beulah's eyes widened as she took in the vastness of it all. Though she had come to the edge a few days ago, she hadn't taken the time to scan the world below her. The road that hugged the mountain wound as far as Beulah could see in both directions. Across the street sat houses and buildings and on the other side of them, a river flowed, broad and healthy.

"Alright. I think a couple of us should go down, then you, Mama, then the rest," Madeline said. "That way, you have people above and below you to help you out."

Beulah looked up at her daughter and saw Beatrice. Nothing about the women's appearance compared, but the wisdom and confidence Madeline displayed in this moment were always visible in Beatrice.

"She gets her wisdom from you," Beulah said.

"If anything, I get my wisdom from her." Madeline chuckled. "I am a mess."

Gwen reached up and tugged Madeline's ear. "Not true."

Beulah flashed a smile at the couple as intrusive jealousy scratched at her skin. She glanced at Stella.

We'll never have that.

Stella's eyes suggested she felt the same.

"Grandmother, I think you and I have done this the most," Forest said. "Why don't you go down and I stay up?" Madeline gave one nod and then, with an agility Beulah didn't expect, her daughter eased her way to the ground.

"Why don't we go together?" Stella asked Beulah. "There will be enough footholds for both of us. I can talk you through it."

Beulah bobbed her head, then watched as Stella turned and scraped around with her boot before finding a solid foothold.

"Come on," she said. "I've got you."

Turning her back to the road was the easy part. Allowing one leg to lower as her arms became responsible for her body weight was terrifying, and she released a squeak.

"Move your leg to the right," Gwen urged, and Beulah followed the command.

By the time her foot landed on solid, secure rock, Beulah's face was covered in sweat, but the relief made her laugh. "I got it!"

Confidence swelled in Beulah's chest as she found the next foothold. Solid and sizable. Unmovable. She continued down, one step at a time. But with the next movement, a rock shifted, pulling away from the earth, allowing gravity to tug her to the ground with rapid force. A scream ripped through her open mouth, but she didn't hear it. Her ears were stuffed with cotton, breath stuck in her chest, legs unable to straighten underneath her.

"It's okay, Beulah, it's okay." Stella's voice pierced through the fuzz. She pulled Beulah to her feet, and this time, when her ear pressed against Stella's chest, she could hear the woman's heartbeat. "You're not hurt. I've got you." Stella pressed Beulah's head away, one hand on each cheek, eyes locked. "I've got you, Beulah." A kiss on the head, and then Stella released her entirely, taking a step back. "You only fell about eight inches. You're okay."

She scanned her body, feeling for any scrapes or bones that didn't feel quite right, and found herself whole. Okay. Just as Stella said. She checked her arms and found that the tight shirt had done its job. She released a long breath, then pumped her fists into the air.

"I did it!"

Everyone cheered. Even Stella's face seemed calmer and excited. Perhaps it would just take them some time to navigate the nature of their relationship. Their beginnings were less than normal, grotesque even. But perhaps...perhaps.

***

A large sign held a white DQ symbol against a red background, and as she drew closer, Beulah could smell grease and sugar.

"What is this?"

"A restaurant. Greasy food and ice cream. You definitely need to taste ice cream."

Beulah followed the others' lead as they settled around tables. A view of the river stretched out before them. The sheer size and speed of it caught her breath in her throat and tears prickled at the backs of her eyes.

"It's beautiful." How long had she yearned to get off the mountain? Glancing at Madeline, she recalled the night they packed up all their things, determined to leave together. Her daughter smiled at her, then went about turning on her phone.

Beulah stayed back as the others gathered round her. "Hi, Mother!" Beatrice's voice sounded so very far away. "How is everyone? Is it cold there?"

"It's still mild here for now. The weather apps show it getting a bit warmer before the cold comes."

"Is everything alright at home?" Beatrice asked.

Madeline looked up from the phone and smiled at Beulah, who shifted from foot to foot. Perspiration wet her palms, and she tried to swallow her fear down a too-dry throat.

"Well—"

"Grandmother, let me take over," Forest insisted, centering the phone to his face. His eyes were bright as they landed on the screen. "Are you ready for this story?"

"Is it a good one?" Beatrice asked, and Beulah remembered the day that her granddaughter had climbed into her nest of roots and told story after story about Madeline.

"Absolutely." Forest told his mother of their uneventful drive and climb up the mountain and how easily the Hedge opened for them. "But when we got to the grove of grandmother trees..." His face fell, but Beulah gathered the impression that his intention was to add drama to the story. "They were all dead. Their

118

bark was dark and dripping sap. Branches had fallen. None of them spoke."

"All of them?" Beatrice asked, horrified. "Even First Mother?"

"Yes. All of them."

"How? What did you do when you realized?" The panic in Beatrice's voice brought a pang of guilt, and Beulah took her gaze up the mountain for a moment. "I need to come home."

"Shh, Mother, listen. We kept walking. What else was there to do?"

"Forest, you were smiling at the beginning of this story. Is there a good part?"

Forest smiled but didn't answer. "As we walked closer to the house, we heard a rustling in the woods."

His mouth refused to do anything but smile, and his eyes were light and joyful. He gave a little laugh but struggled with the words and looked away from the screen.

"I didn't realize it was him at first," he said, bringing his attention back to his mother. "But the closer he came, I recognized him. Mother, Arcas is alive."

Beatrice was speechless. Tears were forming at the corner of Forest's eyes, and he could no longer speak.

"Alright, my turn," Gwen said, taking the phone from Forest. "Arcas comes bounding through the forest, knocks Forest down, and nuzzles all over him. He is laughing and crying at the same time. It was an exciting moment."

"Then we realized we weren't alone on the mountain," Madeline added over Gwen's shoulder.

"So, we spread out and searched," Gwen said, making large gesticulations with her arms. "Madeline and I made our way toward the greenhouse. Forest and Dani went to the Rock, and we left Stella to search the buildings."

"We found nothing," Madeline said, "and neither did they. When we came back to the house, we couldn't find Stella. We searched—"

"Is Stella alright?" Beatrice interrupted forcefully.

"I'm fine, Bea." Stella poked her head over Gwen's shoulder. "Hi."

Gwen handed the phone to Stella.

"Oh, umm, yeah, I guess it's my turn." Stella tucked the hair escaping from her ponytail behind her ears and glanced at Beulah, whose heart flopped like a fish in her chest. "I found her in the bathhouse." Beulah covered her mouth with her hands and stifled a sob. "It worked, Beatrice. She's here. She's alive."

Silence lasted so long the group exchanged glances.

Stella placed the phone in Beulah's trembling hand. Beatrice appeared before her, her face small on the screen. She gasped when she saw Beulah. Then her eyes brimmed with tears, and Beulah's own chin began to quiver. A longing swept over Beulah as her granddaughter managed a smile.

"How is it you're there and I'm here?" Beatrice asked.

If you were here, I would be okay. You would help me trust myself.

"Oh, I miss you, Bea." Beulah tried to calm her shaking voice, but it was futile. "Will come home soon?"

"I've missed you, too, Grandmother. More than you will ever know. We'll have to see if the snow will hold off long enough after Ben's meeting. But I promise I'll be home as soon as I can be. It worked. Goddess, it worked." Beulah felt her heart harden at Beatrice's love of the deity. "Stella must be so excited to see you. She was a mess without you."

Beulah turned toward Stella, who nodded at the truth. "I was a mess without her, too."

"Wait, Grandmother." Beatrice rubbed her forehead with her fingertips. Her eyebrows furrowed. "What happened to the trees, and to Arcas?"

"Well," Beulah exchanged glances with Stella, sorting the story she would tell in her head before speaking again. "My gift finally decided to show up." Beulah watched Beatrice still then focus on the phone. "I can breathe life and death into things."

"You killed the trees?" Beatrice had focused on the death, not the life, and there was a quiet fear in her voice that pricked Beulah's heart.

"No, of course I didn't kill them, Beatrice," Beulah reassured, filling her throat with the voice she'd used to soothe Beatrice for years. "Well, not for long anyway. I needed them quiet so I could talk with my mother alone. They're all fine now."

"Oh. How did that go?" Beatrice asked. "Talking with Ola, I mean."

"Well, there's quite a bit for us to deal with, but we're working through things."

"Make her some spiced orange tea. It's her favorite." Beatrice gave a small, sheepish smile, and Beulah scoffed.

"Do you really think I never noticed you sneaking her gifts?"

"You never said anything."

"It wasn't my place to get in the way of your kindness." Beulah finally eased onto a bench, relaxing into the conversation.

"Oh, Grandmother, I wish we were together. Your gift sounds…terrifying, but also brilliant! How did you realize—"

"I'll tell you all the details when you're home. Now, tell me about Ben. You're in a relationship?"

"This isn't a mixed company conversation." The pink hue on Beatrice's cheeks made Beulah smile. "But, umm, yes. He's taking me to a Broadway show this evening."

"Oh! Which one?" Gwen asked, popping over Beulah's shoulder.

"*Wicked*," Beatrice deadpanned, and Gwen and Madeline both laughed. "He's determined to expose me to every American portrayal of witches he can think of."

"Haven't you reminded him you aren't a witch?" Dani asked with a chuckle.

"I'm not a witch, Dani."

"I know. I know."

As Beulah listened to Gwen, Madeline, and Dani banter, loneliness crept into her bones. She'd only been gone for two months, yet she'd missed so much. Stella reached for Beulah's free hand and squeezed.

"I can't wait to hear about the show, Beatrice," Beulah said, wanting her granddaughter's attention back.

"Has Mother made you biscuits?"

Beulah nodded. "And I've made her pie."

"I love you, Grandmother."

"We'll talk soon."

"Wait, Bea." Stella jerked the phone from Beulah's hand, then touched Beulah's arms and whispered an apology for interrupting. "Are there herbs that could help me get my sight back? I haven't had new visions since…"

Beatrice cleared her throat and nodded. "Yes. Mugwort, but listen to me, Stella, take only the tiniest bit at first. Otherwise, your premonitions will slide into full hallucinations, and it won't be pretty. There's mugwort at home, but you could stop by Wanda's. She can show you exactly how much."

"Thank you, Bea. I miss you. You doing okay in New York?"

A wide smile took over Beatrice's face. "I'm doing more than okay. Take care of yourself."

The group gathered around with the phone in the center and said goodbye.

***

"Let's go find you some clothes," Stella said. "Then I want to stop by Wanda's."

"I want to visit her as well," Forest said. "Meet you there? We can have lunch with her. Pizza?"

Stella gave Beulah a quick glance, asking for affirmation. Beulah bobbed her head. "We'll be quick." She walked them toward the bridge that crossed the river.

"What's that?" Beulah asked, pointing toward water spilling down from a structure that spanned the entire width of the river.

"A hydroelectric dam. It creates electricity."

"Can I hold your hand, Stella?" Beulah asked. Stella responded by reaching out.

Stella side-eyed Beulah as they walked. "I feel disconnected from them, too. I didn't know how to breathe in a world without you in it." Weight pressed against Beulah's chest at Stella's grief and her own guilt. Oh, the ways she had used the woman. "How do I know, Beulah, if what I feel for you real, or if it's that the bind you've placed on me?"

Beulah considered but couldn't provide an answer. "I don't know."

"Can you take it away?"

"Why would I?"

"Because neither one of us will ever know if I meant it when I said 'I love you' two months ago."

I'm not sure I care if you love me. I need you.

***

The store offered everything—shelves stocked with items Beulah had never seen before. Her hands reached out to fondle flowers that didn't seem alive, curious why anyone would want such a thing.

"Beatrice would hate this," she tutted.

"Come on," Stella said, pulling Beulah toward an aisle of books and pens. She pulled a few books from the shelf along with a pack of pens and handed them to Beulah, then led her toward a circular hanger of clothing.

Stella barely gave Beulah a moment to sort through clothing on her own. Instead, she pulled items she said were practical, held them up against Beulah's frame, and nodded when she found something she found acceptable. Eventually, she sighed. "Okay, that should do it."

Beulah followed Stella, whose arms were full of clothes on hangers, to a bench of some kind where a woman took the tag of each garment and ran it across a red light, making it beep. Tilting her head, Beulah asked, "What's she doing?"

"She's scanning the tags and coming up with how much we owe for everything." Stella turned to the woman, who glared through wrinkled eyebrows. Eventually, she gave them the total, and Stella paid with green pieces of paper with men's faces on them—money, Beulah assumed. Curious as she was,

123

she didn't dare ask until they were out of the store. The threat of embarrassment was too great.

On their way back across the bridges, Stella's phone rang. Madeline told them to join the rest of them at Wanda's home. Beulah's palms sweat again as she thought about meeting another person.

"Will I be introduced as Madeline's mother?" Beulah asked.

"Probably," Stella said. "Wanda believes in the miraculous."

"Why do you want your gift of foresight back, Stella?"

"You saw Madeline this morning. She's struggling. I want to help her. And..." Stella stopped walking and squared her body to Beulah. "I want to know what you're going to do to me."

"Believe it or not, Stella, I don't want to hurt you, but I need someone. And, I'm not convinced you'd want me without the bind in place."

Stella narrowed her eyes for a moment, then continued walking. Beulah's legs complained at all the movement. They were rooted and still for thirty-five years, after all. Stella slowed down at a yellow painted house with pansies filling two big, blue pots.

"We're back here!" Madeline's voice called.

Stella led Beulah through a gate and to a backyard full of small gardens.

"Well, hi." Wanda pressed herself out of a plastic chair and reached out her hand to Beulah. Beatrice had shared several stories about Wanda, stories of congenial rivalry, and Beulah eyed her with curiosity.

"I'm Beulah." She took the woman's warm hand in her own.

"Well," Wanda said, "it's awfully nice to meet you. I've heard many stories about you. Nothing surprises me anymore." She chuckled. "Don't be nervous. You're safe."

"We should get lots of pizzas for Beulah to try," Gwen said. "Several options with different toppings on each half." The woman pointed a crooked finger into the air at her idea.

"That's a good idea," Stella said.

"May I ask how?" Wanda asked, her eyes returning to Beulah.

"They didn't tell me specifics."

Beulah locked eyes with Stella, unsure what to say.

"Can we just say that it was magic?" Stella replied.

"And it was more like our magic than anything like theirs," Forest added.

"What do you mean?" Madeline asked, her eyes narrowed.

"Great-grandmother—Beulah—used blood and words, and her sheer will," Forest explained, and Beulah flushed at her grandson's awe. He was proud of her, and something about the way she'd brought herself back aligned her with his magic.

"Three very powerful ingredients," Wanda said.

"How do you..." Beulah didn't finish the question.

"We're witches." Wanda took a long drink of water. "We work with the earth and the land and the spirits. We can see futures and heal and bring abundance to some and harm to others when necessary. We just can't bring fire or vines to our palms." She smiled and sipped her own water. "Beatrice doesn't like our way of magic much."

"She's coming around," Forest said and took a sip.

"Is blood something that you use?" Beulah mind and heart whirred, both curious and hopeful that perhaps she owed the Goddess nothing for the change. She wanted it to be all on her own.

"We use all sorts of ingredients, and yes, blood is one in some cases. I don't think that this just came from your blood and words and will, though. You're from a line of demigoddesses. I could be wrong, I 'spose."

"I'm not sure the Goddess cared enough about me to help me out."

Beulah swallowed, wishing she could sip that confession back inside of her. Her eyes darted to Madeline, who gave an understanding smile, then to Forest, who glared at her incredulously.

"Have you never questioned it all, Forest?" she asked.

Forest's mouth parted, but before he could answer, the pizza arrived. Stella helped Forest bring them to the backyard, where they ate and talked, and everyone watched Beulah's face with each bite of pizza.

"I don't like that one," she said, in response to ham and pineapple. "Too sweet."

"Most people don't," Stella said.

"I just love it!" Wanda chuckled, and Beulah could imagine Beatrice offering a playful retort.

The conversation that bounced back and forth exhausted Beulah, and relief filled her when it was time to leave.

Before they left, Stella asked Wanda about mugwort. The older witch brought her a satchel of tea to show just how much to use. The interaction brought a shiver to Beulah's spine.

Climbing up the mountain proved less scary than going down. Once they were home, Stella nestled the bag of clothes she bought Beulah into a corner.

"Take a bath with me, Stella," Beulah said.

Stella's face paled.

"You don't have to. I'd just like to feel close to you."

Stella said nothing but followed when Beulah made her way to the bathhouse.

"Please don't be afraid," Beulah whispered as she closed the door. "I won't hurt you. And if there's anything you don't want to do—ever—please tell me."

Stella remained silent. Beulah watched as she undressed. When the woman finished, she approached Beulah and pulled at her shirt. Beulah allowed Stella to peel off her clothing her, and released the illusion she'd placed on herself, allowing her scars to show. Stella eased into the bath and encouraged Beulah to join. Beulah nestled herself onto Stella's lap, feeling the woman wrap her legs and arms around her. "Can I trust you, Beulah?"

Beulah leaned the back of her head against Stella's chest, thinking of all the times she took blades to her skin to prevent herself from hurting her mother and then her daughter. She would use the same methods to protect Stella if it came to it.

"I will never use my breath on you again. I promise you."

"You're right to question the Goddess."

"You think so?"

"You can't be the only one who didn't want to be a tree."

"Do you think she helped me return?"

"No." Stella's answer came quick and emotionless. "I think you're strong enough on your own."

Beulah wanted to turn to see Stella's face to get a sense of what thoughts swirled within the statement.

"Is that a compliment?" Beulah attempted to infuse the question with a laugh but choked on the words.

"It's a truth."

"Beatrice called it terrifying and brilliant. Is there any good that can come of it?"

Stella shifted in the water, encouraging Beulah to turn and face her. "You have to decide that, Beulah. No one else."

They repositioned themselves again, and as Stella stroked the skin on her shoulders and her chest and her belly, questions ticked through Beulah's mind.

Do you hate me?

Have I ruined your life?

Would you be better off if I were gone?

"Will you make love to me?" Beulah asked, desperate to change the voice in her head.

"I'm not ready, Beulah. Let this be enough."

"Can we talk, then? My mind is..."

Stella paused her movement for a moment, then returned to the gentle caresses. "What was your favorite pizza?"

"Thank you, Stella."

CHAPTER 12

Beatrice

Beatrice sat on the toilet of Ben's bathroom as wave after wave of cramps rolled over her body. If she were home, she'd make herself a cup of chamomile tea and curl up in a blanket next to a roaring fire. Ben, an avid coffee drinker, didn't keep tea of any kind in the house. So she sat, allowing blood to drip into the porcelain bowl, feeling more disconnected from the ground than ever. She leaned her elbows on her thighs, rested her head in her hands, and squeezed her eyes tight as if it could push out the pain. A sob filled her throat, and she released along with a flood of tears.

"Grandmother."

Until the last few hours, Beatrice hadn't regretted her decision to stay in New York. But now, she was alone in a world she didn't understand, and her grandmother was alive and well and home. Envy, a strange and unfamiliar emotion, constricted her chest. She clucked her tongue at her own feelings.

As much as she trusted Ben, she hated having to ask him for help with her current predicament. With a groan, Beatrice wrapped a wad of toilet paper as neatly as she could, tucked it into her underwear, and left the bathroom.

She plopped down on the couch and grabbed her phone from the coffee table. She'd spent an hour that morning enjoying the music Ben shared with her, pressing the heart when she liked a song. The technology was easy enough to navigate, but she hesitated before pressing Ben's name. The phone rang three times, but just before Beatrice ended the call, Ben answered with an excited "Sweetheart!" and Beatrice couldn't help but smile.

"Hi. I hope I'm not bothering you."

"No, no. I'm in between meetings. Is everything okay?"

"I, umm." Beatrice closed her eyes and bit her lip, embarrassment creeping into her chest. "I need you to get something for me on your way home."

"Of course. What do you need?"

"My cycle started, and I don't have anything to use. And I'd like chamomile tea, for the cramps."

"I can place an order and have it delivered." Ben's matter-of-fact response comforted Beatrice. "I need direction on what product you use, though."

"I don't use a product. I put fabric strips in a cloth bag."

"Something reusable then! I can work with that." Beatrice could hear Ben's smile on the other end of the call. "Do you feel up to the show?"

"I will. I promise."

"Listen, there's ibuprofen in the cabinet. Eat a snack and take two. There's a heating pad under the bed you can use. I'll be home as soon as I can."

It felt so strange, being taken care of. After her mother, Gwen, and Ben left the mountain, the trees had done their best to nurture her. Still, Beatrice loathed the feeling of helplessness.

"Thank you, Ben."

"Rest. I'll see you soon."

"Bye."

By the time Beatrice ate a piece of toast and reluctantly took two ibuprofen with a glass of water, the order arrived. She opened the box and found reusable fabric pads and a giant box of chamomile tea. While water boiled, Beatrice hand-washed the pads, wrung them out, and draped them over the towel warmer in the bathroom. She consumed her cup of tea, then decided to ready herself for the evening. Beatrice knew her nature. Though she didn't cry often, she wouldn't be able to talk about her grandmother without sobbing, so she decided to tell Ben later, after the show.

In the shower, she turned the water up hot and took the time to shampoo and condition her hair. She had brought her own bottles from home, and with her eyes closed, she imagined soaking in her own tub. Here in New York, Beatrice was a fish out of water, and Ben a bird. How did the saying go? A bird may love a fish, but where will they build a home?

After drying off and moisturizing, she took the dry pad and tiptoed from the ensuite into Ben's bedroom. It was easy enough to snap on, and the cotton felt soft against her skin. She pulled the plum jumpsuit she'd purchased for the occasion from the closet. This fabric felt strange on her body, and staring at herself in the mirror brought a sense of self-consciousness. Beatrice had never thought about her appearance until this trip to New York, when she realized most women shaved their armpits and legs and wore makeup every day.

What does he see in me?

She tsked at her weakness.

Too much time alone. Too much time to think.

A few moments later, Ben opened the door. Beatrice pinched her cheeks to bring a blush to them, wiped her palms against the jumpsuit, and headed for the living room. He paused for a moment in the doorway, handsomely clothed in a long wool coat with a scarf around his neck. Any regret she had disappeared. Beatrice, depleted and slightly nauseous, made her way to him.

"You look stunning." Ben brought his hands to Beatrice's waist and pulled her close.

"So do you."

"I need to change, then we can head to dinner."

Beatrice followed him to the bedroom and leaned against the doorframe as he changed, appreciating how comfortable he was with her watching.

"Feel better?" he asked her.

"A little nauseous, but I'll be alright."

"You sure you're up for this? We can stay home and watch a movie instead."

"I want to go, Ben." Beatrice's words were true. She would take every opportunity that the city offered joy. Those moments brought her hope.

Ben finished dressing, checked his hair in the mirror, then offered his hand.

"Let's go."

***

Dinner, a turkey sandwich from a diner, settled Beatrice's stomach. Ben had insisted the experience was a New York must. A shiver of excitement ran through Beatrice as the lights in the theater dimmed. Patrons filled every seat in the theater, but Ben's firm, warm hand kept her grounded. Music swelled around her, and deep within her body, organs vibrated with the intensity of it. She gasped, and Ben squeezed her hand.

"Are you alright?"

"Yes. It's..."

The words lost themselves to the music and movement. The green-skinned witch, Elphaba, perplexed Beatrice, and she scrutinized the depiction through furrowed brows. She couldn't help but compare Elphaba to the family of witches in the movie Ben had shared with her the night before—one about a love curse handed down the generations from mother to daughter. Her mind pressed the depictions—along with those of the witches surrounding Wanda's table at her autumnal equinox party—into

131

a triple Venn diagram.

Hollywood sure takes its liberties.

Yet, she had witnessed these different magical existences: the grounded connection to the earth, and the miraculous infusion of a supernatural deity. She, in truth, was the manifestation of both.

When Elphaba mounted the broom and shot to the sky, belting lines about defying the laws of nature, tears burned behind Beatrice's eyes. The Goddess had given her gifts just as powerful as flight, but Beatrice knew they weren't enough to keep her and Ben together, and for a moment, her divinity felt useless. The tears didn't care about her embarrassment at being seen crying; they flowed down her cheeks, searing her skin, and intensifying as Glinda and Elphaba sang words of friendship to one another. Beatrice cursed herself as a sob ripped from her. She longed for her family and her friends. Ben handed her a handkerchief and rubbed circles on her back, but she was too shattered to feel them.

Finally, the curtain drew closed. Ben leaped to his feet with applause, and Beatrice followed the gesture.

"Oh sweetheart. You're a mess." Ben took her face in his hands and grazed his thumbs against her cheek. "Too much?"

"No," Beatrice said, but her lower lip trembled despite her best efforts at squeezing her mouth tight. "I'm ready to be home." The look in Ben's eyes conveyed he didn't know which home Beatrice meant. In truth, neither did she.

On the ride to Ben's apartment, energy whirred around them, all electricity and motion, while Beatrice withdrew into herself. The medicine she'd taken for her aching womb had run its course, and a headache brewed at her temples.

"What are you thinking about?" Ben kept his voice low.

"I'm wondering why the Goddess never gave us the gift of flight." Beatrice tried to cover the lie with a smile, but Ben cocked an eyebrow and her smile fell. "I need to talk to you when we get back, but first, I need to get rid of this headache."

"Of course." Ben moved to pull his hand away, but Beatrice tightened her hold.

Beatrice, used to going to bed early and waking with the sun, rubbed her eyes, which were heavy with exhaustion, and the two didn't speak the rest of the way home.

***

As soon as they entered the apartment, Ben brought Beatrice a glass of water, a cup of chamomile tea, and two more ibuprofen. They showered together, Ben unconcerned by Beatrice's bleeding. She changed into a pair of his buffalo plaid flannel pajamas, and they moved to the couch.

"Those look better on you than they do me. Talk to me."

"I probably should have told you before dinner, but I wanted to keep the night light." Beatrice picked at the black and red fabric. "My grandmother's spell worked." Ben's eyebrows lifted, and he scratched at his goatee. The reality of the words landed on Beatrice's heart, which filled with heavy homesickness. "She's alive. They called me this morning. I saw her face. She's young and..."

The surprise left Ben's eyes as he took a recentering breath. "We can get you on a plane tomorrow."

Beatrice's gaze moved toward the coffee table, her lips pressed into a thin line. "I want to go. And I want to stay. I'll be homesick either way, Ben."

He took her hand and kissed her gently on the cheek. "I don't want to keep you from your family."

She met his gaze. "I don't want them to keep me from you."

"Do you love me, Beatrice?"

Before answering, Beatrice took in all of him. The hints of gray in his hair. His neat mustache and goatee. She remembered how it felt to hold him in her vines and stare into those eyes. "If I speak it, I'll make it real. And I'm terrified of losing something so beautiful." Ben's eyes softened, but he stayed quiet. "Even if I stay now, home is in West Virginia, and yours is here. I don't know how we..."

Silence thickened the room, and Beatrice sat still, desperate for him to say something. When he didn't, she stood from the couch, then straddled his lap. She kissed Ben deeply, then nibbled around his neck and ears. Eventually, she made her way to her knees and tugged playfully at his pants.

"My body may not want it tonight, but I can still take care of you."

Ben lifted off the couch, slid his pants off, and repositioned. She hoped the pleasure she brought him, a respite from the outside world, spoke the words her lips could not. In silence, they moved to the bedroom and tucked into bed.

"There's more, Ben." She explained Beulah's gift to the best of her understanding, imagining the resuscitation of Arcas's body and Forest's broad smile when he saw his friend again. Ben responded with wide eyes, furrowed brows, and questions Beatrice couldn't answer. "She didn't go into details. I'd love to talk to her alone. It worries me. Ola told me once that Grandmother is the strongest of us all and not to estimate her. She's on the mountain with my mother, who can be…"

"Anxious."

"Paranoid," Beatrice emphasized. "And wrong."

"In that case, I'd prefer you to stay with me, Beatrice."

She canted her head. "Why?"

"If you go, I suspect you'll be put in the middle. Asked to prove your loyalty. And with Madeline's drowning visions, she will be on edge. They'll all look to you to keep the peace. You don't have to be responsible for this. Rest here with me."

Beatrice pressed her body as close to his as possible.

Rest, huh?

"I'm not used to this much alone time. The quiet gets to me."

"I'll work from home as much as I can. And you can explore the city if you like."

Beatrice lifted her eyebrow and glared at him. "I'll get lost in this place."

"You could use your gift to help you. Scatter flower petals

along the streets to track on your way back."

Beatrice scoffed at the idea, though it was worth considering. "Ben, do you believe there are good and wicked witches?"

"Hmm." Ben pressed his lips together and scratched his chin, eyes squinted with deliberation. "Every villain has a backstory."

"Which one am I?"

"You know better than to ask that." His crooked smile made Beatrice blush. "I used to play this game called D&D in high school. It's a lot to explain, but there are character alignments. I would consider you lawful good. You have a temperate set of values that you honor, and you use them for the good of everyone."

"And my mother?"

"Hmm." Ben released a chuckle. "She's a bit more chaotic. Somewhere between chaotic neutral and chaotic good. She doesn't always see the forest for the trees."

"Mmm. My grandmother is one of the most compassionate people I know. I hope Mother remembers that."

"All humans have the power to take life away. Many have the power to give it back. I could imagine it making Madeline nervous. It could be a corrupting power."

Beatrice tsked. "My grandmother is not a wicked witch."

"So will you stay?"

In the background, a siren wailed, drawing Beatrice's attention to the window. She moved toward it and pushed the curtain back, revealing the glittering city. It would never be her home, but she could stay a little longer.

CHAPTER 13

Madeline

Madeline's restless body flipped her over and over in the bed like a fish washed up on the river's edge, her mind continually taunted by visions of drowning. Gwen lay beside her, sleeping peacefully. Madeline bent down to give her lover a kiss between the eyes, then gently rolled out of the bed, pulling her covers back up so she wouldn't feel a draft.

Three days had passed since the five of them made it back to the mountain, and each day, the sensations of drowning brought Madeline more and more unease. She paced back and forth through the living room, which was lit only by a fire. Her mind whirred with the questions she couldn't quiet. Why, for instance, was the liquid she choked on each time she closed her eyes hot and viscous? And who was its victim?

Fear, Madeline's least favorite emotion, propelled most humans to make bad decisions. She finally wrapped herself, reluctantly, in her mother's quilt and lay beside the fire, and the warmth of it lulled her to sleep.

The dream started with a creamy orange sunrise.

Stella, Gwen, Dani, and Forest ran beside her along the bridge that crossed the river, each of them taking turns glancing over their shoulders to see how close her mother and Beatrice were behind them. They made it to Wanda's house and into the shed, but the rusty doors wouldn't close behind them. Her daughter wrapped vines around them one by one. Gwen and Forest were the first to die at the touch of her mother's breath. Madeline ran away from the shed until Beatrice's vines found her ankles and dragged her to the ground. They wrapped around her tightly as Beulah drew closer. She felt her whole body ignite with flame as she railed against the vines, but Beatrice, just as she had been before, was stronger than her mother. Madeline couldn't fight as Beulah breathed her to sleep.

Madeline's eyes flew open to see her mother hovering over her. The flames tingled at her fingertips before they shot out of her hands toward Beulah, knocking her to the ground, her skin sizzling. Madeline leaped from the couch, her brain realizing that she was not in her nightmare and that her mother was on fire. Beulah's bewildered mouth widened, but she didn't scream. Madeline took the quilt in her hands and beat the flames until they were out, then surveyed the damage. The flames had licked her mother's arms and singed them a crisp black. Her body convulsed.

Madeline rubbed the golden healing to her hands and placed them first on her mother's chest and then drew them down her arms. Unmistakable silver trails left by old scars revealed themselves on the spots of skin that weren't burned, but she said nothing. The bottom of Beulah's hair was burned, and Madeline found her energy to work on that as well. Feeling guilt and embarrassment, she looked up and around her to make sure no one else was coming.

"I'm sorry," she said, helping her mother sit. The woman's pajamas smoked. "I was having a nightmare." The words "I didn't mean to" almost escaped her lips.

Beulah's quaking reduced to occasional shivers, and Madeline wrapped the quilt around her mother and led her to the couch.

"What did you do, Grandmother?" Forest's voice came from the corner of the room.

"Go to your room, Forest," Beulah said. Madeline had never heard her mother's voice so grave.

"But Great-grandmother..."

"I need time with my daughter alone. Now, go to your room."

"No." Forest took another step into the room. "I'm not a child, and Mother told me to take care of things in her absence. Now, what did you do?"

"I was having a nightmare, Forest. Mama woke me from it, and my body responded."

Forest's nostrils flared. "Thank the Goddess I wasn't there when you used them against my mother."

For the longest time, Beulah said nothing, and Madeline, unable to take the silence, stood and paced again. "Can I make us tea?"

Beulah nodded, her wide eyes focused on the flame flashing in the fireplace.

Madeline stood. The spike of adrenaline left her shaky. She ran her fingers through her hair, then sat the kettle on the stove. She didn't know what to make of the dream or the image of her mother's charred skin. Breathing in through her nose and out through her nose, she scooped Beatrice's calming tea into a mesh ball and placed it in the kettle once the water came to a boil. She retrieved a tray from a lower cabinet and placed the kettle and three teacups on it. Then, swallowing her shakiness, she made her way back to the living room.

Her mother didn't look up at her. "How many times have you used it?" she asked, keeping her eyes fixed forward. "Have you burned anyone else?"

"It only comes when I get angry," Madeline replied, swallowing the memories of her flames and Beatrice's vines dancing in the winter air. "I have come close," she admitted, placing the tray on the table and sitting next to her mother, whose calm repose made Madeline squirm. "But I've never burned anyone like that."

"Did you come close to burning Mother?" Forest asked.

"I thought she was killing Gwen. It exploded from me. I can't control it."

Forest grimaced like he'd swallowed sour milk, the disgust on his face bringing brought a tingling sensation to all of Madeline's extremities.

"Do you remember the first time you healed me?" Beulah asked.

Madeline took a sip of tea before answering. "You broke your leg in the middle of the forest. It started to rain. You were terrified for me and tried to teach me how to do all sorts of things like you weren't going to make it."

"You told me to be quiet. You felt something in your hands. You took care of every scrape, bruise, and sneeze after that." Beulah placed her hand on Madeline's back. "Want to tell me about the nightmare?"

"Forest, can I please speak with my mother alone now?"

Before leaving the room, Forest turned back to Madeline. His jaw clinched and released before he asked, "Has she forgiven you for it?"

"I hope so." *Goddess, I hope so.* "Perhaps you can forgive me, too."

"You've used your power against my mother *and* your mother, who I've known my whole life. I—"

"Forest, she was scared. I'm alright. Your mother is alright. Now, please let us talk." Once Forest was out of the room, Beulah turned to Madeline. "He's protective of us."

Spurned by the loneliness Madeline felt at the interaction, her mind's eye returned to her nightmare, and the fears she had repressed flooded her chest.

"What about you? Who have you used your breath on? Have

you used your breath on Stella?"

Beulah's furrowed brows kept a sense of softness. "That's what the dream was about?"

"Have you hurt her?" Madeline's voice rose as dread rattled her insides.

Now the furrows grew deeper, and Madeline could smell the anger on her mother's breath.

"No," she responded curtly. "I haven't hurt her."

"Understand this," Madeline continued, and she felt her eyes glow hot again. "That woman adores you—worships you—blindly. She will do whatever you ask of her. Do not use your breath on her."

"Madeline, answer the question now," Beulah demanded through gritted teeth. "What happened in your dream?"

"I saw what you are capable of."

Madeline stood and took quick steps to Stella's room. Beulah didn't follow. Stella lay alone on the bed, and Madeline moved next to her.

"Stella," she whispered and watched the woman's eyes open and widen.

"Is everything okay?" Stella asked, pressing herself up.

"Yes, shh. Listen," Madeline said, looking behind Stella's shoulder to make sure Beulah wasn't in the doorway. "Has my mother hurt you?"

Stella responded with a moment of empty silence before sighing and sitting all the way up. She turned around to check the door herself, then turned her attention back to Madeline.

"What she can do is terrifying." Stella's throat bobbed in the moonlight. "But Beulah's going to become what we make her. If we choose fear, she's going to become fearsome." Madeline felt her shoulders relax at the wisdom of Stella's words. "She's scared, too."

Madeline considered telling Stella that she had once again wielded fire against her mother, but for a moment, it felt as if the two of them were on the same side.

"I wish Beatrice were here," Madeline said.

"Where is Beulah?" Stella asked.

Before Madeline could reply, her mother was in the room, her chin tilted, eyes looking down her nose, scrutinizing the situation.

"Goodnight, Madeline," she said, holding the door wide for Madeline to leave.

***

"Gwen," Madeline whispered, gently jiggling Gwen's shoulder. "I need to talk. My mother. I don't trust her."

Gwen groaned, stretched, and rubbed her eyes. "What happened?"

"I had a dream. She and Beatrice killed all of us."

No worry or concern flashed over Gwen's face.

"Did you hear me?"

Gwen propped herself up on her elbows. "Madeline, sometimes dreams are just dreams. You're still half human, you know. Not every nightmare is a premonition." Madeline felt a flush of anger wash over her. "And if this is your divine side seeing something coming," Gwen continued, placing her hand against Madeline's cheek, "remember that the visions you see of your own life don't always match what ends up happening. If you hadn't trusted Beatrice—"

"I don't know if I can trust her right now, either."

"Madeline." Gwen pressed herself up all the way, crisscrossed her legs, and stared Madeline down with reprimanding eyes. "She's in New York City, falling in love with my brother."

Madeline pressed her eyelids together, then ripped them back upon at the feel of hot, thick water pouring down her throat. "I cannot manage two violent visions happening at once," she growled through gritted teeth.

"Have you tried Beatrice's tea yet? The one that makes dreams go away?"

Madeline shook her head.

"How about I make you some?"

Madeline nodded, then sat on the edge of the bed, keeping her eyes open. How long could someone go without sleep? She didn't stand a chance at defeating the adrenaline weaving lightning strikes throughout every cell of her body without help, and she prayed the tea would work.

Though Gwen had a point, everything Madeline saw happening between Gwen and Beatrice did come to pass, and if any part of this new vision was accurate, something horrible was approaching.

Gwen returned with the tea and handed it to Madeline, who offered thanks.

"Beulah's sitting by the fire. She looks terrified."

"I burned her, Gwen," Madeline said, then sipped her tea.

"You what?"

"I was fighting her in the nightmare, and when she woke me up, my body just..." Madeline recoiled from the mortified look on Gwen's face. "I didn't mean to."

"Drink your tea." Gwen slipped between the sheets next to Madeline and turned her back to her. "We'll talk about it tomorrow."

"I said I didn't mean to, Gwen."

Gwen rolled over and touched Madeline's arm. "I'm so tired. Drink the tea and try to sleep."

CHAPTER 14

Beulah

After Stella fell asleep, Beulah spent the next half hour staring into the fireplace. She was no longer confused. No longer doubting the truth: she needed to remove herself from her family. She had betrayed Stella, and now Madeline was having visions of Beulah doing something so heinous that her daughter was prepared to turn her to ash. Again.

She had expected to travel down this path, anticipated it, even. Her desire to die had driven part of her desire to return to flesh. But her family surrounded her now, and the touch of Stella's fingers had given her hope that perhaps there was a place for her. Perhaps everyone could be happy and safe.

Beulah smiled into the fire.

It was a nice thought.

She stood and inhaled deeply. The smell of her burned skin lingered in the air. She considered checking in on Stella, or even waking her, but she didn't want the temptation of a life she could have had to distract her from what she knew needed done.

Beulah didn't bother with a coat or shoes as she dragged a kitchen chair and a lantern outside with her. In a crate on the front porch, she found a length of rope that she knew would be strong enough.

I can't wait for this to be over.

She draped the rope on the chair and dragged it beside her as she walked toward the trees. Eyes opened, including her mother's, which after scanning Beulah's face grew wide with worry.

"What's wrong, Beulah?" she asked.

"I don't want to do this anymore, Mother. I came to say goodbye. You were so much more than what I deserved."

"Beulah, don't say that. Listen..."

Beulah turned and hurried away from the trees, who shouted her name behind her and sent roots to chase her, but they weren't fast enough.

They'll wake the others...

She thought about turning around and sending them all to a temporary death, but then realized she wouldn't be around to wake them again. Her legs propelled her deeper into the forest and closer to The Rock. By the time she made it to the flat stone, her feet bled from scraps and splinters.

Scanning the surrounding trees, Beulah cursed her height. Finally, she found one that would work. She worked the rope into a noose, the thrill of rest encouraging each loop of her hand, each twist of her wrist. Occasionally, she smiled at the idea of existing in that place of nothingness again. She checked the loop, found that it slipped as it was supposed to, then slung it over a large, sturdy limb. Once she had knotted the rope to the tree, she stood on the chair and slipped the loop around her neck. A brief thought of Madeline's husband passed through Beulah's mind, but she squeezed her eyes shut.

This is right. They won't be afraid of me anymore.

Beulah gave the decision no more thought and jumped from the chair.

A grisly cracking sound came from her neck, and almost instantly, she couldn't breathe or feel her legs. Her eyes bulged as though they would pop out of their sockets at any moment. How long she hung like that, she didn't know, but eventually she realized the truth.

I cannot die.

***

The morning sun crept up the mountain, and Beulah watched the shadows of the trees lengthen. Every part of her body below the neck was numb and her swollen eyes ached from the pressure. Just like the time she spent with the earth pressing in and all around her, she didn't breathe, but somehow, her heart kept beating. She cursed The Goddess.

I hate you. I hate you! I didn't ask for any of this. None of us did!

March warmed a bit, teasing the world before the upcoming storm, but the breeze that blew across Beulah's face did little to comfort her. She knew, even as the blood continued to drip from her sliced open soles, that her family would find her. The idea would have made her shudder if her body could have moved.

They can't see me like this. Please don't let them find me.

The sun sat straight overhead by the time Beulah heard her family calling for her. Forest's booming "Great-grandmother" echoed in the woods still bare of trees. She tried to move her jaw but couldn't even wiggle her plumped tongue which hung from her mouth.

"Great-grandmother!" Forest cried and ran toward her. Beulah couldn't move her eyes in their sockets enough to look down at him. "Oh, god. What did you do?"

Forest righted the chair, stood on it, then lifted Beulah so that she balanced on one of his shoulders. She heard what she could only assume was his pulling out a blade and sawing through the thick, scratchy rope.

"Hold on, I'll get you off of here." Forest continued sawing, grunting as he worked, and finally, he laid a freed Beulah on the ground and worked to loosen the noose from her neck. "Are you alive?" His panicked face broke Beulah's heart. This isn't what she wanted, but what else did she expect? For the Goddess to send vultures to clean up her mess? "I'll be back," Forest said as he scrambled to his feet.

No, no, no, no, no, no, no, no.

The forest was quiet for some time, and Beulah's body remained equally as still. She remembered the first time she threatened to use her breath on Ola, and the woman's strong hands tied her to a chair so tight she couldn't move. The two of them had sat staring at one another for the longest time.

Madeline's agitated voice pierced the silence.

"Mama!" she wailed as she kneeled next to Beulah. "What happened? Forest, I can't tell if she's alive."

"Try," Forest insisted.

If Beulah had been able, she would have said no. She tried to shake her head. They could bury her back in the earth, and while she would be cold and so bitterly alone for eternity, her family would be safe from her. But Madeline's hands were glowing golden, and Beulah couldn't so much as whisper.

Madeline worked from her head down, allowing her palms to move over Beulah's face and neck and chest, all the way down her legs and toes. Her breath came back first, filling her lungs until they felt they might burst. Her eyes could move again and the ability to swallow returned. Feeling returned and spread from her center to her extremities. When Madeline seemed finished and Beulah gained the strength to speak, she whispered, "Please don't tell the others."

"Why?" a pale-faced Forest asked. Tears welled in his wide eyes.

"Is it because of last night?" Madeline asked, and Beulah nodded. Madeline stood, pressed her hands against her lower back, and paced back and forth a few times. A sob worked its way from Madeline's throat and the heat of guilt flushed Beulah's skin.

"Please," Beulah groaned as she began to sit up. "Please,

Madeline. Don't tell anyone else."

Madeline and Forest locked eyes.

"Let's get you home," Forest said as he reached down to help lift Beulah to her feet. "Great-grandmother, don't—"

"Forest," Beulah interjected, throwing Forest a reprimanding glance, "call me Beulah."

Forest's eyes shadowed with the same look of annoyance she'd seen so many times on Beatrice's face. "Listen, I understand what it's like to hold a secret," he told her, "But sharing it with others might lessen the burden."

Beulah turned and found her daughter's eyes, which leaked regret. "Will you tell me what the nightmare was about?"

After a beat of hesitation, Madeline agreed and looked to Forest. "Could you go on ahead? Give us a moment?"

Forest gave a nod and quickened his pace, running his fingers through his hair as he walked away.

"I'm sorry," Madeline said, placing a hand on Beulah's back.

"I'm sorry you found me like that. I should have done it a different way."

Madeline squared her body with Beulah and took her by the biceps. "You shouldn't have done it at all."

Beulah lifted her face and demanded, "Tell me, Madeline. Tell me what I'm capable of."

"Mama, I...I saw you and Beatrice killing all of us."

"How?" Beulah implored, then turned her gaze to the ground as Madeline explained her dream of Beatrice wrapping the family in vine and Beulah using her breath to kill them. When Madeline finished, Beulah simply gave a nod, eyes unmoving from the spot. Silence weighed heavy and thick between them.

"Say something," Madeline urged.

"How do you know I was killing you?" Beulah asked without making eye contact.

"I don't know for sure, Mama. Listen, my flames came because I was fighting you in my dream and then you were there and—"

"I didn't know what you were dreaming about, Madeline, I—"

"Of course you didn't. I'm just explaining myself." Madeline reached up and touched Beulah's neck, a shimmering golden glow shining. "There." She lowered her hand and took Beulah's. "I scare easy. There's so much in my head right now. I absolutely hate it. I'll do my best to keep it together."

A squeeze from her daughter's hand brought Beulah's eyes up from the ground.

"Beatrice doesn't need to know what I've done. Nor what you've done." An unsolicited image of Beatrice, anguish filling her brown eyes as she heard the truth, took over Beulah's vision.

"I agree," Madeline said. "Will you tell Stella?"

Beulah shook her head. She knew full well telling Stella would only drive the woman further away, and the idea of anymore distance tore at her nerves.

"I need to get home. She will worry."

Madeline's sniffles were the only sounds between the two as they made their way through the forest.

***

Gwen and Dani's panicked voices filled Beulah's ears as the three of them entered the house.

"Are you okay? Wake up." Dani shouted.

"Stella, what happened? Can you tell us?" Gwen said, her voice calmer.

Beulah picked up her step, though she was too tired to run. Stella lay on the bed, covered in sweat, skin the color of the paper in the journals she bought. She reached for Beulah, and Gwen moved to make room.

"What did you do, Beulah?" Stella asked.

"I...I went for a walk."

Madeline, on the other side of the bed now, rubbed her hands, building a golden glow.

"Here. Let me help."

Her daughter pressed her palms against Stella's neck, and the woman's breathing regulated, and her face filled once more with a pinkness.

"What happened, Stella?" Madeline asked.

Stella swallowed and shook her head. "I need to talk to Beulah alone."

Madeline, Gwen, and Dani exchanged glances, then made hesitant steps out of the room.

"You tried to kill yourself, didn't you?" Stella asked but didn't give Beulah time to answer. "I know, because I went with you. My breathing changed and my heart rate slowed. I blacked out, but I was with you somehow. Hanging from a tree."

CHAPTER 15

Stella

"I won't do it again, Stella."

"You keep saying that."

Beulah slipped next to Stella in the bed, sending a shiver down her spine. Death still soured her mouth with an earthy mustiness, and her limbs felt full and heavy. This was not like the time before when Beulah used her breath on her and she became nothing. No. This time, Stella hadn't been able to breathe. She had felt her tissues succumbing to the lack of oxygen, but her heart kept beating at a slow pace. And she could see Beulah, swinging beside her.

"I'm not a demigoddess," Stella said. "You could have killed me."

"I said I won't—"

"Why did you do it?" Despite efforts, Stella couldn't bring compassion to her voice.

"Stella." Beulah sat up and turned her gaze toward the floor.

"I hate that you fear me."

"I fear you because I know you're lying to me. Tell me the truth, and maybe I can grow to trust you again."

Beulah sighed and swallowed. "Madeline had a nightmare about me. She saw me using my breath on all of you."

"You promised me you'd never use your breath on me again."

"I don't plan to, Stella. I'm just telling you what she saw. I'm scared. I've used you in multiple ways, and I keep secrets I'm too ashamed to share. This power, Stella...I just wanted to keep my family, including you, safe."

Stella chewed on the flesh around her thumb until she drew blood. At the taste of it, her eyes moved to the veins on Beulah's forearm.

My blood. Beulah is strong, but perhaps I'm the one who made her that way.

"I'm going to make myself a cup of tea now and see what I see. I have to help Madeline, because she can be dangerously wrong."

"What if you see the same things she sees?"

"I don't know, Beulah." Stella shrugged and opened her palms. "I guess the good news for you is that you have me on your side, even if I don't want to be."

Is there no way out of this for me? Think, Stella.

A violent thought stabbed into Stella's mind. "I wonder, what would happen to you if I died?"

Beulah's lips trembled at the question. "I didn't realize the binding would be like this. I thought maybe things would be... that we could be..."

"You can't force me to love you. I'm here because you cursed me. Now..." Stella stood and towered over Beulah. "I'm going to get my sight back and figure out exactly what you're going to do and how the fuck I can break this spell."

Beulah rose from the bed and took a step toward Stella. "I'm regretting my promise not to breathe on you."

Stella brought her face so close to Beulah's she could feel the woman's breath.

"Is that what you want to do? Just get rid of me. How will you explain it to them? Hmm? And how will your body feel if I'm six feet underground?" A shuddered breath escaped from Beulah's lips. "You're just as stuck as I am."

"Then can't we try to make it better between us?" Beulah grabbed Stella's hands. "Can't we try to love each other?"

Stella pulled her hands away and, without tenderness, pressed them against Beulah's cheeks. Her eyes took in every inch of Beulah's blue, determined to find the soul she knew. She recalled the words she said to Madeline.

If we fear you, you'll become fearsome.

"I am going to make tea."

***

The two didn't speak as Stella settled on the floor and crossed her legs. Beulah hovered around, busying herself by taking the tags off her new clothing. The irritation made Stella's skin crawl, and she finally had to ask Beulah to leave the room, although the moment she left, Stella's bones started to burn. A few pictures popped into Stella's mind's eye, but with very little focus or clarity.

Closing her eyes, Stella drew in a deep breath and released it, paying attention to the way the rhythm made the sound of the ocean moving up her throat and out her nostrils. The images began with a shimmer, a deep forest green and light dusty pink swirling and mixing. Then a flash of curly red hair. Women laughing. Waves crashing, skirting froth along the shore. Various landscapes flashed in rapid fire. A desert. A snowcapped mountain. An East Asian village. Scandinavian fjords. More red hair. Gray eyes. The image of two hands clasped together. Giggling and moans that come with passion.

What am I seeing?

Stella struggled to keep up as layers upon layers of memories pancaked upon one another like documentaries on human civilization spliced to form a plot out of sequence. Sweat broke on Stella's upper lip and though she remained entranced, somewhere in her core a worry sprouted that she had ingested too much mugwort.

What am I seeing?

In her mind, the question came as a scream, but her lips remained still.

The beginning.

Stella's eyes flew open, and she whispered, "The beginning of what?" She swallowed, rubbed her sweaty palms on her jeans, and wiped her brow with the neck of her shirt. Beside her sat a jar of water. Stella took a giant swig. She grabbed the notebook and a pen she had bought and started to write. No matter how much she tried to coagulate the words, sentences just wouldn't form, so she settled for a fast stream of consciousness without worrying about flow or grammar.

By the time she finished, she had filled five handwritten pages. Then she tucked the book under the mattress, unprepared to share her experience with the others just yet. Especially with Beulah. What would she say, anyway?

Alice. Perhaps Alice could clarify what she saw, but not at this moment. Right now, Stella needed to be near Beulah.

She finished chugging the water and took care as she stood. After shaking her hands and stretching her neck as if to cleanse the confusing energy from her, Stella left the bedroom.

Beulah sat by the fire, chatting with Gwen and Madeline. All eyes pointed to Stella as soon as she entered. Expectation, excitement, and fear filled the room.

"So?" Beulah asked.

"I think I took too much mugwort." The statement lived somewhere between truth and a lie. As confusing as the visions were, Stella suspected they were puzzle pieces she just needed to spread on a table and piece them together. "The images made no sense. Too fast."

"Maybe you should take some time to recover from..." Gwen glanced from Stella to Beulah and back again. "Whatever that was."

"No drowning in the images?" Madeline asked, disregarding Gwen's suggestion, and somehow, this made Stella relax a fraction.

"No."

She sat down at Beulah's feet, frustrated at the way her shoulders released, and her body purred at the closeness. Beulah ran her fingers through her hair and, despite her mistrust and the others in the room, arousal flittered through her body.

Did Beulah bind me to this, too?

"What time is it?" she asked.

Madeline twisted her wrist to check her watch. "Six. You hungry?"

Stella shook her head. "No. I think I do need to rest." Stella looked up at Beulah. "Come with me?"

"I'm not tired, but I'll tuck you in."

Beulah stood and helped Stella to her feet.

"So, we're just going to disregard the ET, Elliot moment the two of you had?" Gwen asked.

Stella's eyes scanned the faces in the room and landed on Forest's. His eyebrows were furrowed with not only worry but sadness. Helplessness, perhaps?

"Not right now." Stella's voice came out stilted.

"I do need a moment with the two of you," Madeline said. "Right now." She stood and followed Beulah and Stella to the bedroom. Once the three were behind the closed door, Madeline whispered, "Stella, are you feeling okay? You were out cold."

"I'm okay. Tired, but okay."

Madeline's attention turned to Beulah. "Mama, you can't do anything like that again. The two of you are tied together. What you experience, Stella experiences."

No shit, Madeline.

Stella locked eyes with Beulah, who held her chin firm and eyes level.

"I didn't understand the nature of the spell fully. I do now. And I won't do anything like that again."

"It's not just about Stella. We just got you back. Beatrice hasn't seen you in person yet. She would be devastated if you…"

The three stood silent for an uncomfortable amount of time, Madeline's eyes darting back and forth between the two women.

"I really do need to lay down," Stella voiced and tugged Beulah's hand. Madeline gave a nod and turned away.

Beulah had appeared revived when sitting with her family, but by the time they'd made it to their bed, she had released the illusion. Her shoulders bowed, and she rubbed her red-rimmed eyes. "Were you telling the truth? Are you okay?"

"Physically, yes. I just wish I could see things more clearly."

The two sat for several quiet minutes, stealing glances at one another, but never locking eyes. Stella heard chatter from the other room, but she couldn't make out exactly what was being said. The voices ended after the opening and closing of the kitchen door.

"When did the binding take effect, hmm? And, please, if you have any respect for me at all, be honest."

"The spell started long before you ever came." The words trembled as they left Beulah's lips, which were now wet with her flowing tears. "I summoned you to the mountain. I brought you to me."

Bile rose in the back of Stella's throat and her eyes burned. Had every minute on the mountain resulted from the workings of a witch, even her friendship with Beatrice and Forest?

Did the spell cause my visions? Did they really bring me to her? Could it all be a lie? A manipulation?

"There are more sheets from my journal in Beatrice's room," Beulah continued. "They're in the farthest right-hand corner if you're facing the bed under the floorboards. Go get them."

Stella turned from Beulah and pulled open the door to see Dani tiptoeing away. A glance at Beulah's hardened face confirmed that she, too, had seen Dani sneak away.

Stella raised a palm up to stop Beulah from taking a step. "I'll handle it." She strode down the hallway with brisk, long steps, and placed a hand on Dani's back, which stiffened at the touch.

"Hey. Can you help me? Beatrice said there was something in her room that would bring back my visions."

After glancing back at Beulah, Dani gave one quiet nod and followed Stella, who closed the door behind her.

"So, how much of that did you hear?" Stella forced nonchalance as she moved a plant stand off the floorboards Beulah had described.

"Enough to know that she put a binding spell on you and its contents are under there."

Stella's gaze followed Dani's extended finger that pointed toward the floor. She didn't answer right away. Instead, she dropped to her knees and pried at the floorboards, which were more difficult to loosen than those three months ago.

"Could you give me a hand?" While she was indeed struggling to free the board, Stella also wanted Dani closer. They glanced at the door before joining her on the floor. "Listen, Dani, I will not ask you to keep this secret from Forest, but Madeline cannot know about this."

"No, I know. Especially not after she set Beulah on fire."

"She did what?"

Animalistic muscles contractions Stella never experienced in her life rippled through her. She became a lioness, ready and willing to disembowel Madeline the next time they were in the same room. Her nostrils flared and her teeth ground painfully into one another.

"Shit. Beulah didn't tell you? Madeline had a nightmare and when Beulah woke her up from it, Madeline used fire on her. Okay," Dani said, lifting their hands to placate Stella. "It wasn't her finest moment, but Beulah doesn't seem morally superior now, does she? Let's see what's in there."

The two of them wiggled and pried until finally, the board popped up, revealing journal sheets like those Stella found months ago. Without glancing at the words and taking great care to ensure Dani couldn't read them either, Stella knocked the wood back into place with her fist and stood.

"Thank you."

"You're not going to show me?"

"This is between Beulah and me. And I need time."

"Do you know what it was like to find you unconscious?" Dani crossed their arms and regarded Stella with fearful frustration. "I know we don't know each other well, but you mean a lot to Forest and Beatrice, so you mean a lot to me. And how do I know she won't come after me now that I know about the spell?" They pointed to the door as if Beulah was standing right behind it.

"Let me handle it. Where is everyone else, anyway?"

"Taking a walk. Probably mulling over what happened with you and Beulah. I needed to rest."

"Go somewhere you can't hear us. Okay?"

Dani left the room, then the house entirely. Once they were seated on a rocker on the porch, music pulsing through earbuds, Stella returned to her room. Beulah sat on the chair in the corner, rocking, her face streaked with salty tears. Stella positioned herself on the edge of the bed and turned her back toward Beulah to be alone with the words.

You will come to me willing and giving.
Kind, pliant, and amazed by the enchantments.
Along with your blood, you will give me your loyalty.
You will be my protector and my friend.
Forever by my side, under my care and keeping, to be my comfort.

Stella reread the words multiple times, then engaged her journalist brain, grabbed a notebook and pen, and scribbled all that she understood. Beulah didn't demand a woman. She didn't ask for attraction or lust or romantic love. The bind she placed on Stella tied her to loyalty, protection, friendship, and physical closeness. Nothing else. Beulah intended to keep her near and in her favor.

"Could I see it? I don't remember what I wrote."

Stella handed the papers to Beulah, who slumped onto the

floor, drew her knees into her chest, and read. Then she covered her face in her hands.

"The spell wasn't all that evil and sinister, you know?" Stella kneeled and placed her forehead against Beulah's. "You knew you'd need someone in your corner. I might rip Madeline's limbs off for burning you again. Were you going to tell me?"

"I don't know," Beulah answered without taking her hands from her face. "Will you tell me what the tea showed you?"

"Like I said, I'm not sure. Images of different places and different times. Laughter. Love making, maybe."

Beulah tightened the ball her body was in, and Stella could feel it—the desire to run. To leave. To die.

"Be honest with me. Have you told me everything about the incantation?"

"Yes."

"I have feelings that aren't part of the spell. Can I show you?" Beulah uncovered her face and peered up. "This." Stella leaned forward and pressed a chaste kiss on her lips. "Come on." She encouraged Beulah up and into bed. Stella faced her and ran fingers through her golden hair. "You petitioned the universe for a friend, and here I am, for your protection and comfort." Beulah screwed her face up and tears came again. "Shh. It's okay. You vowed to protect me, too. We're in this together."

"Do you resent me?"

Stella offered a small smile. "Not right now, but I'm sure the feeling will come and go."

"Hold me," Beulah commanded, and rolled over, pressing her back into Stella's body.

"Goodnight, Beulah."

Stella lay there and considered where she'd be if Beulah's incantation hadn't beckoned her. If she had written the story about the West Virginia witches and came home to her heels and high-rise apartment. To Roger.

She snuggled closer into Beulah and tried to name the emotion that came with holding her. But there were so many. Fear.

Tenderness. Affection. Lust. Bewilderment. Respect. Awe. The woman in Stella's arms had changed herself, a forced metamorphosis, just like Gertrude. Beulah had a power that could change the world, but her psyche lived under the influence of sadness and anger. Everyone wanted Beatrice to be here and help them navigate the world, but this thing between Stella and Beulah seemed too unwieldy even for Beatrice to wrap her vines around.

What will you think of what your grandmother has done?

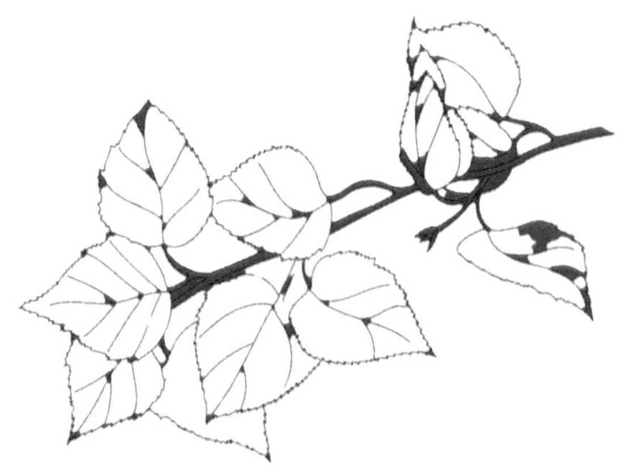

CHAPTER 16

Beatrice

"Where are you taking me now?"

Beatrice felt better, her mood much improved by a good night's sleep, substantial breakfast, and their current route away from the city. Ben had woken at five to respond to emails and kissed Beatrice awake at six, explaining he had a long day planned for them. He took great care in packing medicine, tea, and all the things that would keep her menstrual pain away.

"It's a surprise, my love." Ben took her hand and kissed it. "One of two, actually."

There's that word again. Love.

"Really?"

"Mmhmm." Ben hadn't stopped smiling since waking. "Very long day, though."

"So you've said."

"You might need to use your vines."

"Oh! Exciting."

The playlist Ben had created for the trip filled the car with rhythm and he sang along and tapped his fingers on the steering wheel. Beatrice took turns laughing with him and staring out the window, watching the landscape change. Hills grew larger until finally, an expanse of mountains, rounded and old just like the ones Beatrice knew, took over.

"Ben..."

"They're a subrange of the Appalachian Mountains. Your mountains."

Evergreens covered much of the mountain and a dusting of snow rimmed the top. Ben navigated the curves with ease, but Beatrice's stomach still swirled at the movement. As the car climbed upward, the nausea eased, and her heart grew peaceful. Bare trees still in the grip of winter filled the spaces between the firs and pines, but Beatrice could distinguish between birch, maple, and ash. This wasn't her forest, but she could almost feel the ancient line that ran between these mountains and her own.

Ben pulled the car into a gravel parking lot and turned to her. "Ready for a hike?"

"Absolutely!"

"I've packed us a picnic. I was hoping you'd conjure up some fruit."

Beatrice cocked her eyebrow at the word conjure but then grinned. "Of course."

Ben didn't allow Beatrice to help empty the car of its contents, claiming there was a surprise hidden in the trunk for later. He handed her a lightweight hydration pack and pointed out the various things he'd stowed for her. She strapped it on and followed him to a trail map board.

"A little over five miles. Perhaps three hours. What do you think?"

"I would love to be in this forest for three hours."

"We have somewhere to be at eight, and it'll take us an hour to get there."

"You did tell me it would be a long day."

Beatrice hiked alongside Ben, breathing in the cold March air and fighting the urge to take off her shoes.

If we could spend time in these mountains now and again, maybe I could stay in New York with him.

She allowed her mind to wander as they continued upward, hand in hand, occasionally sneaking glances at him and wondering if he was performing similar calculations in his mind. Their legs propelled them at a quick pace, and a light perspiration popped out on Beatrice's lip. She needed this. These trees. The ground underneath her feet. Her eyes roamed over the forest, and she thought of home. How quiet it was here. No grandmothers chattering. No Forest or Stella. Only Ben, wordless beside her, the swish of her pants, and the scurry of a squirrel.

"Do you think we can call them tonight?" she asked.

"Of course we can. Missing them?"

"Terribly."

"Me too."

An awkwardness unlinked their hands and pressed them away from one another until two feet separated their bodies. The quiet gave Beatrice too much space to think, but instead of filling the void with chatter, she gave in to the worrying. Her mother had predicted Forest's near death and hadn't told her. And Beulah. Did Ola know about the breath? She had to. Why else would she tell Beatrice that Beulah was the most powerful of them all?

But Grandmother said it was new. She wouldn't lie. Not to me.

Another hour of hiking passed with few words between them before they came to an overlook providing expansive vistas of the hills and valleys below them.

"It's gorgeous in the fall." Ben wrapped his arm around Beatrice and drew her close.

Conflicting emotions pulsed through her heart and problems with difficult solutions shot rapid-fire through her mind. In his arms, she was both home and homesick, but amid the confusion, one truth ground her.

"I love you, Ben," she said, leaning deeper into the one-armed embrace.

He swallowed beside her and tightened his squeeze. Then her belly rumbled, and he chuckled. "Hungry?"

"Ravenous."

After rolling out a blanket, Ben produced a thermos of hot tea, crackers, cheese slices, prosciutto, an assortment of spreads, pickles, and olives from his backpack while Beatrice's upturned palms birthed apples, pears, and grapes. She sat down and surrendered to the urge to expose her feet to the chilly morning air. Ben stared at her wiggling toes for a moment, then doffed his shoes and socks as well, stretching his legs out next to hers.

"I don't have to live in the city, you know?" he said.

Beatrice forced her body not to jerk in surprise. She surveyed his face and found nothing but open honesty there. No sadness or disappointment. A smile began to spread across her face, but just before it widened completely, Ben spoke again.

"But I love my job, Beatrice. Interacting with people. Finding them great places to live. It means something to me. And there's not a lot of opportunity in the town at the foot of your mountain."

Beatrice lowered her head and gave a slow, understanding nod. She took a sip of tea, popped a few grapes in her mouth, then scanned the mountains around them. They would never release her, these hills. Nor did she want them to. Her eyes stung and her throat constricted, and she looked to the sky, hoping to see Gertrude.

Come get me, Gertie. Fly me away from here.

Rejection tightened the muscles around her heart, and her palms sweated. She wanted to be as far away from this man and this place as possible. Pressing her hands against the rock below her, she muttered, "I need to walk."

"Beatrice." Ben placed a gentle around her wrist. "There are thousands of towns and smaller cities between your spot on the mountain and New York City. Let's find a place that serves both of us. Look." He withdrew a map full of green, yellow, and brown. "Here," he said, circling the brown, wrinkled ridges, "these are the mountain ranges of the United States. I'd prefer to stay close to the Eastern seaboard, which would mean staying in the Appalachians. But look how far they run." His finger traced from Maine to Georgia, then he locked eyes with her. "I'm serious, Bea. I know there's a middle ground."

Beatrice took the map into her own hands and spread it on her lap. Soon after her mother, Gwen, and Ben had left for New York, she had purchased an atlas to understand how much distance there was between them. She pointed to an arbitrary spot between New York and West Virginia.

"Somewhere in between."

"Maybe. I don't want to go further north, that's for sure! But I would consider farther south."

"And be farther away from Gwen?"

"Gwen and I are like this." Ben crossed his fingers. "Inseparable. I could move to the moon, and we'd still be this close."

Beatrice scanned the sky and saw her sister perched on a tree branch. True, they weren't twins. They didn't even share a father, but she and Gertrude shared the same bond. Her stomach smarted. Ben smirked, then slid a piece of cheese onto a cracker and handed it to her. They filled their bellies with nuts, fruit, cheese, and hot tea, chatting all the while about what they each needed in a home.

"I want to have enough room for everyone to come stay from the Solstice all the way through New Year's! And I need enough of a yard for a greenhouse. Maybe not as big as the one I have now, but big."

The words tumbled out of them, and they interrupted one another, finishing each other's sentences and laughing. Beatrice grew from excited to anxious when the conversation turned to interior decorating.

"Let's slow down," she said, raising her palm. "I knew Forest and I probably wouldn't live together forever, but I never imagined I'd be the one leaving the mountain."

Ben rubbed his palm against her back and kissed her hair. "We can take as much time as we need to decide. However, we need to get back down this mountain so we can move on to the next surprise."

The two of them packed up their picnic and headed down the mountain. As they went, Beatrice named every tree, and when she came to a tulip poplar not yet ready to bud, she whispered, "This is the one I want to be when I die."

"Don't be so anxious. We have our whole lives ahead of us."

***

Beatrice snuggled deeper into the warming passenger seat.

"We're not going back the way we came."

"Nope." Ben shook his head. "We are not."

"Where are we going?"

"You just sit back and enjoy the ride." He leaned forward and turned the music on. A light mix of stringed instruments paired with melodic voices encouraged Beatrice to sink deeper into the seat. "You can take a nap, if you'd like."

"I don't want to miss a minute with you."

She chattered on about plants, sharing vivid details about her favorite flowers, tomato varieties, and green beans. He asked if she'd ever studied books on plants. She hadn't, and a flash of embarrassment at her lack of education whipped through her. But Ben displayed no judgment and went on to explain courses she could take, like botany, plant ecology, and horticulture.

A flush bloomed on his face as he seemed to realize who he was talking to. "I'm sure you could teach them a few things."

Beatrice lifted her chin and gave him a smile that faded as she considered the impossibility of it.

"I don't have a high school diploma." A sudden pang of guilt and panic that Forest didn't either assaulted Beatrice.

"Adults go back to school all the time." He placed a reassuring kiss on her hand.

Beatrice pondered her divinity as they drove away from the mountains. Her attention focused on the way they changed, reduced to smaller hills, and so she didn't see it coming. She didn't see the cherry red truck speed through the stop sign. Didn't see Ben's face as he braced for the impact.

The crash came first in waves of sound. Ben screamed her name. Metal squealed against metal. Glass shattered into a million pieces. The force slung her against her door, and the car tilted violently. The airbags deployed just in time to buffer the full blow of Beatrice's body against the door, but momentum wasn't finished. She closed her eyes so she didn't see the world spin through the windshield as the car continued rolling down the hill. A sickening crack vibrated from Beatrice's clavicle throughout her body, and vomit rose to her lips. When the tumbling came to a halt, the car lay upside down. Beatrice opened her eyes and turned to Ben. A piece of glass the size of a cell phone stuck from his throat. Blood sputtered from his mouth and the wound. His glassy, wide eyes searched for her face.

"Ben." Beatrice reached for the glass, desperate to pull it out, but thought better of it, remembering the way Forest's blood spilled from his body and the actions it took for her to put him back together again. She dug around in her gut and her mind and her soul, willing the vines to come, but they refused. She was too broken.

"I love you," sputtered out of Ben's lips, then a rattling breath scraped from his throat. His body went limp, and all signs of life evaporated.

"Ben!" Beatrice's body thrashed against the seatbelt which was now so tight it dug into her. Her shaking hands fumbled for the latch, and a sharp pain tore through her body. She refused to relent and eventually unlatched the belt, only to tumble headfirst against the top of the car. "Ahh!" Adrenaline pushed the pain away as she scrambled to kneel, aligning her face with Ben's. She pressed her hands against his graying, cold skin and kissed him on his forehead. "Come back, Ben. Please." She gritted her teeth and pleaded to her vines and to the Goddess and to all the big and great things that made the world spin.

"Please." She broke into a sob.

Then it slipped from his mouth.

His silver soul.

Beatrice.

His voice filled her ears and her heart.

I feel nothing. Nothing. Nothing. All around me is nothing.

"Are you in pain?" She thought she knew the answer—once you're dead, nothing hurts anymore, but she wanted to be sure.

Am I dead, Beatrice? So much of nothing. Dark. Am I dead Beatrice?

Beatrice dug her nails into her scalp.

Am I dead, Beatrice? Am I dead? Am I dead?

"Yes, Ben. Yes. Don't be scared."

I am dead. I'm not scared. I am okay. I love you.

Beatrice wrapped her arms around her quaking body as the silver ribbon moved toward her and hovered around her chest.

May I?

It took a moment for Beatrice to understand the request. Releasing the bind around her chest, she opened her heart

"Yes."

Ben's soul slipped into the skin at the base of her throat, and Beatrice shivered at the chill of it. Fear consumed her for a moment before warmth spread through her body.

I'll stay until you tell me to go. There are plane tickets in the glove compartment. Let's go home.

Before injury and fatigue could overtake her, Beatrice rearranged her body, wincing at the pain, and opened the glove compartment. Documents spilled from it. She clutched them all to her chest, then collapsed on the car's ceiling.

***

A shrill beeping sound and bright lights woke Beatrice, who tried to swallow, but her mouth and throat were too dry. The rancid taste of vomit lingered on her tongue. Before she could bring herself to look at her body, she scanned the room. The wooden door was closed, but an open window allowed Beatrice

169

to see people in white jackets chatting outside her room. Smells of antiseptic and latex burned the back of her throat. The walls were cold, too white.

Just like Ben's house.

Beatrice tried to move her hand to her heart to rub the place where his silver soul had slipped into her body, but a pinch at the inside of her elbow stopped her. A tube, stabbed into her flesh and taped to her arm, traveled to a bag full of clear liquid that dripped slow, methodical drops into her. She ripped at the tape with frenetic panic, but pain seared through her ribs, forcing her to relent.

Be calm.

Ben's voice reverberated through her body, and she shivered.

"Ben."

Get to the airport.

"How?"

You only have a few hours.

Beatrice had never wanted to be home more than she did in this moment, and she closed her eyes, imagining her feet on the forest floor. How was she to do it? She had no clue where the boarding passes were now, much less how to get to the airport and find her way to the right gate.

Two people wearing white coats and pity in their eyes entered her room without knocking, and she realized that only a thin hospital gown covered her. She dragged the too-white sheet further up her body.

"Beatrice Woodson, is it?" the person with a long ponytail draped over her right shoulder asked. The stitching on the person's lab coat read "Dr. Adams."

Beatrice frowned in confusion at first, forgetting that she'd taken on her mother's adopted name to navigate the world. A small nod was all she could provide.

"You were in an accident. Do you remember?"

"Yes," she croaked. "I want to leave."

"That's understandable. Could I take a listen?" The doctor

pressed the stethoscope ear pieces into her ears, thumped the round flat metal disk, then moved it toward Beatrice's chest.

Beatrice, who had never been to a doctor's office, asked, "Listen to what?"

"Your heart and lungs. So far as we can tell, you have two broken ribs, and a cracked collarbone. We want to make sure your lungs are safe."

A flashback of knitting Gwen's lung tissue and ribs and chest muscles back together pulsed through Beatrice's brain. Now, she was the broken one with a doctor moving closer and closer. When the cold metal pressed against her chest, she snarled and grabbed the woman's wrist.

It's okay, Beatrice.

Closing her eyes, she relented. The doctor asked her to take deep breaths, and with each, sharp agony sliced through her.

"Your lungs are fine. I'll want to do some imaging to make sure you aren't bleeding internally."

"How long will that take?"

The doctor gave a sharp smile. "I've found it's never worth it to speculate about how long things will take in the hospital."

"I have a plane to catch. I can't stay."

"We have to determine if—"

"No." Beatrice returned her attention to the tape on her arm and, fueled by adrenaline, tore it from her, taking the tube with it. "I'm leaving now." Swatting the sheets from her, Beatrice turned and found the floor with her feet. Lightheadedness swept over her and prevented her from standing.

"I have to insist—"

"No. You can't make me stay here." The words came from Beatrice's mouth as sure as she knew the sun rose from the east and sat in the west, though she had no clue if they were true. "I have rights."

The woman's lips pressed into a thin line, and she turned on her heels to leave the room. The man she left behind closed his eyes and scratched his fingers through his wispy gray hair.

"Doctor Adams lost any sense of bedside manner she once had when her partner died last year. The man you were with, Ben Murphy, he was found d—"

"I was there." Beatrice stood now. "Where are my clothes?"

"In the garbage."

Her eyes widened.

"You were cut out of them, but you're right. We can't make you stay. Doctor Adams will be back with documents affirming that you've declined medical care."

"How long will that take?" Beatrice glanced at the stitching on his coat. "Doctor Sharpe."

"I'll see if I can push it along. You were holding a few things when they found you." He pointed toward a plastic bag labeled Patient Belongings on a table.

"What about his things?"

"Are you his next of kin? His spouse? Sibling?"

"No. He has a sister. Gwen Murphy." Beatrice brought her hand to her throat. What would she say to Gwen?

"I suggest you let me stop the bleeding, Ms. Woodson."

His expression had changed to one of concern, and Beatrice's eyes followed his pointed finger. Hot liquid splashed in drops on Beatrice's feet. The sight of her own blood made her dizzy, and she slumped onto the bed. The doctor smiled politely as he taped gauze around the crook of her arm.

"That'll stop it. Doctor Adams should be back soon. Take care, Ms. Woodson."

The blood on Beatrice's foot brought a flash of Ben's final moments into her mind, his blood gushing from his throat.

I'm here, Beatrice.

Though a tingling lightheadedness flittered throughout her chest, she stood, tied her gown a little tighter, then moved toward the bag. The boarding passes, her identification, and the debit card her mother set up for her were all together. She glanced at the clock, which read five. She had no idea how far she was from the airport, and there wasn't enough time to figure it out.

Beatrice strode toward the window and glanced downward. She could make it down in one piece if she used her vines. Searching the room for something to break the glass, Beatrice settled for the IV pole, then gathered her strength and ran with what force she had toward the window. The impact of the blow against the shatterproof surface brought Beatrice to the ground, pain reverberating throughout her body. She scanned the room again.

Nothing's going to break that glass.

She considered running down the halls and right out the front door but knew the energy of fighting other humans would destroy her.

Help me, Goddess.

Her palms opened and she gathered every electrical pulse of energy to the center of them, calling on her vines. She closed her eyes and sent them forward, coaxing them to tendrils so thin they slithered into the impossible spaces between the molecules of glass and polycarbonate. Once she'd penetrated corner to corner, she jerked the vines toward her, and shatters of sharp, clear beads scattered across the floor. Sweeping away the glass as she walked, Beatrice made it to the edge and peered down. The process had depleted her, emptied her gut and divine powers, but she could do this. She had to.

She leaped, trusting her vines to catch her. Then everything went blank.

CHAPTER 17

Gertrude

Never in her twenty years of life had Gertrude watched her sister do something so stupid as to break through a hospital window, her body broken into pieces, and try to use her vines to help her down. Now Gertrude plummeted toward Beatrice in a desperate effort to save her.

The sun had drifted lower, painting the city in a dusky twilight, but even so, the lack of light was enough to impact the eagle's vision. Her old body had to fight the wind, which was growing colder and angrier. Just before Beatrice made impact with the concrete, Gertrude sank her talons into the vines Beatrice had wrapped around herself and lifted her to a rooftop.

The woman who had raised her and who she had helped raise lolled her head and cracked open her eyes.

"I have to get home, Gertrude."

"You're hurt! You don't have the energy to get home. Snow is coming. You'll freeze!"

"I'll die in that place."

Clad in only a thin hospital gown, Beatrice shivered. Gertrude knew what the cold could do to humans. She scanned the streets, searching for a poor soul she could snatch a coat from. Leaving Beatrice on the roof, Gertrude swooped toward a person who was covered in layers and layers of warmth. She lifted the human with her talons and let them fall, not far enough to injure, but enough to knock paralyzing bewilderment into them.

"Sorry." The creature, who trembled out of fear instead of cold, couldn't understand her, of course. Using her talons and her beak, Gertrude gathered up a hat, ripped gloves from hands, moved the body this way and that until socks and shoes, coat, and one layer of pants came free. She left the remaining under-layer and trusted that they would cross the street and tuck into the hospital without damage.

She ascended to the rooftop and found Beatrice unconscious. Her beak pecked at her sister's ears and pulled her hair. Beatrice groaned, but her eyes fluttered open.

"Get dressed."

Beatrice frowned but followed directions mutely, her eyes lolling in their sockets from exhaustion. She swallowed and croaked, "Airport," then she wove a green cocoon around herself. Gertrude entangled her talons in the vines and hoisted Beatrice into the air.

***

Beatrice was much heavier than the first time Gertrude had carried her to safety all those years ago, and her wings had to pump harder than ever. She felt old. No. She was old.

The eagle understood that her next actions would be the last offerings of help she could give her sister before her avian body released her spirit. The thoughts were as heavy as the weight of her sister's body.

If Beatrice had stayed conscious long enough, Gertrude would have explained that there were several airports nearby and that snow would fall soon, heavy and fast. She lugged Beatrice just over the forest canopy and scanned for lights.

This is impossible. Goddess, you gave me grace when I wanted change. Please help me now.

With the last words of her prayer, Gertrude felt the winds shift, lifting her and pressing around her, dictating her flight.

Thank you.

Gertrude rested as the flow of air carried her for quite some time. Their journey ended outside Albany airport where she placed her sister on the unyielding concrete and poked her awake. Beatrice stroked her feathers.

"Thank you," her sister whispered. "Will you meet me in Charleston?"

"Yes," Gertrude promised, and she pressed her beak against her sister's cheek.

CHAPTER 18

Madeline

It wasn't a nightmare that shook Madeline awake well before the sun rose, but the absence of one. She cracked her eyes, and the realization slammed in her chest that the rushing water had claimed its victim, then it evaporated, leaving no trace, not even vapor to moisten the air. All was barren, cracked earth.

Her eyes traveled to Gwen, who wore a frown even in her sleep. Before she woke her wife, Madeline wept. Gwen's phone chimed on her bedside table, startling her wife awake, and she answered without checking the number. Madeline's heart clenched.

"Hello. Yes, this is Gwen. Yes, Ben's my brother. Okay." Gwen's breathing intensified, her mouth parted, and she jumped from the bed. "No." She shook her head, as she circled the perimeter of the room. "No. Please, there must be some mistake. Can I put you on speaker?" Her eyes locked on Madeline, who covered her face to stifle a sob.

The officer relayed the report in straightforward but compassionate detail. There was an accident. Someone speeding ran a stop sign and T-boned them. The car flipped and tumbled someways down the mountain. Officers found Ben dead on arrival.

"We're not in the city. We're in West Virginia and…" Gwen scrambled to the window and pressed back the curtains, and through it, Madeline saw at least eight inches of snow blanketing the ground. "Are the airports in New York closed?"

"Not yet, but if this storm hits as hard as predicted, they will be soon."

"I don't know what to do. What do we do?" She turned her panicked face toward Madeline.

"You'll have to direct other questions to the hospital staff. I'm very sorry for your loss, Ms. Murphy. Take care."

Gwen let the phone fall from her hand and onto the floor. Madeline scurried to pick it up and call the hospital. Her fingers shook, her synapses misfiring. Finally, she made contact with a nurse.

"I'm Madeline Woodson. I believe my daughter Beatrice may be there."

"Let me see." Madeline heard typing in the background. "It looks like Beatrice was admitted, but she's no longer here."

"What?" Madeline stood. Fury flamed through her. Fury at the hospital for letting her go. Fury at Beatrice for being stubborn. "How bad was she injured?"

"Ma'am, I cannot disclose patient injuries."

"I am her mother."

"I'm not supposed to say this, but she left AMA—against medical advice. I'm sure she will get in touch with you soon."

"Damn it!" Madeline threw the phone onto the bed before remembering Beatrice now had one, too. Her anxious fingers fumbled around the screen before her thumb finally pressed her daughter's name.

The phone rang and kept ringing until Beatrice's voice came through the phone. "Just because your call went to voicemail doesn't mean anything is wrong, so don't worry, family. I'll call you back. I love you."

Madeline moved to Gwen, who sat on the floor with her back against the wall and knees drawn into her chest. She could see her lover's breaking heart through her skin and through the cage that wrapped around it. She wrapped her arms around Gwen and rocked her side to side. A warm wetness permeated through the fabric and into her pajamas top. "I'm here, Gwen. I'm here, I'm here."

The woman's body grew limp in Madeline's embrace, only moving with the sobs that undulated through her, sobs that grew into wails and then screams. Her own eyes filled with tears, and their voices of intertwined grief filled the room and the whole house. A frantic knock pounded on the door and, without receiving an invitation, Beulah entered the room. Those blue eyes were wide and her skin pale.

"What's happened?" Beulah kneeled in front of them and ran her fingers across Madeline's wet cheek.

Her mouth parted, but her throat was thick with disbelief and nausea. Ben was gone, and Beatrice was missing. She tried to swallow, opened her mouth again, but all she could produce was a choking sob that threatened to bring vomit to her lips.

Beulah's eyes traveled to Gwen, but the woman kept her face tucked into Madeline's shoulder.

"Let me get you some water."

Beulah made it to the door just as Stella, Forest, and Dani arrived.

"What's wrong?" Stella asked.

"I don't know," Beulah said. "I'm getting water."

Stella and Dani sat on the edge of the bed while Forest took Beulah's spot in front of Madeline. As his worried green eyes searched hers, she could see that her grandson knew someone was gone. Liquid welled just at the edge of his lower eyelids but didn't drop, and he swallowed deeply before asking, "Has something happened to Mother?"

Beulah hurried in with a glass of water, and Madeline gulped it down. The iciness of it shocked her system and brought with it painful brain freeze. It was enough to bring her back into the room. Back into her body. Gwen's sobs had subsided to whimpers.

"There was a car accident. Another vehicle struck them and sent their car flipping down the mountain. Ben didn't..." At the words, Gwen drew her knees closer and pressed harder against Madeline's body. She stroked the woman's hair and rocked her body again. "Your mother was admitted to the hospital but refused care. I can't get her on the phone."

"Try again!" Forest grabbed the phone Madeline had placed beside her on the floor and handed it to her.

Madeline did as Forest asked, placing the call on speaker so everyone could hear, ending just as Beatrice's voice started. She did it again. And again.

"Okay," Dani said, raising their hand. "Forest, if the wreck was that bad, she probably doesn't have access to her phone."

"We have to get to her."

"Have you looked outside?" Gwen said, pressing away from Madeline. "There's no way, Forest."

"There are other ways for us to find her," Stella said, then stood. "I'll get in touch with the police if I can get service."

"Here." Madeline reached Gwen's phone toward Stella, who pressed it back toward her.

"I'll use my phone. You keep trying to Bea."

"Right," Madeline replied, annoyed by her scrambled thoughts.

Forest and Dani followed Stella out of the room, and Beulah's eyes followed.

"Go," Gwen told her. "There's nothing you can do for me."

Madeline watched as her mother swallowed. "There's nothing I can do for them, either. I can sit here with the two of you."

"Do you think the trees could help?" Madeline asked.

"No." The finality in Beulah's voice sent a shiver down Madeline's spine. "At least, they said they couldn't help me get to

New York when I first…came back."

Madeline's eyes narrowed. *New York?* Her mother barely had the courage to make it down the mountain, much less get on a metal bird and fly to an unknown place. She wouldn't even know how.

"But maybe they can connect with her if they try hard enough," Madeline suggested. "They can communicate with—"

"Yes, Madeline. I know. I could, too." Madeline's jaw clenched at the bite in Beulah's voice.

"Go ask them." Gwen's vacant eyes stared into nothing.

"I'll stay with you," Beulah said.

"Then I'll do it."

Madeline stood, and Beulah took her place beside Gwen on the floor.

***

Madeline had packed for a blizzard. Her fleece-lined boots kept her feet warm as she trudged through the snow, and the balaclava protected her face from the wind. She tucked herself into the trees, pressing her back against one of her grandmother's trunks.

"Ben died last night." One by one, sets of eyes opened. "A car accident. Beatrice was hurt and should be in the hospital, but she left. And now, she's missing."

"Oh, Goddess."

"She never should have stayed."

"Why did you let her stay?"

"Enough." The voice came from Ola, whose deep brown eyes opened and locked on Madeline's. "This is not Madeline's fault. Beatrice is a grown woman, and she chose to stay." The words were a stark departure from the time at the Rock when the tree hung Madeline upside down and shook her for abandoning Beatrice. She opened her mouth to voice as much, but Ola interrupted. "There has to be a way to find her."

"The hospital let her leave. Either she won't answer her cell phone, or it was lost in the crash." Tingling dizziness spread throughout Madeline's body as she imagined it. Imagined her daughter being tossed like a rag doll around the car, and Ben.

It was blood. He choked on his own blood.

She sank her knees into the snow and pressed her forehead to Ola's bark. Then the tree did something remarkable. Roots lifted and wrapped around Madeline. "I was hoping you could communicate with her."

"We can't connect when she's this far away," Edith said.

"We've even tried turning all our thoughts to her at the same time. Nothing works," Alice said.

"Try harder!" Madeline felt her skin warm as her anger rose.

"Careful, granddaughter," Ola said, but she kept her embrace around Madeline. "You've got to get your anger under control." The tree released a sigh. "Beatrice has been through too much."

Unlike before, Ola's voice held no accusations, no malice. Perhaps Beulah's return had softened her. Madeline remembered the relief and joy she felt at having a second chance with Beatrice. Redemption, it seemed, was the common ground she and Ola walked.

"Please, try harder."

"We have to try," Ida insisted. "We have to break through to her."

Alice began to hum, and the others joined her. The sound hit all the notes woven through Madeline's grief, and she broke into a sob.

"Join us," Ola whispered.

Madeline wiped the snot from her nose with her gloved hand, repositioned herself in Ola's arms, and hummed along with them. How long they spilled their song into the sky, Madeline did not know, but an abrupt, collective gasp ended it.

"We have her," Ola said, and she released her hold on Madeline. "Where are you, Beatrice?"

Madeline pulled away to see every eye closed tightly, and brows of bark furrowed.

"She says she's coming home." Alice's voice boomed through

the forest with the blizzard wind and every tree trembled.

"She can't get here in this blizzard. There's no way." Madeline choked on her words.

Ola's eyes peeled open. "You don't know your daughter as well as we do."

Sparks flew to Madeline's fingertips.

"I'm not trying to be cruel," Ola assured. "She's so strong."

"And stubborn as a mule!" Edith added. Trees chattered in agreement.

"There's something else." Ida interrupted them with a tremble in her voice. "She said 'fly.' Nothing else, just fly."

"But the airports are going to be closed, and how will she get a ticket and—"

"Beatrice has an oversized eagle for a sister, Madeline," Ola responded.

Madeline's fear compounded exponentially. Both of her daughters were in the storm. She wrapped her arms around herself. Her teeth chattered.

"Make yourself a little fire. Sit with us for a few more minutes."

"I don't know that I can. It only comes when I'm angry." She thought about the smell of her mother's burning skin.

"Then think of something that makes you angry."

Despite the kindness Ola had shown her, Madeline's mind went straight to the scars on Beulah's arms.

"What did you do to my mother?" She locked eyes with the tree. "She has scars all over her body." It was working. Flames rose to Madeline's palms. Without answering the question, Ola used her roots to assemble a stack of twigs and small logs for Madeline to set aflame, and she did so without saying another word about it. When she looked back at her grandmother, she found sap trickling from her eyes and down her bark.

"I hope she'll tell you everything one day, but she has to feel safe enough."

"I burned her." Madeline sat down beside the fire, her back against Thelma—at least, she thought it was Thelma. "I was having a nightmare. She woke me up from it, and I threw flames at her."

"Tell me about the nightmare." Ola's sap-tears were dried up now, and her voice held an edge to it, as if she stood ready to protect her daughter. "In detail."

Madeline's voice quavered as she explained the vines and her mother's breath, ending her story with a panicked defense that she would never hurt Beulah that way. Then she added the visions she'd had about drowning, the way the hot liquid felt flowing down her throat, and how she didn't discern the victim until Ben died.

"Well," Alice said, and Madeline prepared for a lecture about how her visions were never quite right. "Your premonitions of your family seem to stop just short of the full picture. You know that."

"I know." There was no use arguing the point. Madeline wiggled on her sitting bones, grounding herself more firmly to the earth. "What if I close my eyes and let them come?" Though it was a practice she engaged in with every customer she served, Madeline had never approached the violent visions of her family's future this way. "I could share what I see. Maybe if I feel safe, I can follow it longer."

"I think it's a good idea," Ola said.

Madeline took a moment to survey her surroundings. She cataloged each sensation she felt in her body, the feeling of her seat supported by the earth, the weight of her clothes pressed against her skin, the wind chilling her face. She inhaled the wood smoke in the air and the smell of cold, fresh snow. Her eyes scanned the forest and up and down the trees where the tiniest buds considered poking their gold-green heads into the world but were now capped with white powder. Then, determined to face what she saw with curiosity instead of fear, she closed her eyes.

"I see Beatrice. Her palms are open, and vines are pouring from them."

"Can you see what happened before then?"

In her mind's eye, Madeline tried to rewind the image, but she could only freeze it.

"I can't," she huffed.

"What's the look on Beatrice's face?"

Taking a deep breath in and expelling it into the air, Madeline urged every part of her to embody the moment, to transport her psyche—her very soul—into that place. Beatrice locked weary, exhausted eyes with her, and when she had bound them all tightly, she stood back and lowered her eyes. Madeline opened her eyes and reported her findings to the trees, who all agreed that Beatrice couldn't hurt a fly even if she had to. So, was her mother forcing her to comply then?

Madeline stretched her neck one side at a time, then rolled her shoulders and stretched her hands in front of her, cracking her knuckles.

"Oh, I miss that feeling," Alice said with a small chuckle.

"I'm going back in," she said and let her eyelids lower.

Encased by a constricting cocoon of vines, Madeline felt her adrenaline rise along with the heat in her body. Her gaze transitioned from Beatrice to Beulah, whose face revealed what Madeline could only describe as glee.

"She's happy to do this to us!" she shouted to the trees, her eyes still closed, her body still in the moment. "My mother wants us to die."

"Breathe, Madeline." Madeline heard the attempt at soothing in Ola's voice, but it only caused her to thrash her body around even harder, both in the vision and in real life. "Give the vision time to show you more."

Madeline breathed deeply in through her nose as she watched Beulah whisper Forest and Dani to sleep first, then move to Gwen, whose eyes were wide and sad, not unlike Beatrice's.

"Why are you doing this?" Madeline asked.

Joy no longer brightened Beulah's face; instead, a fierce determination mixed with something of hope lived in her tightened jaw, lifted chin, and those bright blue eyes. Without answering, Beulah released her breath in a puff and the image deepened to darkness. She sat in meditation for several more minutes, but when nothing else came, she opened her eyes. "I can't see anything else." Madeline's voice scratched her throat.

"Was it really glee?" Ola asked.

Madeline sighed. *My god, this is exhausting.*

"I'll look again."

This time, Madeline focused all her attention on Beulah and the way she moved her body. What Madeline mistook for glee now appeared an eagerness, like a boxer bouncing from side to side, preparing for a match. Then there was the way her face fell when it came time to breathe on her family. Once again, Madeline asked, "Why are you doing this?" And once again, Beulah didn't answer.

Madeline opened her eyes and asked Ola, "is she still angry with you?"

"I'm sure she is. I was not the best mother to her."

Eighteen years old with no understanding of the world other than the top of this mountain. We were all too young to be mothers.

"Maybe she and Beatrice weren't killing us in the picture I saw. Maybe they are protecting us, but from what?"

"Not us," Ola reassured.

"I believe you. I need to get back. Gwen is suffering, and when Bea gets home..." *Oh god, she's going to make it home.* The realization sparked an electric jolt of excitement through Madeline. "I saw her at home! She's going to make it home!" The trees all responded with a variety of "of course she will" and "we wondered how long it would take you to figure that out." Ola finally insisted that Madeline finish her statement. "Beatrice will be suffering, too. I need to be calm. I need you." Her gaze traveled from one set of eyes to another.

Stiff and cold, Madeline pressed herself from the ground, grunting as she stood.

"Sometimes I feel as stiff as a tree," she huffed. "Thank you," she offered, her eyes roaming from one face to another. "This has been helpful. Can we try it again?"

"Of course," Alice said. "And, Madeline, take the time to practice with your own gift. Get it under control."

Madeline's head bobbed. As she walked away, she considered that the only two women she knew of to use their gifts against others were herself and Ola, and while so much remained a mystery, she knew her responsibilities. She would sit with the terrifying images and know there could be more to them. She would find quiet moments to practice with her fire, and never again would she use it against her family.

***

It didn't take long for the visions of vines and fire and breath to replace the waterlogged images of what Madeline now knew was Ben dying. Flashes of writhing green and flashes of flame and her mother whispering them all to sleep fueled her terror as she looked down at her mother sitting next to Gwen.

"They made contact. She told them she was flying home."

"The airport will be…"

"Gertrude." Beulah pressed herself up to stand. "She's carried her before."

"Not this far, Mama."

Beulah's eyes narrowed and her lips curled into an almost smirk, mischievous and impish, the way Beatrice looked when she knew something you didn't. "I did not do a great job of teaching you about our family." She lowered her voice to a whisper. "We're demigoddesses. Have faith."

Though Beulah's words were confident, the shudder in her breath as she left the room revealed her true feelings.

She's worried.

Madeline drew Gwen to the bed, enveloped her into a spoon, and pulled the covers over both of them. She waited until Gwen's breath became sleep-soft then gently climbed out of bed. Her mother sat by the fire mending a quilt she didn't recognize;

the quilt Beulah made for her was neatly folded on the couch. Madeline sat down and pulled the quilt to her lap.

"Beatrice loves this one."

"I made that one for you. Ida made this one." She nodded at the one her fingers worked over. "She and Beatrice have a special bond." Beulah looked up, and Madeline shifted her gaze to the fire. "The dream. It's turned into a vision, hasn't it?" she asked.

"It's gotten worse."

Beulah stopped mending. "Really?"

Madeline nodded, still looking into the fire.

"Are you seeing anything different?"

Madeline shook her head, and Beulah clicked her tongue.

"Maybe I should leave the mountain."

Madeline lifted her eyes to Beulah's, and she recalled the way the woman lay limp with no heartbeat yet somehow alive.

"Where would you go?"

"Would it matter?" Beulah asked.

Gwen was right. The woman was confused and scared and willing to do anything for her family, just as Madeline was.

"Mama, I'm never wrong."

"You were wrong about Beatrice."

"About her intentions, yes. But not about what happened."

"I will never do anything to hurt you." Beulah stood, placed a hand on Madeline's shoulder, then moved to the kitchen.

Madeline stared into the fire, tracing the stitching on the quilt with her finger.

What would you be protecting us from?

CHAPTER 19

Alice

I've lived too long. Much too long. All I want is rest. My limbs shiver in this cold March blizzard. I've always hated this fickle month, which is always more winter than spring. Bear, raccoon, and chipmunk have yet to poke out their heads, and the night is silent with only the occasional, piercing hoot of an owl.

Watching one granddaughter pry her soul from her fleshy body and press it into a feathered one, then another one claw through the earth, determined to return to humanity inspired me. For the first time, I wondered if I had the choice to change. I considered asking Stella for her blood, since she knew the process, or Dani, but I suspected neither of them would engage. Especially not now, with Beatrice missing.

It's been decades since I've called the Goddess to me; she's always come without invitation. I've asked very little of Her, so perhaps She'll grant my wishes tonight. Or destroy me for them.

She's coming.

I know Her by the energy vibrating throughout every cell of my being, by the shimmering green glow that floats in the air, a magic dust, and by the song She sang those days when She courted me.

She materializes. Wild red hair. Gray eyes.

"You called me, Alice."

"I want to speak to you, Hazel." When our relationship started, she asked me to give her a name that only I would use, and I chose Hazel. "Alone."

"Of course, my love." Her voice is a melody powerful enough to give birth to planets and stars and propel comets through the air. "Now, let's get you out of this bark."

Unbeknownst to the rest of the trees, she comes to me several times a month. She brings me back to kiss my lips and caress my skin, and I wish that were enough to be content. I've fallen out of love.

When I was eighteen and abandoned by my family, institutionalized for my presumed madness, She came for me. Swallowed me into Her. Loved me in ways I never could have imagined. Gave me family and immortality. But my vows to Her were shortsighted, and now, at over one hundred and fifty years old, I face hard truths.

For a moment, I am everything. The sun. The moon. The earthworm. The rain. All of time and space and history—everything. So different from the nothing I was when Beulah put me to sleep. I prefer the nothing. Everything is too overwhelming. It makes my heartbeat too quickly and brings drops of sweat to the surface of my skin. Time stretches and contracts, and in what seems both eternity and a single breath, Hazel and I are atop another mountain. My legs are underneath me. My arms by my side. I'm young again, and my smooth, dark skin gleams in the moonlight.

"I've missed you," Hazel says again and brings Her lips to mine. I'm not sure when the gesture turned from warming to chilling, but a shiver runs down my spine. "Why have you called me?"

My mouth grows dry.

"Beatrice." I say her name because, as the oldest grandmother, I should put her first. "She's lost."

"Not to me. I know exactly where she is." Hazel trails Her fingers down my arms, and I shudder.

"She's safe?"

"As safe as any of the rest of my daughters." She tilts Her head closer and nibbles at my neck. "You know I don't interfere."

My insides twist at the lie.

"Please interfere this time. It's Beatrice." My heart thuds against my chest. Hazel's never understood how much Beatrice means to all of us, nor how much She means to Beatrice.

Hazel regards me, then smiles. "My darling, I'll do anything for you."

"Anything?" I choke out, and Hazel's right eyebrow lifts.

"Just ask me."

"I don't want to do this anymore, Hazel."

The human body sheathed over the all-powerful deity stiffens, and her eyes narrow. "Which part of it, my love?"

Searching for the words leaves me stammering, and I curse myself for not thinking of what to say before I called.

"Any of it."

Instead of pulling back, the Goddess squeezes my upper arms, and I can feel heat pulsing from Her and into my flesh. Her eyes glow the way Edith's did, and the way Madeline's eyes do when she summons fire.

"You don't love me anymore?"

No. No. No. I don't love Her anymore. She's no longer beautiful to me, and neither is the view atop this mountain.

"Please don't be angry," I say, because how do you look at someone and tell them you no longer love them in the way they desperately want you to?

"What is it you want, Alice?"

"I want my soul back." My lips tremble as I speak. "I want to move on the way human souls move on."

"You're asking to die?" I watch Her grow taller, wider—watch Her expand until her glow is everything, the intense heat radiating from her burning my tender skin. "You want to leave your family?"

"Don't take this out on the rest of them," I beg, struggling to keep my voice calm. "They don't all feel how I feel."

"But some of them do? Is that what you're saying?"

When She asks questions knowing full well the answer, it's a punishment, and instead of Her lover, I am Her child. I swallow.

"I know Beatrice doesn't feel the same way." My granddaughter's beautiful face comes to mind, and my stomach seizes at the thought that my selfishness could bring her harm. "Please."

"No. I will not grant you this."

"Then, I'll ask Beulah to breathe on me." I say this as much to see just how strong of a power the Hazel has given Beulah. "And I'll be nothing."

"You think Beulah is stronger than I," Hazel sneers. "You think she resurrected with no help from me?"

I wince at her words and pull away.

"Beulah, Madeline, Beatrice—all of you are nothing without me. And now you're telling me you'd rather be nothing than be with me?"

Now, there is anguish in her voice, and as much as I want free, I can't bring myself to say yes. I can't call up any words.

"All the trees will suffer the fate you've requested. I will rebuild you as bone and muscle and flesh—return you to the age you should be. As far as Madeline and Beulah, they have one week to leave the mountain. And if Beatrice has the strength to make it home and the courage to challenge me, let it be. Perhaps she will take your place, since she's the loyal one."

The whirring of wind whips around me, and I'm scooped up and driven back into the ground, back to my place next to my daughter and granddaughters, skin hardened to bark, arms forked, growing long.

She's gone.

***

When I tell them of the Goddess's plans, my daughter Imogene weeps sap that drips down the length of her.

"You'll live on in stories," I promise. "Stella will write them."

"Just because some of us were okay with the state Beulah's breath put us in doesn't mean we're ready to be a stack of bones!" Thelma, the quietest of us all, cries into the sky.

"Shh. They'll hear you."

"Well, we need to tell them anyway! They only have a week to get off the mountain. And what of Beatrice? Maybe she'll take your place. What does that mean?" Thelma continues.

"I don't know. Look, I wanted those of us who want to move on to have a chance. I didn't mean to make Her so angry."

"Are you really that tired of it all?" Imogene asks, sounding like a child. "Not just tired of Her, but tired of us?"

"Oh, sweetheart. I could never be tired of you."

"Do not lie to her," Ola said. "And for those of you so upset, I challenge you to stop lying to yourselves as well. The Goddess loves Alice, but to hell with the rest of us."

A wailing erupts among the trees, and I see movement at the door.

"They can hear us. Shush now."

But it's too late. Forest runs towards us, his goofy bear by his side. "Is everything okay?"

"We're crying for Beatrice," I say, and his shoulders slump in response. "Let's quiet down now, all of you. Give Forest and the rest of them some peace."

Forest thrust his hands in his pockets and turned back to the house. Once he was out of earshot, Ola speaks again.

"Listen to me, when Beatrice makes it home, she will need tended to. This will come as a shock to her, and she may not have it in her to help us. We should tell Beulah first. She's the only one who has a chance of fighting the Goddess."

"Fighting her?" I'm appalled at the suggestion, both because it seems completely absurd, but also because I still care about Her. Then, I remember the look on her face. "And then what? She destroys the Goddess and we're all stuck here for eternity."

My children threaten to wail again, but Ola's voice roars, "Silence! Oh, I don't think the Goddess will leave us here. She'll keep her promise of destruction. Our souls will go on. We can't cry about this anymore. We only have a week, so let's come up with a plan that only involves Beulah and consider how Beatrice can help if she can."

I acquiesce. Together we form a plan that will at least keep Madeline, Forest, Gwen, Stella, and Dani safe.

Chapter 20

Beulah

Beulah couldn't stop moving. No one else could either. They sent messages. They called, but Beatrice wouldn't answer. They paced. Stella filed a missing person's report, but the police made no promises.

Fly…what were you thinking, Beatrice?

While she had done her best to lift Madeline's worries, Beulah couldn't keep her own mind from worst-case scenarios. Tired brains and hearts made a petri dish for irritation to breed, and small spats broke out. Madeline and Beulah both grew frustrated at their partners for not being more concerned about Beatrice. Moments of isolation passed in rooms with closed doors, or silent contemplation, staring quietly into the fire.

The time for breakfast had come and gone. Beulah knew hunger wouldn't help any of their endeavors, so she went to work cutting potatoes to fry. Stella joined her in the kitchen and focused on making coffee, and in no time, Forest stood at the stove frying bacon while Madeline worked the biscuit dough. Gwen had stayed tucked away in the bedroom. No one spoke. No one could.

The house smelled like breakfast and woodsmoke, and Beulah wished Beatrice was home to share it. The urge to cry, the urge to break things, and the urge to pull Stella into their bedroom and take her all swirled within Beulah. The knife she'd been wielding violently against the potatoes slipped and pierced her skin. Blood drew quickly to the surface.

"Damn it." She grabbed a cloth and wrapped it around her hand. Madeline moved quickly to rinse the dough off her hands and tend her mother's wound. She hadn't intentionally harmed herself since she tried to die. The pain and irritation of the cut surprised her.

And then, silence again. Beulah's eyes traveled to Stella who stood in a pair of blue jeans and a button-up shirt just the right shade of green to bring out the intense color of her eyes.

She doesn't understand. She doesn't know what it's like to have a grandchild.

Grinding her teeth, she went back to slicing potatoes.

"I don't think you're remembering who Beatrice is," Stella finally said, pouring hot water over coffee in the French press. "She's strong and resourceful. She's—"

"Injured," Madeline interjected.

"She wouldn't have left if she didn't think she could get home safely."

Beulah shot Stella a look, and Stella looked defiantly back. To Beulah's surprise, she felt herself soften and her arousal stir. The woman's pushback suggested some level of trust.

Now is not the time.

"What if she didn't care if she got home safely?" Madeline asked with a harsh breath, prompting a suspicious glance from Beulah.

"What do you mean, Grandmother?" Forest asked.

"Nothing," Madeline said and cut the dough into circles,

plopped them onto the pan, and then moved to check on Gwen, calling behind her, "Those will be ready in about fifteen minutes."

Forest pulled the slices of bacon out of the frying pan and onto a plate and went to wake Dani. Beulah put the potatoes in to fry in the remaining grease. The kitchen was empty, save her and Stella. Blood pulsed at Beulah's temples and in between her legs. *Stop it, Beulah.* Stella hadn't touched her in so long, and Beulah ached despite the stress, or perhaps because of it.

She shifted the pan off the fire and shortened the distance between herself and Stella. Stella's eyes widened as Beulah gripped the back of her head and crushed her lips with her own.

"Beulah…" Stella said, pressing a hand against her chest.

"It won't take much, Stella. I need a release. Please."

Stella's eyes shifted from no, to defeat, then to defiance again, and Beulah wished she had the gift of vines to tether the woman's face against her sex.

"They could be back in here any second."

"Come."

Beulah took Stella by the hand, led her into their room, and locked the door behind her. She tugged Stella toward her, pressing her own back against the door.

"Kiss me."

Stella followed the order, and as she did, parted Beulah's legs with her thigh, applying pressure where Beulah wanted it the most. Beulah rocked her hips against the jean-clad leg, groaning against Stella's lips. The feeling that erupted from her core and shot all the way to her crown and down her toes reminded her that living wasn't so bad. She broke the kiss, leaned her head against the way, and encouraged her heart rate back down.

"Thank you," Beulah told her. "I really needed that."

Stella stood stiff, her face blank and emotionless.

"What's wrong, Stella?" Beulah asked. "Do you feel like I forced you?"

"The bind forced me to."

Stella took a step back, and Beulah took a moment to

straighten her own clothes. "What do you mean the bind forced you? I thought you had feelings for me that weren't part of the bind. I thought you were attracted to me."

"I am, Beulah. But sex isn't what I want right now." Stella waved her hand between the two of them. "My best friend could be dead on the side of the road somewhere covered by a foot of snow, and I can't…" The woman's eyes filled with tears. Beulah wrapped her arms around Stella, relieved that her lover held her back. "How are you thinking about sex at a time like this?"

"I don't know. I guess I wanted to escape for a moment."

"Did it work?"

"Mmm." Beulah nibbled on Stella's ear. "It worked. I'll show you later, if you'll let me."

Stella sniffled and pulled away. "It just feels crass. Maybe there's a word we can come up with if I just can't give you what you want. A word that means no negotiations."

A small sliver of Beulah, the piece that reveled in her power, wanted no part of this contract, but just like Stella, her feelings were greater than the binding.

"What word?" She crossed her arms and shifted her feet.

"I'll think about it." Stella leaned in and placed a kiss on Beulah's forehead before heading toward the kitchen. "I need to wash up," she said before tucking herself in her winter coat.

"Wait, Stella. You didn't answer my question. What do you mean the bind forced you?"

"It's like my system knew what you needed, and I had to provide it."

"Come up with a word," Beulah said, and Stella nodded in agreement before leaving the house.

***

Beulah rinsed her hands before returning the potatoes to the fire. Now and then, she glanced out of the window and into the woods to see the eyes of the trees moving and the mouths whispering. Once the potatoes were crispy, she began scrambling eggs in a bowl.

199

"You forced her?" Dani leaned against the countertop, their arms crossed, eyes dark as ever. "She said the spell made her do it. I haven't told anyone about the bind yet, not even Forest, but if you don't break the bind, I will."

Beulah set her jaw and straightened her back.

"I don't know how to break it, Dani." On its face, the statement was true. She didn't know how to break the bind, but she also had no intention of trying.

"You took her blood and worked a spell so strong that it rewrote your DNA, and you expect me to believe you can't figure out how to do this?"

Beulah balled her hands by her sides.

"Wanda and I can try, okay?" Dani's voice softened, but Beulah's nostrils flared at the suggestion. "Look, I know with one whisper you can kill me, but you're hurting my friend."

Weakness overtook Beulah, and she stumbled to sit at the kitchen table. "Since when was she your friend?"

Dani tutted. "Don't try to kill yourself again," they whispered, looked behind them to make sure no one else was around, and sat down beside Beulah. "Beatrice will hate what you're doing to her, and she'll figure it out without any of us saying a thing."

Beatrice.

Beulah closed her eyes and covered her face. "Ask her first," she said. "She may not want you to break it."

Stella came through the kitchen door, her eyes darting between Beulah and Dani.

"What's going on?" she asked Dani.

"I heard you. You said the bind forced you to…Listen, I could work with Wanda and Forest. We could beak the bind."

Stella shook her head and looked down at Beulah. "Not yet."

Yet?

"She forced you to—"

Madeline entered the room with Gwen shuffling behind her and interrupted the vile accusation Dani intended to throw at Beulah.

"There's food." Stella gestured at the stove and island. Her eyes locked on Gwen as if she would reveal too much if she made contact with Madeline.

The group circled around the kitchen table and pushed food around their plates. There were even leftover biscuits at the end.

"I'll clean up." Madeline stood and stacked plates.

"It's okay, Madeline. I need to move," Beulah said.

Madeline gave a half smile. "Seems to be a family trait."

Once again, Beulah was left in the kitchen alone. Stella's words and actions were so confusing, and for a moment, she considered what it might be like to have her without the bind. She looked out the kitchen window to the tree line and saw her. Gertrude!

***

Beulah kept her gaze focused on the bird as she ran, coatless, against the snow.

"Gertrude!" she shouted, expelling and ingesting lung-burning breaths in heavy pants. "Are you alright? Where's your sister?"

The eagle released small, gentle coos.

"I don't know what you're saying." Beulah leveled her eyes at the trees. "Do any of you know what she's saying?"

"Beatrice was the only one gifted with the ability to speak to animals," Alice said.

"I have to go get the others."

At Beulah's words, Gertrude flew down and flapped her wings, keeping her at eye level, creating a breeze that moved Beulah's hair. The sounds she made now were frantic, desperate ones. After several moments, Gertrude landed at Beulah's feet and cooed again.

"You don't want me to tell the others you're here?" Beulah asked, and Gertrude rubbed her face against her leg. "Is Beatrice okay?"

A soft sound squeaked from Gertie, then she took flight once again and left the forest. The trees were awake now and staring at Beulah.

"Should I follow her?" she asked them. "What are we supposed to make of that?"

"Beatrice said she was coming home. And I, for one, have faith she'll make it," Alice said.

Beulah's shoulders slumped and she shivered. "Have you heard from her?"

"Not recently."

"Beulah," Ola said, "we need to have a conversation about what you tried to do."

Beulah dropped her gaze to the ground and swallowed deeply. "I don't want to talk about it."

"We have to, Beulah," Ola insisted.

"She'll freeze out here. At least let her go get a coat," Edith said.

"Start a fire, Ma." Ola shifted her roots to give Beulah a place to sit while Edith and Ida worked to start a tiny flame. "Beulah, what were you thinking?"

"I'm so tired, Mother." Beulah leaned into the cradle Ola had created for her. "I keep hurting the people that I love. It's been my entire existence."

"That is simply not true," Ida rebuked. "You helped raise Beatrice and saved her life many times. She loves you. Stella loves you."

Bitterness slipped through Beulah's lips in a sardonic laugh. "I can't be sure of that."

"It's time for us to tell them the truth, Beulah. There's something coming. Something we can't tell you just yet, but we may need your gift when the time comes. So, let's get it all out."

"Not unless you tell me what's coming."

"Beatrice is involved, too," Alice said. "It seems simpler to tell you both at once."

A frustrated sigh that turned to a growl rumbled through Beulah. "I'm so tired of being scared."

"I know, dear. I know."

With Ola's help, Beulah confessed all her sins, explained the illusions she'd placed on her mother and recalled every living thing she had breathed breathless. Every tantrum she had as a child. Every time she wished she'd never had Madeline. All the darkness came spilling from her mouth along with tears down her cheeks, and though with each word she relieved another rip of her flesh, she felt lighter, as though removing stone after stone out of her pocket.

"Don't you see?" Panicked desperation filled Beulah's voice, and she stood, turning to the face the trees. "I'm a monster."

"No, Beulah. The Goddess gave a child way too much power," Alice said.

And deep in the pit of her being, in the nucleus of her cells, she knew. The Goddess had made her an equal, and what a fool She had been.

CHAPTER 21

Beatrice

Beatrice hobbled out of the airport, still clad in the oversized clothes her sister had picked off a stranger. She shivered, pulling the coat tighter, but it was no use. More layers were necessary to protect against the winds and snow that howled around her. The plane had landed just as the blizzard whipped up. The flight itself had been horrendous. Turbulence knocked Beatrice around in her seat, and she couldn't get the air vents to blow just right. A headache and chills set in. She knew it was a fever. The flight attendant gave her ibuprofen from the first aid kit and a warm cup of weak tea. Now, she searched the sky for her sister. Not seeing her, she scanned the street for taxis. She stumbled toward a black car and knocked on the window.

"Could I get a ride to Hinton?"

The man's eyes raised. "Hinton is under about a foot of snow, and it's headed this way. I can get you down about as far as Dry Branch, but then I've got to get on home."

"Do you take a card?" Beatrice asked as she pulled her false driver's license and debit card from her pocket.

"Sure. Let me help you with your luggage."

"I don't have any." Beatrice swallowed as loneliness, and perhaps fear, crept into her chest. Something about the man reminded her of the hunter and of Sam.

"Climb on in."

Beatrice hesitated. "If you have any intention of hurting me..."

The man's eyebrows furrowed, creating a fuzzy caterpillar across his forehead. He stared at her for a long moment, then his face softened. "Climb on in," he said. His warmth caused her shoulders to relax, so she opened the car door and eased in, careful of her injuries. "May I ask what happened?"

"Car accident."

The driver's head bobbed. "You sure you don't need a hospital?"

"I've already been."

"Uh huh."

Leaning back and closing her eyes, Beatrice channeled all her energy toward connecting with Gertrude.

I'm on my way!

I'm taking a cab to Dry Branch. Meet me there.

"Take a nap if you want to! I'll wake you when we get there."

"You're very kind."

The words barely left her lips before she drifted to sleep, but a nightmare met her instead of rest.

Naked in the woods. Guts spilled to the ground. The sound of eagle wings. Roots glowing gold. Healing. The putrid taste of partially chewed fish forced down her throat. Velvet roots. Fluids. Sweat. Screams.

Back pressed against gray rock. A green glow on the belly. Writhing. Contracting. Opening. Pain. Birth. Progeny. Green eyes. Fluids. Sweat. Screams.

Skin to skin. A soft bed to bed. Words spoken through touch. Eye contact. An honest giving. Vulnerability. Pleasure. Control. Fluids. Sweat. Screams.

Green shimmer. Shining eyes. Silver antlers.

A ripping in two. A painful expansion.

Beatrice, shattered, woke in a fit of hyperventilation, panting the words, "Too big too big too big."

"You okay?"

Beatrice couldn't answer as she tried to put together the scenes. The first was the hunter. The second, conceiving Forest. The third, Ben.

Breath stopped moving entirely as she choked on vomit that rose to her throat. She covered her hand over her mouth and slammed on the door. The man steered the car off the road and Beatrice wasted no time opening the door and spilling the contents of her stomach onto the road.

I'm with you, Beatrice.

Ben's voice, along with a warmth that spread across her chest, calmed her, and in only a few moments, she'd regulated her breathing. Around her, snow fell like rain, piling on the ground in front of her. A wind twirled it in wisps. She looked at the driver. "Are we close?"

"We're about ten miles out. Here." He tugged a bottle of unopened water from the cooler and handed it back to her. "I have some chewing gum, too. The mint might help. It's against company policy, but if it would help your stomach to ride up front, I don't mind."

Beatrice sipped her water before taking the gum from him and sliding it into her mouth.

"I'm okay back here but thank you."

Instead of closing her eyes, Beatrice watched the snow fly as the car pulled back onto the road. That last image. The green shimmer and the pain. She allowed the details to sharpen in her mind. The being with the antlers her was creation energy itself. A deity. A Goddess. And just as she had been decades ago when the hunter claimed her body, in this dream she at the mercy and whim of something much larger than herself.

She took another sip of water.

It can't be Her.

Her family's Goddess didn't have silver horns or talons to dig into skin. She had held the felt doll her mother made in her hands, touched the wool red hair. *You're not a seer, Beatrice. You had a nightmare. That's all.* Nightmares weren't new to her, after all. She wished she had her tea to sip on instead of water, which sloshed in her stomach despite the tiny sips she took.

The driver took an exit and turned into the parking lot of a diner.

"I can drop you off here or find a place for you to stay. Looks like you could use a hot bath." The man's eyes roamed over her face. "Course, you may be stuck here for a while."

Are you close, Gertrude?

I'm going as fast as I can. I never should have let you do this.

Beatrice thought back to the last time a blizzard of this proportion had slammed the area over a decade ago. It took twelve hours to move through completely, leaving drifts of snow against the cabin. Tucked inside their charmed home, Beatrice and Forest went about life as usual. Pragmatism won over her need to be home when the car gave a little shimmy as a blast of wind knocked against it. "Finding a place to stay seems the best idea."

The man removed the phone affixed to the dashboard and his thumbs flew over the screen until he finally released a sigh. "No hotels anywhere near here. There's a vacation rental home down the road. Let me make a call." After communicating with the owner for a few minutes, the driver ended the call and turned back to Beatrice. "The owners rent out one room in the home and live in the rest of it. They're willing to collect payment once you get there."

After ten minutes, the car pulled up in front of a split-level with an exterior of yellow clapboard and brick.

"Are we still in Dry Branch?"

"No ma'am. Montgomery."

Beatrice opened the door, then turned back to the man.

"Thank you."

Pressing her body against the assaulting wind, she trudged towards the house, and when she opened the door, a gust caught it, forcing her to fight against her pain to press it closed. Two women inside the door rushed to help her, and when it was secure, they all stepped back from it, breathless.

"That wind is something!" The woman, clothed in all silver and black pajamas, had a head full of wild black hair with more silver streaks in it than Beatrice's own and wore thick mascara and red lipstick. She extended her hand and said, "I'm Circe and this is Callisto."

Beatrice couldn't keep her overactive right eyebrow from arching.

"We had an eccentric mother." Callisto, too, wore all black, though hers was embossed with gold. "She passed last week." She stretched out her arms to emphasize the clothing, then dropped them by her sides. "We're in mourning."

"I'm sorry to hear that."

"Enough about us. You're hurt," Callisto said, letting her eyes roam up and down Beatrice who tightened her arms across her chest only to be stabbed with pain. "Let us help you."

Beatrice thought about Gwen looking up at her with hesitant eyes but choosing trust in the end. Trust that Beatrice's intentions were pure and that she could, in fact, help her. The three of them exchanged cautious glances until Circe finally said, "Bathroom is upstairs. Go wash up."

"We'll make you something to eat while you shower." Callisto pointed up a steep staircase. "Follow the hallway to the right."

***

Chartreuse covered the entire tiny bathroom—chartreuse tiles, toilet, bathtub, and even the bathmats. But it was clean and smelled of lemongrass. Beatrice grimaced as she took in the sight of herself. A stitched wound across her left cheek throbbed, and seeing it allowed the pain that adrenaline had numbed to overwhelm her. Sour sickness slid up her throat, but she swallowed it. How long had it been since she'd eaten?

She unwrapped the coat around her, then unbuttoned the long, white dress shirt Gertrude had pilfered from the man on the street.

Poor guy.

With mindful, measured movements, she opened the shirt, revealing a purplish, red bruise that spread along her left side from just underneath her breast all the way to her hipbone, and toward her navel. She brought her hand close to her skin but didn't make contact. Next, she removed the trousers, let them fall to the ground, and surveyed her legs, which appeared unharmed. She turned on the water until it was almost hot and stepped in. The shampoo and conditioner were homemade and comforting, at least for a moment. The minute she closed her eyes, memories of the crash assaulted all her senses, but instead of fighting them, she let them in. The painful beating her body took. Ben's eyes as they went from desperate to accepting, wild to dim. The blood.

I'm with you.

A stinging formed behind Beatrice's eyes, but she forced back the tears. Crying would only make her more miserable.

Washing and conditioning her hair and taking care of her private areas seemed all Beatrice could handle. Her face stung as the shampoo suds slipped down the torn flesh, and her side was too sensitive to touch. She turned off the water and reached for a towel, using her right hand to avoid pain, and she shivered as she wrapped herself in it.

Fever.

She stepped out of the bathroom and cracked open the door.

"Go straight down the hallway. Bedroom's to the left!" She thought it was Circe's voice, but she wasn't entirely sure.

The bedroom made up for the bathroom's small size. Double the size of her own bedroom, it offered an ornate four-post bed and a matching dresser with a hanging mirror, which Beatrice avoided. On the bed lay a pair of sweatpants, a tank top, and a sweatshirt with a hood. She started with the top layers, then, after mentally preparing herself for the pain bending over would cause, she slipped on the underwear and pants. Both women were shorter than Beatrice, and the pants rose between her ankle and her calf. Somehow, a smile formed on her lips. She'd found people like her.

It took time and effort to ease the garments on, and by the time Beatrice was fully clothed, a bead of sweat had broken out on her upper lip.

Definitely a fever.

She had just sat on the edge of the bed to catch her breath when there was a small knock on the door.

"Beatrice? May I come in?"

"Yes."

Callisto entered carrying a tray holding a silver tin, a white plastic bottle, a glass of water, and a steaming cup of tea. She sat the tray on the bedside table and opened the white bottle, tilting two pills onto her palm. "Have you had any ibuprofen?"

"Not recently, no." Beatrice furrowed her brow, trying to recall the information without remembering the details of the past several hours. "I'd say it's been five or six hours."

The woman handed her the medicine and the water, which she gulped.

"Easy, now."

"I didn't realize I was so thirsty."

"I also have some natural remedies here for your cuts, scrapes, and bruises." Callisto's voice brimmed with a hesitant hopefulness, one that Beatrice understood. "The tea will work with the ibuprofen, and I have salves you can try."

Beatrice lifted her chin and eyed the lid on the tin, which read *Three Cs Comfrey, Chamomile, and Calendula.*

"You don't have to try it, of course, but—"

"But you're a smart woman trying to get somewhere, and you want to feel better." Circe entered the room and stood above Beatrice and Callisto, serving them both a raised eyebrow, do-not-question-me stare.

Beatrice's lips twitched at Circe's demeanor, and for a moment, she forgot to be sad. "How do you know I'm smart?"

"Because you're not eyeing the salve like a skeptic. You're evaluating the ingredients like an expert."

Beatrice didn't stop the grin from forming. "I've never thought to add chamomile. What's in the tea?"

"Smell it and tell me." Circe handed Beatrice the cup.

After a brief inhale of steam, Beatrice listed off turmeric, ginger, cinnamon and lemon balm.

"And chamomile!"

"She loves the stuff," Circe said, then reached for the salve and slid off the lid. "Here." The dark-haired sister rubbed her finger over the surface of the salve until enough accumulated, then brought her hand toward Beatrice's face. Beatrice flinched, and Circe froze but didn't withdraw her hand. "I don't like being taken care of either," she said, then she smoothed the salve along the wound on Beatrice's cheekbone. After tending to all the visible bruises and scars, Circe asked, "Where else?"

Beatrice swallowed deeply, then lifted the shirt to show her ribs.

"Oh, darling," Callisto said. "Maybe I shouldn't have given you ibuprofen."

"Damn." Circe gently palpated the swollen skin and tissue all along Beatrice's tissue. "You could have internal bleeding. You need to go to the hospital."

"I've already been to the hospital. Please, just do what you can." The sound of her own voice infuriated Beatrice. Notes of desperation, anger, sadness, despair all chimed together in a plea.

Circe scooped a dollop of salve on two fingers and layered it along Beatrice's flesh. When she was finished, she pulled Beatrice's sweatshirt back down.

"Alright then." Circe stood, then gestured for the other two to follow. "Dinner."

She exercised caution, focusing her attention on each step as her foot landed on it, knowing for certain a tumble down the stairs would surely kill her. The smell of a home-cooked meal wafted from the kitchen, and Beatrice sniffed the air, picking out green beans, bread, and roasted meat of some sort, and once she made it to the table, she found her suspicions to be right, though her nose had missed the mashed potatoes.

"Thank you so much," Beatrice said, taking a seat.

"Let me fix you a plate." Callisto scooped portions of each dish onto a plate and handed it to Beatrice.

"Wanna tell us what happened?" Circe asked as she helped herself to a heap of potatoes.

"Car accident. I'd rather not—"

"Of course, dear. No pressure." Callisto, lips pressed into a line, side-eyed her sister.

The room grew quiet and stayed that way as the women ate. The intense hunger Beatrice felt surprised her, and she allowed Callisto to scoop more servings of beans and another slice of sourdough bread with butter onto her plate. The silence, which felt awkward for Beatrice but normal for the sisters, stretched until their plates were clean. Before returning to her room, Beatrice cleared her throat and stated, "I'm not a witch." Standing at the kitchen sink, the two sisters glanced at one another and released hearty laughs.

"Whatever helps you sleep at night, sister," Circe said, and went back to drying.

Well, now you have to show them. Ben's voice warmed Beatrice's chest.

I can't do that. Beatrice shook her head at the thought. "Goodnight," she said to the women, and she trudged back up to her room.

Beatrice lay her body on the bed, her stomach nauseated from the extra helpings of food, but the most tender parts of her felt some better, and she was able to find sleep.

***

The clock on the bedside table read four thirty when Beatrice woke, panting, covered in sweat, and her mind filled with scenes of Ben choking on his blood.

I haven't left you, Beatrice. I'm here.

Beatrice ripped the covers from her, but when she made to stand up, it felt as if she didn't have enough blood in her body. She was freezing, as if each cell were a snowflake drifting downward to pile at her feet. Glancing out the window, Beatrice took in the storm's impact. Drifts formed hills against the shed she hadn't noticed the night before, and she estimated at least a foot and a half had fallen. Thin, gray snow clouds covered the sky, but it seemed the precipitation was over.

Where are you, Gertrude? Can you get me home?

Meet me outside.

Inhaling a deep breath, Beatrice stood and made her way to the bathroom. Her tortured body roared in response to her squatting on the toilet. After relieving herself, she splashed water on her face. She'd never seen herself look so tired. So defeated.

I'm here.

For a moment, Beatrice resented Ben's voice as it floated in her head, separated from his dead body. She purged herself of the thought quickly, not wanting Ben to sense it. Not wanting him to leave.

She layered the man's clothes over the sweats the sisters had given her, then tiptoed down the stairs to keep from waking them up. But they were already awake and sitting at the kitchen table with steaming cups of coffee.

"Where do you think you're going?" Circe asked.

"Oh, she's not leaving," Callisto replied, swatting her hand at her sister. "Are you cold? We can turn up the heat for you."

"I am leaving."

Callisto's mouth parted for a moment before she protested, "You aren't going to get an Uber in this weather."

Beatrice recalled Ben's words. *Well, now you have to show*

them.

Drawing in a deep breath, Beatrice straightened her spine, rolled her shoulders back, and lifted her chin. "I have a ride. Let me show you."

The women wrapped themselves in coats while Beatrice pulled on the too-large boots and tied them.

"Here," Callisto said, handing Beatrice a coat, gloves, and a hat.

Beatrice considered protesting but accepted the gift with a thank you and a smile.

The snow came up to just below Beatrice's knees and she winced as it tumbled into her boots. She walked away from the house just far enough to do what she had to, then held out her palm. For several seconds, nothing happened, and Beatrice felt a burning in her eyes that she blinked away.

Please, Goddess. Help me.

A tingle started at her feet and warmed its way up Beatrice's body as she felt the gathering of cells congregate in the center of the palm. The vines slithered from it in a slow crawl. Callisto's mouth spread into a smile, while Circe's eyebrow shot up, impressed by Beatrice's work. Green worked its way around Beatrice until a cocoon had shut out the sight of the sisters, and Gertrude's piping alerted her it was time to go. The impact of Gertrude gathering the vine pouch in her talons knocked Beatrice against the side, and she gasped. Dizziness took over again, and her body gave into the cocoon holding her.

"I'd still call you a witch!" she heard Circe call as the world around her faded to black.

CHAPTER 22

Stella

Stella woke before Beulah and left the woman asleep, grateful that somehow the two of them had rested amid the worry about Beatrice. She knew it was early, but her eyebrows shot up as she read the clock.

Madeline paced in front of the fireplace. Dark, puffy circles ringed her eyes and her disheveled hair hung loose and wild.

"No sleep?"

Madeline shook her head. "You?"

"Yeah, we slept a bit. I am going to take some tea. I hate to ask you a favor, but I want to drink it near the trees so I can talk with them. Could you..." Stella glanced out the window and waved a hand. "Burn it away and make me a little fire?"

Madeline's shoulders slumped, and she huffed. "I'll try."

They put their coats on, and Stella followed Madeline out the door where the woman stopped and stared at the blanket of precipitation.

"I'm not sure how to make it come without anger or arousal. I suppose you could insult my parenting and remind me how bad a daughter I am." Madeline's face was impassive and her voice emotionless as she spoke.

She was right, though. Stella could say those things and with conviction, but then Madeline may turn her flames on her. Stella's hatefulness wasn't needed; just the thoughts brought a red glow to Madeline's palms. Fire shot from them, and the woman walked forward, making a dry path. Stella didn't follow, choosing instead to let Madeline work while she made herself tea. Just as the kettle whistled, Madeline trudged into the kitchen, appearing even more depleted.

"Thank you."

"I need your help to figure this out, Stella, so I'll help in whatever way that I can."

Madeline returned to pacing the den.

Stella took her mug and followed the path through the snow where Madeline had built a small fire. A log sat close enough to the flames for Stella to feel warmth, and she settled in.

The mugwort skipped Alice's life, and instead, Imogene's story unfolded before her. Prompts for Stella's writing. It seemed fitting that the first round of stories should be of the family weaver and writer. A part of her wished it was ethical to ask Beulah to put the rest to sleep so that she could have one-on-one time with only Imogene. Instead, she settled for asking for as much privacy as the others could provide.

"Tell me about it," she told the tree, though she kept her eyes closed, focusing on each image.

"I realized we were different," Imogene started, "when I started reading the books Mother brought up the mountain with her. Different, but not magical. Not enchanted. *The Legend of Sleepy Hollow. Frankenstein.* I still don't see us as any more magical than the people in those stories! Victor Frankenstein created life. The Bible is full of magic. I pulled thread from thin air; Jesus turned water into wine."

"You know that *Frankenstein* and *The Legend of Sleepy Hollow* weren't true stories, right?" Stella asked, a smile playing on the corners of her mouth. "And the Bible...well, wars are fought over that one."

"Beatrice has told me as much." The tree diverted her eyes. "But that doesn't mean she's right!"

"There is truth in fiction, too," Stella deduced. "Did reading ever make you want to leave the mountain?"

"Oh yes," Imogene said. "Once in a while. Then Mother would remind me of her childhood and how cruel people could be. So, I made my own stories!"

Stella smiled, recalling the *Adventures of Solomon the Owl*, a collection of stories she'd read in Imogene's journal.

"I've never written made-up stories before," Stella confessed. "Any advice?"

"Well, you're not making our stories up, are you? You'll just tell the world they aren't real."

Stella nodded, then spent the next hour listening to Imogene describe how she learned of her gifts of weaving. The need for clothing revealed the talent for creating thread and designing clothes, and the need for adventure spurred Imogene's love of storytelling.

When Imogene had supplied Stella pages worth of notes, she closed her eyes slowly and whispered, "I don't want to go."

Stella's brow furrowed and she leaned in closer.

"Go where, Imogene?"

"Wherever you go when you die."

"That won't for a very long time, now, will it?"

Behind Imogene, Ola's brown eyes opened wide. "Well, trees do die, eventually. Or, at least, that's what we assume."

Stella turned her attention to Alice, the first tree, the companion to the Goddess.

"Alice," she said, "can you help me understand the first images the tea showed me?"

Alice's eyes opened and they seemed brighter to Stella

somehow. "I'll certainly try, dear."

Stella explained the pictures that came to her, the different landscapes and laughter and wild, red hair. When she finished speaking, Alice hummed.

"You've seen the beginning, Stella."

"Of what?"

"Of the Goddess's interactions with humans—with women. We aren't Her first family, you see."

"I wonder if we will be Her last," Ida said.

The trees grew silent, and Stella glanced around from trunk to trunk. Some eyes were sad, others excited; Alice wore resignation on her face.

"What's going on?" she asked. "Do you all understand Madeline's nightmare?"

"Not the details," Alice said. "But we know the events will come to pass. Madeline's visions always do."

"So Beulah will use her breath on me."

Wind whistled and rattled tree limbs, but no one spoke for several minutes. Stella's eyes moved from tree to tree.

"Answer—"

"Not out of malice," Ola said. "She cares for you. And her breath may be useful."

Stella closed her eyes, pressed herself up, and brushed dirt from the bottom of her pants.

"Thank you."

As she walked to the house, she heard Ola call, "She loves you, Stella!"

***

She roused Beulah from her slumber and told her what Imogene had shared.

"Something is going to happen to the trees. Imogene told me she wasn't ready to go."

Beulah worked her jaw and swallowed hard but couldn't seem to speak. Stella moved toward the woman.

"They're certain that you will use your breath. Ola said it

may be useful." An invisible rope tightened between Stella and Beulah, pulling her closer as she said, "But you promised me."

The muscles in Stella's chest tightened, and her stomach roiled. A barrage of thoughts erupted at once, the predominant mantra becoming *you promised me*. But she was learning how to talk with the women of this family. The more she pressed, the more they closed off and defended their hearts like longbowmen shooting arrows at those down below. It wasn't worth it. And, after all, what did Beulah owe her? In the end, her family would always come first even if Stella's blood flowed through the woman's veins.

Words wouldn't make their way to Stella's mouth as she stared into Beulah's eyes, and she did her best to remember what she had been so drawn to. What was it about Beulah that made her willing to give so much of herself? The two versions of the woman seemed incomprehensibly difficult to reconcile, but she searched for the connection, nonetheless. And in the quiet, sifting through memories of being held and napping within the cradle of roots, Stella considered perhaps she didn't love Beulah at all. Perhaps the enchantment of it all, the magic itself, had spurned her decision to help. And perhaps Beulah's motivation had little to do with companionship and more with desperation.

Regardless, the two shared blood and a bed, and being in Beulah's presence righted all the physical, mental, and emotional pain that being separated from the woman had created. Stella knew that resisting the unholy link between them would be detrimental to her health, as Beulah's attempt at suicide had proven.

"Beulah, I'm not sure I can live without you. I'm not sure you can live without me. And I don't mean that in a silly, romance novel way. My blood and your magic have bound us to one another. Wherever you go, I go. When you were gone and I went to New York, my body almost shut down completely."

Beulah said, placed her palm on Stella's cheek. "I feel it, too."

"But is it love?"

Beulah tucked her chin. "Perhaps when all this is over, we can figure that part out. Until then," she said, lifting her eyes once more, "we are one another's lifeline."

"What will be will be," Stella said, taking the woman's hand and kissing the top.

Stella pulled Beulah close to her and held her heart-to-heart, feeling the synchronous rhythms, and prayed.

Goddess, help us.

"I will have to test my breath on Beatrice to make sure Madeline and Forest will be safe if I use it on them."

This added information set Stella's teeth on edge, and she ground them before taking a deep breath, schooling her face, and saying, "I'm not sure why it wouldn't work. The four of you are still half human."

"I have to know for sure." Beulah said. "It will be alright, Stella."

You don't know that.

"I need a little break. Coffee?" she said as she stood. She needed a moment away from the conversation with Beulah to reset herself. To focus.

"Wait. Can we make love first? You can say no. I won't protest, I just…miss your touch."

"I haven't come up with a word yet."

"Well, how do you feel right now? Does it feel wrong to think about it right now?"

Yes, of course it feels wrong now.

The frightened parts of Stella divided themselves and gave her two different sets of instructions. One reminded her that Beulah could kill her on the spot and that the safest bet was to give in. The other demanded she stand her ground, lest this bind with the woman become even more demanding.

Beulah lifted her fingers and traced Stella's jaw.

You are so beautiful…and so damn terrifying.

"I'm afraid you'll be mad if I say no." Stella hated the sound of her voice almost as much as she hated those words. "I think

I need to say no right now just to practice saying no to you." Unexpected tears sprang to her eyes, and she wiped them with her shirt sleeves. "And I need for it to be okay."

Beulah withdrew her hand. "I meant it, Stella. I'm not angry. Don't get me wrong. I want you. Desperately." Her eyes fell to the floor for a moment and she squeezed her hands together in her lap. Then she looked up and locked eyes with Stella. "But I want your trust more than I want your body."

Stella's shoulders released at the words, but the tears returned. "Thank you."

"No, Stella. Thank you. Thank you for being honest."

"I do want to come up with a word..."

"I'm thinking we're too complicated for just one word." Amusement laced Beulah's voice.

Stella couldn't help but smile. "Coffee?"

"That should not be the word," Beulah said.

"Well, it could be an affirmative answer. 'So, Stella, are you in the mood?' 'Yeah, I could go for a cup of coffee.'" The two laughed at thought. Stella allowed the laughter to subside before she said softly, "I am up for affection." She tilted her head, leaned in, and kissed Beulah one time on her lips. "Now, coffee?"

"Okay."

Without another word, Stella left the bedroom and made her way to the kitchen. Beulah followed and sat down at the table. Stella joined her as the coffee steeped, and the two took in the sight of the snow. Stella's eyes welled with tears again and a lump formed in her throat as she thought of her friend trying to make her way home. The swooping down of something green and brown and noisy into the trees caught Stella's attention, and both she and Beulah stood and made their way to the porch.

"What was that?" Beulah breathed. Gertrude, her large wings pumping her toward the house, her throat full of eagle's cry, answered. "Get Madeline!" Beulah said, then took off toward the trees.

CHAPTER 23

Madeline

Madeline had heard Stella's voice this panicked before months ago on that late morning in December when Gwen had fallen, and her cracked ribs had pierced her lung. Without stopping for a coat or even a pair of shoes, Madeline ran behind Stella toward the trees as a frantic Gertrude squalled overhead. The voices of her grandmothers layered on top of one another, but instead of the usual chaotic chatter, their words were measured and coordinated.

"We've got you, Beatrice," Ola soothed.

"Beatrice!" Madeline scurried closer and saw her daughter tucked in a vine-woven womb.

She worked with the trees to pull the vines away and grimaced as she surveyed the scars on Beatrice's face, the clammy perspiration that glistened on her ashen skin. The smell of sweat and other bodily fluids emanated from her dirt-encrusted clothes. Madeline used her palms while Ola used her roots to bring healing energy around and over her.

A hand pressed against her shoulder, warm and gentle. "It's working," Beulah said. "Look."

Color returned to Beatrice's face. She swallowed, and her eyelids parted slightly. She released a groan but made no effort to move.

"Can you sit up, sweetheart?" Madeline asked.

"No." The word was just a breath on Beatrice's lips, and her eyes closed at the end of it.

"We'll clean her up just like we did before," Ida said. "And tuck her in for a nap. She needs rest."

How many times will we have to save my daughter?

Madeline stood and stepped back to allow Ida more room to cradle Beatrice up in her roots and sweep her to the bathhouse.

"Wait." Ola's voice, deep and firm, rumbled in Madeline's chest. "We have to tell her about Madeline's vision. She needs to know what's going on."

"She can't even hear us right now, Ola," Madeline spat.

"Madeline's right, Mother," Beulah replied, and the words of affirmation straightened Madeline's spine. "We will tell her as soon as possible. But look at her." Beulah's voice wavered and Ola's eyes grew soft.

"She needs rest, but the moment she's able to hear you, you must tell her."

"Stella, can you get her clothes?"

Stella nodded and took off, but Beulah stayed behind, looking at Madeline with questioning eyes.

"Will you help me?" Madeline asked, and her mother took her hand.

Ida weaved a cocooned Beatrice to the bathhouse and offered support as Madeline and Beulah worked together to peel cold, wet clothes from her body, revealing wounds and bruises Madeline and her grandmother hadn't mended. Pressing her lips together, Madeline brought her golden light to the swollen bruise that covered her daughter's side. She hovered her hands above the skin, wishing she could divert her eyes from the scars scattered along Beatrice's body. With enough time, energy, and encouragement from Beulah, Madeline returned her daughter's body to wholeness. She prayed the transition to the warm bath would rouse Beatrice back to consciousness, but her head just lolled to the side as she sank into the water.

Madeline sat back on her heels, covered her face, and pressed her fingertips into her eyelids. "Jesus," she whispered. She could hear water sloshing as Beulah went about washing Beatrice's hair and body. The healing had depleted her own body, so she remained still until Stella arrived with a change of clothes. Tree roots and human arms and hands lifted and tugged and rearranged until Beatrice was dressed, then Ida cradled her again.

Madeline, along with Stella and Beulah, followed behind the vines holding Beatrice as Ida eased her through the house and tucked her in the bed. The noise woke the rest, and Forest, Dani, and Gwen all filled Beatrice's tiny bedroom.

"Ben!" Gwen cried and climbed into bed. Her hand hovered over a space behind Beatrice, stroking air. "Ben."

Madeline moved toward Gwen, took hold of her shoulders and, with tenderness, made to pull her from the bed. Gwen jerked away.

"He's here, Madeline. He's with her."

Madeline took a step backward as Gwen kept repeating her brother's name, eventually lying down facing Beatrice and stroking her face. Beatrice remained unconscious, but her chest moved with steady, deep breaths.

"Is she alright?" Forest asked behind Madeline, who turned to face her grandson.

"Ola and I healed her. Mama and I cleaned her up and changed her clothes. She's as good as she can be, I guess."

"Can I just—?" Forest pointed toward Beatrice, and Madeline scooted to the side to let him pass. Gwen didn't move from her spot alongside Beatrice, leaving Forest to move around the bed to the other side. He sat on the edge of the bed and stroked his mother's hair. "It's alright, Mother. You're home now."

"She'll be hungry when she wakes up," Dani said. "I can't cook worth shit, but I can throw together a fruit salad if someone will go get fruit from the greenhouse."

"I'll go." Forest stood, keeping his eyes on Beatrice and Gwen for a moment before leaving the room. Dani followed.

"I'll go scramble eggs," Beulah added, and Stella followed up with the offer to reheat the coffee, leaving Madeline and Gwen alone in the room.

"I'm not going anywhere. He's here, Madeline. He's smiling at me." Gwen sniffed, and a laugh tumbled together with a choked sob. "Ben." She stroked the air again, then brought her hand to Beatrice's waist. "I'll stay with her. Go make biscuits."

"Okay," Madeline said. She moved to the door but paused, leaning her head against the frame. There her daughter lay, fragile and broken again. She brought up the image of Beatrice wrapping vines around the family again.

I'm missing something. She couldn't hurt us even if she wanted to.

"I love you, Gwen."

"I love you, too."

***

Beulah, tears streaming down her face, stood in the kitchen whisking eggs while Stella made coffee and Dani stared out the window, waiting for Forest. Madeline's mind wandered as her muscles moved together to put together biscuit dough. Forest entered the door, handed Dani a basket of fruit, then moved closer to face Madeline.

"Grandmother, we should give her time to heal, but the rest of us should know the details of the vision you're seeing."

Madeline's eyes darted from Forest's to Beulah's, which were still red and leaking tears. She returned to folding the biscuit dough without responding, but once the dough was ready, she looked back up.

"We all flee the mountain and make it to Wanda's shed, where

Beatrice ties us up in vines and my mother uses her breath on all of us."

"You didn't tell me the nightmare included Beatrice, Beulah." Stella gave Beulah a pointed look before pouring coffee into cups.

"Does that change things?" Beulah asked.

"My mother doesn't have it in her to hurt anyone," Forest said.

Beulah released a sardonic laugh. "But you think I do."

"I didn't say that, Great-gran…Beulah."

Madeline noticed the way Dani glared at her mother. There was heat and intensity in the stare, but their body language, the way they tucked themselves behind Forest, indicated Dani's mistrust, or was it fear? Returning to cutting the biscuits, Madeline breathed through the tension punishing her chest.

"I've gone to the trees with the vision and I'm trying to sit with it instead of avoiding it. I need context. My visions of my family always lack context." Madeline plopped the biscuits on to a pan and slid them into the oven. "I can't say for certain," she said, straightening back up and turning toward her mother, "but I don't think we're running from you or Beatrice. Something bigger is coming."

"Grandmother, was there snow in what you saw?" Forest asked.

"No, I don't think so."

"Then perhaps we have time. It will take a while for the snow to melt."

"It's supposed to be sixty-eight tomorrow," Dani said. "Sunny."

Madeline released a long exhale. "After breakfast, I'll sit with it and see what I can see."

"Or sit with it now. While the biscuits bake," Forest insisted.

Madeline was too tired to say no, so she gave a nod and retreated to her bedroom. She sat on the edge of the bed with little concern about readying the space; the vision would either come or it wouldn't. She took a deep breath and held it before exhaling and closing her eyes.

Madeline's heart pounded and she panted as the sensation

of running filled her senses. Several times she glanced over her shoulder, and a swirl of green shimmer urged her to run faster. The Madeline sitting safe in her bedroom, the observer, spoke the words "look down" aloud to the Madeline sprinting. Indeed, small drifts of snow still lay in pillows around the base of trees, and the grass was wet and slick. Not needing to see more, Madeline opened her eyes and moved back to the kitchen, taking a seat at the kitchen table.

"We have to tell her today. There will still be snow on the ground when this thing happens."

"What if I'm not fast enough?" Dani asked, their eyes locked on Forest's.

"We will leave as soon as we can. We won't wait."

"But that's not what your grandmother sees."

A spark of irritation grew in Madeline's belly. She had watched Forest tend to Dani, fetch them glasses of water and take their plates to the sink. Though the person always showed gratitude, it irked Madeline. Dani moved through the world with a tough exterior and an even tougher mouth but softened to a helpless kitten at home.

"You'll do the best you can," Madeline said, then stood and pulled the biscuits from the oven. "Just like the rest of us."

CHAPTER 24

Beatrice

Beatrice woke to the sight of Gwen's wet face and the feeling of the woman's hand in her own. An initial inclination to console softened Beatrice's features, and she almost wiped Gwen's face and told her it would all be okay. But it wouldn't. Ben was gone. She pushed aside the urge to comfort and joined Gwen in her tears. She pressed her forehead against Ben's sister's and sobbed until snot and saltwater wet her pillow and nausea filled her belly. Gwen's tears slowed, and between jerky, shuddering breaths she said, "He's with you."

A bout of doubt flashed through Beatrice, a cold chill along her chest.

Was it wrong of me to let you in, Ben?

No, darling.

"He's..." Beatrice had to pause and swallow hard. Her voice sounded all wrong, small and rough, as though she had aged fifty years. She pulled further away from Gwen and rubbed her hand to her chest. "He's here. He asked me if he could…and I said yes."

Gwen placed her hand atop the one Beatrice held to her own heart.

Tell her I love her so much.

"He says he loves you so much."

"I love you too, Brother," Gwen said, her eyes traveling past Beatrice. "How are you feeling?"

Now that she'd stopped crying, hunger took over. "Starving."

"Well, I'm sure your mother made biscuits."

"Of course she has." A smile formed on Beatrice's lips, then vanished in an instant. "Can we stay here just for a few more minutes? I'm just not ready to face it all. We can sit with our feelings together."

"Who taught you that?"

"You," Beatrice replied. "Can I talk about it?"

Gwen inhaled a sharp intake of breath, but she nodded, her eyes filling with tears once more.

"He'd taken me to the mountains." Beatrice closed her eyes and remembered how she'd never felt so loved. "And planned to surprise me by bringing me home early. While we were driving, we talked about the future. We were going to find a place where we could both feel at home. He was willing to leave the city, and I the mountain." Beatrice shifted to her back and covered her face with her hands. "Maybe you shouldn't be the shoulder I cry on. He's your brother." She sniffled.

Gwen scooted her body closer, wrapped an arm around Beatrice's waist, and pressed her forehead into her shoulder. "No one will have the same understanding of what we're going through. Did he suffer?" The words came out ragged and shuddering, and they brought sobs to Beatrice's throat all over again.

"It happened so fast. We rolled over and over again, and I must have blacked out for a moment. I'm sure it hurt, but it didn't take long. A piece of glass had…there was so much blood."

The two women allowed the tears to flow again for several

minutes.

"Will you help me pick out an urn for him? I want them to send the ashes to town. I don't know when I'll be ready to go home now."

"Okay." Beatrice pressed herself up and turned to Gwen. "I'd give anything to have him back."

Gwen's brows furrowed and looked away. "No, I don't think you would give anything."

Beatrice felt like she'd been plunged into a bath of ice water. "Why would you say that to me?"

"I'm sorry. I know you loved him very much." Gwen sat up, squared her body with Beatrice, and crossed her legs. "But there's something we have to think about. Your grandmother breathed on the carcass of a bear that had been dead for three months. He's back. Happy and healthy. When his remains come, she may offer. Or, we could ask."

Beatrice's mouth parted at the suggestion, but she couldn't form words.

Gwen's lips twitched, but a smile didn't form. "We shouldn't decide anything on an empty stomach." She moved from the bed and tilted her head from side to side.

"I'll be right there."

Alone, Beatrice recalled the conversation she and Gwen had sitting at the kitchen table creating wreaths for the Solstice. Ben's soul hadn't left to pursue its next incarnation; it stayed tucked in right alongside hers. She reached out to him in her mind. His only words were: *I don't know, Beatrice.*

***

Beatrice found her grandmother and Stella rocking by the fire. They both stood when they spotted her. Beulah made the first move, her feet scurrying across the floor, propelling her until she stood in front of Beatrice. There were no words to encapsulate, no words to crystallize the feelings that swirled through Beatrice's heart, mind, and body. Here was the woman who raised her while she raised Forest, who healed her, who comforted her in the absence of her mother. Neither of them spoke. Instead, they wrapped themselves in a tight hug and stayed that way for several breaths. Beatrice was vaguely aware that Stella had made it to her side, so she pulled herself from her grandmother's embrace.

"I'm so glad you're home, Beatrice," said the trusted voice that had consoled Beatrice all her life.

Beatrice framed the woman's cheeks with her hands and looked down into her eyes that were a deeper blue than Madeline's. She took a step back and surveyed every inch of her. Her body was shorter and thicker than either hers or her mother's, and her left earlobe had a little notch in it as though an earring had been ripped out.

"Look at you." Beatrice brought Beulah into a hug again, this time leveling her eyes with Stella, whose smile warmed her heart. "It worked. The two of you..." The enormity of magic—yes, magic, there was no mistaking it—that stood before her stole her breath. When she let Beulah go, Stella wrapped one arm around the woman's waist and kissed her forehead.

"Beatrice." Beulah's voice reminded her to breathe. "Do you want to sit a bit?"

Beatrice blinked several times and gave her head a shake. "No." She moved to the kitchen door, turned the frigid metal knob, and pushed the door open. Bundled from head to toe and with blankets on their laps, Forest and Dani sat in rockers on the porch sipping tea and cracking walnuts. Her son stood and wrapped her in a hug.

"I'm so sorry, Mother," he said.

Beatrice stayed in the embrace until her mother whispered her name.

Madeline, eyes misted over with the threat of tears, stood with her hands clasped in front of her. Gwen stood beside her with her hands balled by her sides. Even though she had just been talking with Ben's sister, making eye contact with the woman who looked so much like him caused Beatrice's heart to seize.

"Let me take a look at you. Make sure I didn't miss anything." A gold shimmer rose to Madeline's fingertips, and Beatrice cried as her mother placed her hands on her throat, chest, abdomen, all the way down to her toes. "All is mended." She hovered her hands over Beatrice's heart. "I wish I could heal this for you, but I can't."

"We were all so scared," Beulah said. "None of us have slept."

"How did you get here?" Madeline asked.

"Gertrude helped me to the airport. I took a taxi to a bed-and-breakfast." Beatrice's gaze wandered and landed on the trees. She thought of Callisto and Circe. *I should write to them.* "Gertrude carried me from there."

"Can you eat?" Beulah asked.

Beatrice nodded. "I'm very hungry."

Beulah, Madeline, and Forest brought breakfast to the table, and they all stood around it. Grandmother looked to daughter who looked to daughter. No one could muster the faith to bless the food.

"I'll do it again," Forest offered, and his jaw clenched and released.

Beatrice bowed her head and listened as Forest thanked each grandmother, and her eyes burned when he spoke of Beulah and Madeline.

Why have I never asked him before?

And when he voiced gratitude for her, Beatrice's eyes flew open and she watched his face, his brow furrowed, tears slipping silently down his cheek. An awkward silence slid around the table before Stella finally urged them to sit and eat.

"So, your sister, she—" Beulah started.

"My vines cocooned me, and Gertrude lifted me up and down the countryside and under bridges that crossed rivers. I slept through most of it," Beatrice said. Her eyes turned dark for a moment but brightened again as she buttered a biscuit and smiled Madeline.

Gwen took a bit of her biscuit then looked around the table. "We have to tell her," she said, brushing her hands off over her plate.

Beulah at once looked toward Madeline, who shook her head slowly.

"No," she said. "Not yet."

"All of it," Gwen insisted. "Now."

Madeline shifted in her chair. "Not now," she insisted. "She just got home."

"I agree with Madeline," Stella said, drizzling honey on a biscuit. "She needs to rest."

"I heard Ola saying something about a vision, Mother." Beatrice watched as eyes glanced around the table. She could see the heat that rose to her mother's skin in red patches. "You don't have to protect me. I'm not fragile." That last part was true. Beatrice could shoulder anything. She always had and she always would until the day she died. But Goddess, she was tired.

Beatrice listened as Madeline detailed the images of her wrapping the family in vines and Beulah breathing the breath of death. When Madeline confessed to using her flames against Beulah, the idea of it froze Beatrice's insides. "Mother!" Her voice bore admonishment.

"She was panicked, Beatrice," Beulah said. "She just had this awful dream, and I was standing over her. It's not her fault."

"What happened to the vision of the waterfall?" Beatrice asked.

Silent moments stretched between them. "It stopped when Ben died," Madeline replied, and Beatrice covered her face with her hands for a moment.

"What possible reason would Grandmother have for killing the entire family?" Beatrice asked. Truth be told, the drama of it all did serve to take her mind momentarily from her grief. "And why on earth would I help her?"

"I don't know," Madeline said, shaking her head while looking into Beatrice's eyes. "But I'm working with the trees on how to process the vision and gaining control over the fire. I will never do that again."

"Do you feel like going for a walk after we eat, Beatrice?" Beulah asked.

"Sure." Beatrice made note of the way Stella glared at her grandmother, as if the request were absurd.

"Is that alright?" she asked Stella, who swallowed deeply, her face pale.

"Of course." Stella reached for a glass of water and took a drink, averting Beatrice's eyes.

Few words passed as the family finished eating. The salty, hot biscuits revived Beatrice's spirits enough for her to glance around at the faces and take it all in. Gwen's sadness. Madeline's anxiety she was fighting so hard to tamper. Forest's worry. Dani's exhaustion. Something unsettling pulled at the space between Stella and Beulah, something magnetic and cold that made Beatrice shiver. When they were finished, Madeline and Stella did dishes, and Beatrice followed her grandmother out the door.

***

Beatrice walked briskly beside Beulah, finding the woman's pace too quick for her weakened body.

"Where are we going?" she asked, panting.

"I'm not sure," Beulah responded. "I just need to tell you some things."

Beatrice pulled ahead of her grandmother for a moment so that she could face her.

"Can you slow down, for just a moment? I can't walk this fast." The woman charged forward. "Stop, Grandmother. Please."

Those blue eyes were wild, and Beulah was breathless. Beatrice touched her grandmother's hair and put her palms against her cheeks.

"Your body is not seventy years old. Mother looks older than you. I still can't believe it. How do you feel? How does your body feel?"

"My body feels really wonderful, for the most part." The woman's face seemed to soften, and the impatient nervousness eased for a moment. "Better than I remembered. I touch and smell and taste everything that I can. I take all the colors in."

"How are you and Stella?"

"We need to hurry," Beulah said, then started walking again. "And that isn't what we need to talk about."

"It's what I want to talk about." Though Beatrice wasn't sure why. She had just lost her love. But she just wanted to know. "Are the two of you romantic?"

Beulah's cheeks warmed a rosy-red, and for a moment, Beatrice didn't think of death.

"It's very complicated," Beulah said, then drew a deep breath in and released it. "And I don't know how to talk to you about it."

Protectiveness permeated Beatrice's heart. "Well, she's loved you romantically for a long time."

"Maybe." Beulah snorted.

"No, I know she does, Grandmother. She's told me so."

Beulah faced Beatrice, her eyes sharp and narrow under furrowed brows. "I said it is complicated."

"But you were talking about all the sensations and how good it felt to be back in your skin. I guess it's none of my business, but she's my friend and you're my grandmother."

Beulah nodded and tucked her hair behind her ears on both sides. "Stella and I share blood and a bed. And yes, we are intimate."

"It's wonderful, isn't it?" Beatrice asked.

"It's overwhelming. And beautiful. And terrifying."

"Cherish it. Hold her and kiss her as often as you can." Beatrice squared herself fully to her grandmother. "And do your best not to hurt her. She was in a horrible place without you."

"How about the greenhouse?" Beulah asked, ignoring Beatrice's last comment.

The two didn't speak until they were in the expansive space that somehow seemed grander than when Beatrice left.

"I want more privacy," Beulah said, and Beatrice watched her look overhead at the tall glass ceilings of the greenhouse. "I feel like She can see us."

"She?" Beatrice asked. Beulah locked eyes with her, but once again avoided her question. "There's shed over here." Beatrice pointed.

Papa had built it to hold the gear he needed to cut down trees and chop wood, and Beatrice and the trees built the greenhouse around it. The oppressive darkness wrapped tightly around her ribs as she entered the shed.

"Grandmother, it's too dark in here for me. Please, can we just—"

"I feel safer in here."

"Well, I don't."

Beatrice felt the woman take her hand and realized the woman was trembling.

"Beatrice, I'm afraid. What if..." She paused. "What if what Madeline keeps seeing comes true? What if I...do you think I could actually?"

"Shh," Beatrice said, and she massaged the woman's hands. "I know you, Grandmother. You're the woman who healed me... twice. You've shown me nothing but kindness and tenderness."

"You don't know everything about me. They tell me her visions always come true, one way or another. And what do you think your role is in all this?"

"There is nothing that would bring me to the point of killing my family."

"And then there's Madeline's anxiety." Beulah jerked her hands away. "She gets out of control with these things, Beatrice."

"I know. I've been on the other side of her fire." The memory of the heat licking at her vines flashed through Beatrice's head. "I'm so sorry she hurt you."

"Beatrice, I don't think she's wrong." Beulah's voice was stern. "I believe I will use this power."

"How often have you used it?" Beatrice felt her heart beat

harder. The silence in response made Beatrice impatient. "Grandmother, be honest with me. What have you killed and what have you brought back to life?"

"I don't want to tell you everything," Beulah said, then paused. "You already know I've killed the trees and brought them back. And…I don't like it when predators play with their food, when they kill them with no intention of eating them. Especially bunnies. I can't stand to see dead baby bunnies."

Beatrice chuckled. "So, you've used this formidable power to bring dead baby bunnies back to life?" Beulah nodded. "Well, now I am terrified," she said, and felt relief when her grandmother joined her in the laugh. Another sound came slithering through the corner of the shed.

"Shh," Beatrice said, "do you hear that?"

A glow emerged revealing a root uncoiling out of the dirt floor. Another shoot of green came through, and then another. Each root thickened into a thin trunk, until eventually the growth stopped, and stillness took over.

Beatrice surveyed the small trees that nestled in this tiny shed with her and Beulah. She touched their bark and along their stems. The trees looked familiar. Then one by one, sets of eyes began to pop open, and Beatrice pulled back. She turned to her grandmother, whose eyes were wide.

First Mother. Ida. Imogene. Martha. Edna. All the trees were there except Ola.

Beatrice glanced at Beulah, then back at the trees. "How?" she asked.

"No matter. We need to speak with you about Madeline's vision," First Mother said. "Away from the rest of the family. Has Madeline told you about it yet?"

"Yes, First Mother," Beatrice said, giving her head a nod. "She has."

"Call me Alice."

Beatrice's eyebrows shot up. *Alice.*

She listened as Alice explained her decision to leave the

Goddess and the consequences her actions had on the family. Somehow, she had never connected that First Mother—Alice—was the Goddess's romantic partner.

How bold to leave the Goddess...

"You've been Her lover for over a hundred and fifty years?"

"Yes, Beatrice."

"I knew you were closest to her, and the first, obviously, but I didn't understand..." Beatrice felt tension tighten into a heavy bundle within her belly. The dream. Her eyes moved toward the floor of the shed. It seemed so much more than a dream. Did she have the gift of foresight like her mother? She imagined herself in front of her home, terrified and alone as the Goddess swept her away to a new land and locked her into some arranged relationship, and this fear spurned her next question. "Why do you want to leave her? Has she been cruel to you?"

"She's never been cruel. Not until now, that is. Oh, Beatrice, my soul is ready to move on."

"And what about the rest of you?" Beatrice's eyes scanned the faces of the trees, who all spoke their opinions at the same time. She returned her focus to Alice. "Every tree will suffer the same consequence, and She's forcing us from home," Beatrice said. Her fingertips and toes tingled until eventually her body grew numb and she slumped down on the cold ground.

"I am sorry, Beatrice. I suggest leaving early," Alice continued. "Before Madeline fully understands what's happening and loses control of her fire. If that happens, Beulah, when you're all safe at the bottom of the mountain, use your breath on all of them. Everyone except Beatrice."

"Why?" Bewilderment etched Beulah's face. "I promised Stella that I would not do that again."

A wave of realization widened Beatrice's eyes. Beulah had used her breath on Stella. As much as she wanted to demand answers right then and there, the trees had more talking to do.

"You have to protect them, Beulah. You have to protect them from The Goddess," Alice insisted. "Beatrice, once they're settled, you must return."

"Why?" Beatrice asked. "If what you're saying is true and we'll all be safe at the bottom of the mountain, why should I come back?"

"Negotiate. Convince her that she doesn't have to force you from your home."

"I want to use my breath against the Goddess." Beulah's words erected the hairs all over Beatrice's body, and she shivered.

"We don't know that your power will work against the Goddess, Beulah," Alice said.

"So, I will be on this mountain with the Goddess alone?" Beatrice whispered, curious how the trees would respond.

"Beatrice," Alice said. "You have been through more than any of us, and that makes you stronger than any of us. And She holds you in high regard. If anyone can convince Her to let you and the others keep your gifts and stay on the mountain, it's you."

Is that even what I want anymore?

Ben's voice chimed in. *Beatrice, home and magic are the most important things to you.*

"It's not magic!" Beatrice voiced aloud, then cleared her throat. "What power do I actually have? What will She agree to?"

"That's for you to figure out," Alice said.

Beatrice's mouth parted, the shock of Alice's indifference toward her safety bringing tension back into her muscles.

"Beatrice, I need to test it on you," Beulah said. "My breath. I need to know if it will work on Madeline."

Not you, too.

Beatrice felt her body sink even deeper onto the cold ground. Her family seemed more than willing to hang her out to dry.

"I'm sure it will work," Alice reassured.

Perhaps the idea of cold, dark nothingness should have frightened Beatrice. Perhaps she should have resisted. But the promise of respite from this human existence was a welcoming thought. "Alright," Beatrice said, laying down on the ground. Beulah said nothing as she kneeled, kissed Beatrice on her forehead, and blew.

***

That evening, Beatrice caught the look in her mother's eyes. Suspicion. Fear. Worry. She tried her best to calm her fears with smiles and compliments over dinner. When it was time for bed, she tucked a satchel of herbs under her pillow to ease her into a dreamless sleep. She couldn't face that green shimmer hovering over her body again. Anger rarely flowed through Beatrice's body, but the betrayal of the trees and Beulah especially brought clenching to her jaw and a tightness to her chest. Her hands squeezed into fists.

On this night, her herbs refused to protect her just as her family did, and she glided through warm air, transported quickly to a new, warmer mountain.

Her body lay naked and flat on a small knoll, light green with new grass. Green. Everything green. A green hand pressed against her womb. Pressure. Screams of childbirth. Screams of being torn in two.

It was these screams that brought her out of the nightmare and into the present. She sat covered in sweat and tears, and the screams bellowed out of her. The door opened and both her mother and grandmother came to her side.

"Sweetheart," Madeline breathed, passing her hand along Beatrice's wet hair. "A nightmare?"

Beatrice nodded her head quickly, her breath caught in her lungs.

"Ben?" Beulah asked, and Beatrice shook her head.

"The hunter?"

Beatrice's stomach turned. The answer to this question was both a no and a yes. "No. Please, I can't talk about it," she pleaded and drew her legs into her chest and squeezed them.

"Can I make you some tea?" Madeline asked.

"I don't want to go back to sleep."

"Beatrice, it's too early to get up," Madeline soothed, rubbing her back. "It's barely past midnight. I'll get a new satchel for you."

"Do you think I didn't try that?" Beatrice stood, made her way to her dresser, splashed water on her face, and rubbed it vigorously with a towel. "It won't work against this."

Against Her.

"Why don't you change into dry clothes?" Beulah said, pulling Ben's pajamas out and laying them on the bed.

Nausea crept to Beatrice's throat. Soon, soon, she would belong to the Goddess.

She slipped out of her damp clothes and into the warm flannel that smelled like him. The breath of the winter in the spring released some of the tension in her neck, her chest, her bowels.

"Do you want to change rooms? Gwen and I could stay here," Madeline said. "A different setting may help."

Beatrice shook her head. "They're going to keep coming."

"Tea now?"

Beatrice crawled into bed and leaned her head back against the headboard. She nodded in affirmation. Beulah pulled up the covers and snuggled in close, and Beatrice nestled against her shoulder.

"Do you think it was a vision?" Beulah asked.

"I don't know," Beatrice whispered. "And I can't tell you about it, Grandmother. It's not all bad. I think you and everyone else will be safe."

"What happens to you?"

"I'll do what I have to do."

Madeline came in with a cup of tea and handed it to Beatrice.

"Will one of you stay with me?" Beatrice asked. Her mother and grandmother locked eyes, then turned their attention back to her.

"We'll both stay with you, Bea," Madeline said and crawled into bed.

The three filled the bed with little space between them. The warmth of closeness and the rhythm of breath slowly rocked Beatrice to sleep. And the Goddess visited no more that night.

CHAPTER 25

Stella

Stella peered outside the kitchen door to see the sun barely peeking over the mountains. After waking to an empty bed, she had slipped on her house shoes and wrapped a sweater around her shoulders. She checked in on Forest and Dani who slept soundly, then made her way to Beatrice's bedroom where she found both Madeline and Beulah snuggled up to Beatrice. In the time she'd known Beatrice, she had never seen her broken, her spirit shattered, her strength diminished. The best thing, Stella thought, was to cook breakfast for them all.

She moved through the kitchen collecting eggs and fruit, then she made her way outside into the chilly March air to the smokehouse for bacon then to the dairy shed for milk. Beatrice had taught her the rhythm of breakfast cooking—when to start the biscuits, fry the bacon, crack the eggs, and slice the fruit. But only Stella knew exactly when to pour water over the coffee.

She started with the biscuits. In the ranking of biscuit quality, hers were not as good as Beatrice's, but certainly better than Beulah's. She slapped the raw dough against the cool counter and cut them out in less than perfect circles. As she moved around the kitchen, she found meditation in her motions.

Beatrice losing Ben was a cruel joke; it wasn't fair that Stella had Beulah, as complicated as the relationship was. Madeline had Gwen, and Forest had Dani. A miracle. That's what so many people would call what happened. The woman she loved was gone forever, and Stella's own body waste away in her absence. Then, a resurrection. Well, if that wasn't a miracle, what was?

Stella kept her cooking as quiet as possible, wanting more than anything for the rest of the household to get rest. The smell would rouse them.

Gwen was the first to enter the kitchen, her red-rimmed, darkly-circled eyes set into a pale face. Grief had aged her and left her without the vigor she once held in her speech, her body, and her eyes.

"Good morning," Stella said as Gwen took a seat at the kitchen table.

"Do you know where Madeline is?" Gwen asked.

"She and Beulah are both tucked with Beatrice. I'm assuming she needed comforting last night."

The biscuits produced the salty wheat smell that Stella had grown to associate with home.

"It's hard, Stella," Gwen said, then placed her crossed forearms on the table and rested her chin on top.

"I know." Stella started frying the bacon in the cast-iron skillet. "I lost my father when I was young, and in some ways, I lost my mother, too. She never was the same."

"And you thought you lost Beulah." Gwen's voice lowered. "I don't want it to change me, but I think it already has."

Forest came in and gave Gwen a rub on the back. "How are you?" Gwen shrugged. "Need help with breakfast?" he asked Stella.

He looked tired, too, but those curls around his face kept

his appearance youthful. Forest still held an innocence Stella envied, even though he had experienced his own losses. Loss, though temporary, of a great-grandmother. Worry over a sick mother. A bullet fired from hatred. But he had never loved and lost, and Stella wondered if the saying was true, if she was truly better for it. How would her life have been different if she had never looked into those blue eyes? Would she have survived if Beulah hadn't returned to the land of the living?

"Ben lives through you, you know?" Forest said as he sat down next to Gwen, and Stella winced at the statement. Perhaps she'd take Forest aside and school him on toxic positivity.

"Of course he does," Gwen said with no attempt to smile. "We shared a home for nine months."

"Want to come chop wood with me later?" Forest asked. "It helps me when I'm upset."

Gwen smiled and nodded. "Taking my anger out on an inanimate object seems like a good idea."

Stella checked the biscuits, transferred the bacon from the pan, and began cracking the eggs.

"At least let me cut the fruit." Gwen stood, made her way to the counter, and began to slice apples and pears.

"Thank you," Stella said.

Beatrice, Beulah, and Madeline made it to the kitchen just as Stella and the others placed plates and food around the table.

"Good morning," Stella said and moved to hug Beulah, the woman her body needed, even if the connection terrorized her heart and soul. "Everything okay?" she asked, pulling away to scan Beulah's face.

"A bit of a rough night," Beulah said, "but I think we're okay."

Beatrice and Gwen embraced and held one another for several moments, and when they pulled back, both faces were wet with soft tears.

"You two were gone a while yesterday afternoon," Madeline said, glancing at Beulah and Beatrice.

"We had a lot of catching up to do," Beatrice responded, then she sat down and looked toward her food.

Dani stumbled into the kitchen, bleary-eyed, and plopped down next to Forest.

"Mm," Beulah said, taking a bite of biscuit. "These are good."

"Agreed," Beatrice said, her mouth full of biscuit. "You've done it, Stella."

Stella's chest warmed as everyone else took turns agreeing. The kitchen was once again full of family, but they were all so tired. So beaten from the events of the past several months. Someone had to be strong. Stella squeezed Beatrice's hand and, in the gesture, made a promise. *I'm here.*

"Where did you do your catching up?" Madeline asked, and everyone's eyes moved toward her.

"We walked to the greenhouse," Beatrice said, with no defensiveness in her voice. "You've had Grandmother for a few days. I needed some time with her alone."

Stella noticed Madeline's face grow long at the mention of Beulah and Beatrice's closeness. She didn't know if it was sadness or remorse or regret or anger, but she could imagine the pain.

"We talked a lot about Ben," Beulah said, and though her face was solemn and sober, Stella knew she was lying.

One glance at Beatrice's flush face confirmed it. Stella didn't know the outcome of the vines and the breath, but she knew the trees were right. Madeline's visions would come to fruition. She scrutinized her friend's expression, noting just how hard it was for Beatrice to lie.

"Does it bother you, Madeline?" Beulah asked, reaching out her hand.

"Beulah." Stella wanted to take Beulah's hand into her own and give it a squeeze to stop the conversation.

Why would you want to rile Madeline up?

"What's that?" Madeline said, withdrawing.

"That Beatrice and I have had more time together than the two of you."

Madeline parted her mouth. Her eyes darted between Beatrice and Beulah.

"Enough," Gwen said, pushing her plate away after eating only half a biscuit. "I need to mourn my brother, and there's no space to do it here."

"Hey, ready to chop wood with me?" Forest asked.

"Finish your breakfast, Forest," Gwen said as she smoothed her fingertips over her brow.

"I can bring it with me." Forest slid the egg onto the bottom of the biscuit and sandwiched it with the top. He leaned to give Dani a kiss on their forehead, looked at Gwen, and said, "Let's go."

Gwen grabbed her jacket and followed Forest out the door.

"I'm going to follow her," Madeline said.

"Madeline, no. Give her space," Stella insisted, pressing her chest forward and raising her voice. "I know your visions are overwhelming and there's tension here..." She waved an upturned palm between Beulah and Madeline. "But she needs you."

Stella stunned herself with her assertiveness toward a woman who could burn her to ash. Beulah's eyes were watery, and Stella placed her hand on her leg. The woman turned those big eyes toward her and smiled slightly.

"Let's finish eating," Beulah said. "These really are the best biscuits, Stella. It's good of Forest to take her out." She turned to Beatrice. "You raised a good man."

"I'm pretty fond of him," Beatrice said. "He and Ben didn't have a chance to get to know each other. I think they would have made good friends." She finished her last bite, then said, "I wish I had told him I loved him sooner."

"Love is difficult for most," Madeline added, finally settling into the calm. "Perhaps even more so for our family."

"I thought keeping the feeling to myself would protect him... and me," Beatrice said.

Stella couldn't help but turn to Beulah, wanting to say the

words for the first time since December there at the kitchen table in front of everyone, but she had made a vow not to say it until the bind was broken.

"Think it's alright to check on Gwen now?" Madeline asked.

"More time," Stella insisted.

Madeline sighed "Okay."

"Do something nice for her," Stella said. "Go to the greenhouse and pick her a bouquet of flowers. Make her tea. Wrap her up in a blanket. Point all your attention toward her even if it's just for a few hours."

"Stella's right on this," Dani said.

"I don't remember asking for anyone's opinion but thank you." Madeline stood with a huff, moved to the sink, and took out her anger on the dirty dishes.

Stella focused on Beatrice. The woman's face held more pain and exhaustion than when she was sick with cancer. "Beatrice." The woman raised her head and locked eyes with Stella. "The mugwort is working, but I'm only seeing the past so far, not the future. Your family's past. Do I have your permission to see your life?"

"No." Beatrice spoke the word without a moment's hesitation and simply went back to eating her breakfast.

"What if I can't control it?" Stella asked.

"If you don't have control over what you see, please stop drinking the tea altogether."

Stella swallowed. "No. I will not stop, but I will do my best to focus."

"I don't want you writing about my past."

Stella reached across the table for Beatrice's hand. "I want to help your mother. That's all."

"I don't want you to see my life, Stella." Beatrice stood and handed her plate to Madeline. "I hate to interrupt Gwen, but I want to get this urn picked out. Would you come with me, Stella? We haven't had time together either."

"So I can't go talk to her, but you can ask her to do *that* right now?"

"That's at least part of the grieving process," Dani suggested. Madeline pressed her lips together and continued scrubbing.

"I'm going to go with her, okay?" Stella asked Beulah.

Beulah pursed her lips but gave a nod. "Sure."

While Beatrice grabbed something from her bedroom, Stella made Gwen and Forest jars of water, then the two donned their coats and trudged through the snow toward the woodshed.

"Why do the two of you ask one another if it's okay to spend time apart?"

The words "we don't" almost trickled off Stella's tongue, but she knew better. Beatrice would see right through her lie, and that would only make matters worse.

"The working Beulah did to bring herself back bound us together. It's hard when we're separated. It's physical. It can be painful or itchy or burning." Not a lie, but not the entire truth, either. *You don't need to know that she summoned me and now I don't know what's real.* "But we're okay. Don't worry about us."

"But how do things feel when you're together?"

Overwhelming. Terrified. Lovely.

"It's beautiful," Stella said, and Beatrice smiled a wide, genuine smile. "I've never felt this way about anyone." Perhaps this was the greatest truth.

"I'm happy for you."

Guilt infused Stella. She had been such a mess when Beulah fell, much more so than she was when her own father died, and Beatrice and Forest had carried her. And now, after losing her love, Beatrice wanted to make sure Stella was okay.

"I'm sorry that I lost myself. You kept me standing." Stella took Beatrice's hand and squeezed. "I'm here for you now. You're allowed to fall apart, you know?" She kept her eyes forward instead of looking at her friend, respecting Beatrice's vulnerability as well as her pride.

"I'm sure I will at some point."

***

Forest and Gwen had worked up such a sweat that they were working without coats. Each grabbed a jar from Stella and chugged.

"Thanks," Forest said, wiping his brow.

"Gwen, can we choose the urn? I want to get his body back to us."

Gwen's eyes fluttered shut. She drew in a deep breath, sighed it out, and offered a reluctant smile. "I could use a break. I don't have my phone, though. And I don't feel like seeing…"

"I have mine." Stella pulled her phone from her pocket, unlocked it, and handed it to Gwen. Then she gave the two women space, joining Forest where he leaned against the wood-pile, sipping his water.

"Have you told her?" Forest asked.

"About the bind? Yes."

Some of it.

Silence wrapped around them, and in that silence, Stella could feel the doubt brew in Forest's mind.

Beatrice pulled a photo from her pocket and showed it to Gwen. Stella and Forest weren't close enough to hear the words being spoken, but Gwen raised her hand to her mouth and stifled a sob. Beside Stella, Forest shifted on his feet and swallowed. Gwen scrolled and Beatrice pointed to the screen, her face filled with something akin to joy.

"Watching others grieve is almost as hard as going through it yourself," Stella said.

"Especially when it's your mother grieving."

"Thank you for taking care of me, Forest."

"Stella…" Forest squared himself to her, blocking the view of Beatrice and Gwen. "Beulah beckoned you to the top of this mountain and has done nothing but use you since. I love her, but I don't like what's she has done to you."

"That's not true. We—"

"I want you to be safe. I think you should leave the mountain. I can help you."

The thought of being that far away from Beulah twisted Stella's gut so hard she swallowed bile. Even now, less than a tenth of a mile away, she could barely stand being in her own skin.

"I can't do that, Forest. And I don't want to." *It's more than a spell. I know it's more. It has to be more.* "I mean...do you want me gone?"

"Of course not, I—"

Gwen and Beatrice approached, handing the phone back to Stella.

"All done?"

"All done."

"I'm not ready to go back yet," Gwen said, reaching down to grab an ax.

"Don't be too angry with her," Beatrice said. "She's scared."

"I know. And I'm sad. We're just not what the other person needs right at this moment. And that's okay. We're surrounded by people to love us."

On the way back to the house, Stella pondered Madeline's role in what was coming. The vision the woman saw only had her running. Stella decided it was on her to make sure it stayed that way. To make sure that Madeline knew her own strength so the woman wouldn't burn the forest down.

CHAPTER 26

Madeline

Madeline followed Stella's suggestions and brought a bouquet of Gwen's favorite peonies back to the house, tied them with twine, and added a small bow. She then began to slice apples and make biscuit dough for apple dumplings, one of Gwen's favorites. Meditations moved through her mind as her hands wrapped the apples with the dough, a series of *may you be well, may you be happy, may you be safe, and may you live a life of peace.* She sprinkled her love with sugar into the dish and slid it into the oven.

"Apple pie?" Beatrice asked as she entered the kitchen.

"Apple dumplings. They're Gwen's favorite."

"Oh!" Beulah exclaimed, entering the room. "Have you had them, Stella?"

"No, not yet."

"They really are wonderful," Beatrice whispered, then sat down weakly into a chair.

Madeline looked at her daughter and found that her face held more than fear and sadness. Instead, her brown eyes displayed weariness and despondency. For several minutes they held each other's gaze, but a stirring within Madeline encouraged her to resist the anxiety and panic that threatened to well up and out.

"They only need about fifteen more minutes." She smiled.

"I think I need some rest," Beulah said and glanced at Stella. Stella's only response was "sleep well."

"I don't even know what I need," Beatrice said and rested her head in her hands. Madeline sat down across from her.

"Maybe you should rest, too, Bea."

Beatrice shook her head. "No, I think I need to move. Maybe I'll make some soap and things for the farmer's market." She stood, slid on her jacket, and left.

Madeline looked out the window and watched Beatrice stride purposefully toward her greenhouse. "She really can't be still..."

The kitchen began to warm with the smells of cinnamon, apple, and buttered biscuits.

"Are you seeing anything else in the visions?" Stella asked.

"You told me to focus on Gwen, and that's what I'm doing." Madeline opened the oven to check the dumplings, knowing that the action did little more than allow heat to escape.

"Please answer me."

Madeline turned to look at Stella, who sat at the table, picking her fingernails.

"Multiple times an hour, now." Madeline folded the dish towel in her hand and placed it neatly on the counter.

"I need to talk to you."

Madeline's eyes narrowed.

"Can you hurry up dessert? Then we'll walk to the Rock," Stella said.

Madeline sighed.

"You told me to focus on Gwen." Even as Madeline pushed back, she used her telekinesis to encourage more airflow around the fire in the oven.

"You're right, but she's chopping wood with Forest right now. You can spare a few minutes."

Madeline knew the dumplings were done by the smell and pulled them from the oven to cool.

Stella said nothing as they walked across the thinning snow. Bare limbs still stood stark against the sky. It would be April before the forest would find the gold that always comes before the green. Here and there, patches of grass that saw the sun were lush, but otherwise, winter still held the wood's breath.

They came to the Rock; the sun brought to it a warmth that Madeline could feel through her pants as she sat down beside Stella. She watched Stella's face and waited for her to start.

"Okay, Madeline, I'm begging you not to get angry..."

"She breathed on you, didn't she?" Madeline said. She felt the heat rise. *Control it, Madeline. Control it. This is not Stella's doing.*

Stella turned to face her, and Madeline found the face before her pale and the eyes within it darted around.

"Yes, she breathed on me. And Beatrice."

At the sound of her daughter's name, Madeline stood and roared, flames shooting from her hands and her eyes. Fire wreathed around her entire body. "You must help her!" she screamed. "I have always come to you, and you've always answered in your time. Please. Please help my daughter."

She continued to wail, and her flame expanded into a conflagration that threatened the whole of the mountain.

When the heat melted the Rock underneath her feet, Madeline remembered Stella, and with a great deal of her energy spent, she brought the fire back within her belly.

Oh god, Stella.

It took a moment for Madeline to return to reality. When she looked over, she found Stella standing at the other edge of the Rock.

"Did I hurt you?" Madeline felt wave upon wave of nauseous panic move from her bowels and into her throat as she ran to her friend.

Stella shook her head quickly. "Madeline, you have to learn how to contain it. Beulah and Beatrice are overwhelmed, and they may need you. If you don't learn how to control it, you're going to hurt someone. Someone you love. I don't know how to help you do it, but you have to keep your feet on the ground." She paused in her admonishments. "Keep practicing." She turned and walked away leaving Madeline at the Rock.

"Please, Goddess." Madeline toward the sky. "Whatever this is, please keep my family safe. Keep me focused. Show me where to help."

A gentle breeze blew across Madeline's face carrying a whisper. *I let my children choose.* She gently pulled off each shoe and sock and felt her feet against the cool rock, then closing her eyes, she held out her hands and allowed them to warm.

***

After what felt like hours of evoking flames and encouraging them to retreat back into her palms, Madeline decided it was time to go back and see Gwen. The apple dumplings would need reheating, and she hoped to be there when Gwen saw the bouquet. Though Stella was much younger, Madeline knew she spoke the truth. Gwen needed her tenderness, and the family needed her fire. Only she could find that balance.

The forest floor sank gently with her steps as she walked along the moist ground. Sweeping sounds of cavernous wings caught Madeline's attention, and she looked up to see her youngest daughter swooping down. Beatrice had taught her to carry gloves, and Madeline pulled one from her pocket and pulled it over the length of her right forearm. Each time she interacted with this daughter, with Gertrude, her heartbeat grew faster and faster until she felt faint from both continued regret and an intense intimidation of a being who could move her soul from one body to the next all on her own. This was the first time Gertrude came to Madeline without Beatrice nearby, and she looked at the bird as she landed on her arm, wondering why she came without a way to translate.

"Hi," she breathed, and the eagle piped. "I don't know how I'm supposed to understand what you're saying."

Gertrude rubbed her beak against Madeline's cheek and tucked her head into the crook of her neck.

"Are you alright, Gertie?" Madeline asked and the bird shifted higher up her arm. She moved toward a large pine and gently sat herself down at the roots with Gertrude still in place. The great golden eagle pressed her side into her mother's body and Madeline gently stroked her feathers. Something clicked in her gut, that place of all creation and knowing of all truths. Ends were coming.

"I can't trust her, Gertrude," she whispered to the bird, unsure if she was talking about Beulah or Beatrice.

With a sudden burst of nervous movement, Gertrude jumped off Madeline's lap and began to pipe at her loudly, modulating between brief and long iterations. Madeline felt tears form and fall.

"I don't know what you're saying, Gertrude."

The eagle's voice only grew louder and her movements more and more erratic until finally, the bird appeared to have enough and flew off into the sky. Madeline sighed, stood, and made her way back to the house.

***

Once home, Madeline found Beatrice on the front porch tying twine around the small satchels of her herbal concoctions.

She looked up and Madeline saw her eyes were still tinged with deflation.

"Calm," Beatrice said and held a satchel out to Madeline.

An attempted smile from her daughter's lips brought Madeline to her knees.

"Beatrice," she whispered and put her hands up to her daughter's face. "Is there anything I can do to help you?"

"I wish there was, Mother. I really, really do. I have to do this alone."

Again. Alone again.

When Madeline left the mountain in January, she knew it wasn't forever, but now, when she looked into Beatrice's face, she couldn't help but remember the fourteen-year-old girl she left behind.

Beatrice glanced over her shoulder, then back to Madeline. "Grandmother is involved but not in the way she thinks she is."

"We found each other after twenty years," Madeline said. "Are we going to lose each other again?"

"We will be apart, but we will never lose each other," Beatrice said, taking Madeline's hand and squeezing it.

"I can fight whatever this is with you. I've been practicing my flames." Madeline held her palm out and encouraged a flame to it, watching Beatrice's reaction. Her daughter's eyes watched the flame for a moment, then flickered up to lock with her own.

"No." Beatrice shook her head. "No fighting in our futures. Only surrender."

The vortex of grief pulled Madeline's heart into a deep sea of confusion, and the pressure mounted against her until she felt her whole being would implode, all while Beatrice held her gaze firmly.

"Everything okay?" Gwen's voice interrupted the tense moment, and Madeline was grateful. She stood and turned to find her partner sweating, dirty, and glowing.

"Feel better?" Madeline asked.

"A little," Gwen responded, and Madeline saw a continued iciness in her eyes.

"I made you apple dumplings," she said, taking Gwen's hand and bringing it to her lips.

Gwen smiled briefly. "I'm going to wash up, and then we can have them."

Madeline followed behind Gwen as she went to the bedroom and found the bouquet of flowers on the dresser.

"I'm locked in now," Madeline said. "I know how to keep my balance now."

Bouquet in hand, Gwen turned toward Madeline.

"My visions haven't changed," Madeline said. "Dark days are coming, Gwen. How they could get darker, I don't know. I don't know where she's going. I'm not sure she even knows, but we're going to lose Beatrice. And I've looked into her eyes, and I see she's resigned to it all."

Gwen's brows furrowed and she canted her head. "Madeline, what is happening? Do you think she knows more than she is telling you?"

"I don't think it matters," Madeline said, holding her arms out to the side. "She's not going to tell me. She's determined that this is her fight and her fight alone. We need to have Ben's rites soon."

"Yes, Maddie." Gwen moved her body closer and pressed her forehead against Madeline's.

"Let's not compete in our grief, okay? There's room for it all."

"Surely the pain has to end sometime. Our family...we've been through too much, and it all comes so quickly."

"It seems that way, Gwen." Madeline rubbed her lover's back.

"What's going to happen to her, Maddie?" Gwen choked.

"I only know that she's going away."

"Forever?" Gwen breathed in less than a whisper.

"I don't know."

Gwen reached for Madeline, who pulled her up and into her arms. "It may sound wrong right now, Maddie, but can you take me away from all this for a moment or two?"

"Yes, Gwennie," Madeline responded, and then kissed Gwen tenderly but deeply. "I love you."

Madeline slowly kissed her neck, nibbled her ears and her collarbone, while Gwen continued to cry softly. Madeline's lips found Gwen's nipples, and within her own body, the stirrings that had been missing engaged.

"This way," Gwen said, and she turned herself so that her back faced Madeline.

Madeline slipped Gwen's shirt off her shoulders, traced her

fingertips down her back, and admired her body, then positioned herself on the bed and slipped her lover's jeans down. She wrapped her arms around her body and rubbed her breasts and licked her ears with her tongue. She pressed her fingers in between Gwen's legs and gently stroked.

"Lift up a bit," Madeline said when she felt wetness.

She eased Gwen's body onto her two fingers and continued to rub with her other hand. Gwen's crying transitioned from soft to hard, shuddering sobs. Madeline stopped her movements.

"Madeline, please don't stop." Madeline continued, and Gwen rocked more and more until her body convulsed in a shudder. She moved to withdraw, but her lover held her fingers inside.

"Stay. Please, stay."

"Okay, Gwennie," Madeline said, and she stayed. She stayed even after the tears stopped and the breath calmed, and the heart found its rhythm again. She stayed. She stayed until Gwen lifted and pulled her hands away. Gwen's red, swollen face threatened to bring Madeline to brokenness. But then she began unbuttoning Madeline's shirt and pulling her pants down. She pressed her onto her back and kissed her. She moved over her body until she also climaxed. Then she pulled Madeline to seated and wrapped her legs around her waist, straddling her.

"My brother is gone now. My mother and father are dead. My grandparents are dead. My cousins are scattered across the country. You and Beatrice and Forest and Stella and Beulah and the trees are all that I have. And I'm not sure I'm safe here."

Madeline's eyes narrowed. "Gwen"—she looked deep into hazel eyes—"I hear you. The visions are coming at a rapid-fire pace. And as hard as I try, watching my mother kill you and Forest and Stella over and over and over again…it's devouring me. But I love you so, so much. I'll keep you safe."

Chapter 27

Beulah

Two days passed. Beulah watched as the visions exhausted Madeline more and more. With the predicted event growing closer, the family struggled to make meals, choosing unintentionally to snack their way through the day. Stella had been more affectionate, though, a needed change from their previous sessions. The two hadn't made love, but Beulah took comfort in kisses and hand holding.

As for Beulah, she took up her daughter and granddaughter's habit of pacing. She felt like an animal in a cage ready to attack the moment the Goddess showed Her face. She and Beatrice had reviewed the plan during moments they had privacy, and each time, Beatrice firmly rejected Beulah's insistence on using her breath against the Goddess.

"Grandmother, you can't come with me. You have to be safe so you can bring the others back."

The plan the trees suggested seemed strange, the more Beulah thought of it. Wouldn't it make more sense to have Madeline, who'd spent hours upon hours practicing her fire, climb back up the mountain with them? She didn't know how to convince

Beatrice to allow her to follow, but she would go. Even if she had to put Beatrice to sleep as well and go by herself.

Madeline's focus had clarified her vision a bit. Beulah would not be breathing her family to death but just to sleep. They'd still be alive. Beulah had tried and tried shift her brain from death to sleep on various plants and animals. Sasha, to her surprise, offered herself up as a guinea pig, but the breath rendered the snake completely lifeless until Beulah revived her.

Beulah tutted and splashed water on her face before turning to Stella, who lay in bed writing in her journal. The movements of her hand and wrist were ferocious and her breathing intense. Beulah hated that she had no choice but to interrupt her.

"Stella."

Stella looked up from her writing, a hint of annoyance written on her face. "Yes?"

"I need to change my breath. I need to be able to just breathe people to sleep. Not kill them. It's the difference between keeping the breath stirring and not."

Stella put her pen down, slipped a ribbon between the pages of her notebook, crossed her legs, and waited for Beulah to continue.

"Can I practice on you?"

Green eyes combed over every inch of Beulah's face until she flushed, angry at her own embarrassment. The woman patted the bed in front of her and Beulah sat down.

"Tell me more."

"I've tried on all sorts of things, but nothing has worked. I'm not sure if it's because I can't get in the right space or if—"

"Why do you need us asleep at all, Beulah?"

"Because we can't risk your involvement. It's too dangerous."

"And you don't think we will just listen to you and stay out of your way?"

"Madeline can't keep from defending Beatrice and you..." Beulah cupped Stella's cheek. "You're spellbound to protect me. I can't put you in that position. I'm very sorry." She took Stella's left hand, flipped her palm upward, and kissed her wrist. "I'm sorry for putting you in this position."

"But even if we die…even if we're dead for days, you can bring us back." Stella frowned. "You're worried that you might not survive this, aren't you?"

"It's possible."

"Beulah, Madeline is controlling her fire. Don't you think she can help you?"

"I can't risk it, Stella. Now please. Let me try."

Stella moved her pen and journal off the bed, lengthened her legs, and asked, "Want me to close my eyes?"

"It may help for me to imagine you're sleeping."

Stella nodded and fluttered her eyes closed.

Beulah closed her eyes, too, and brought to mind all Stella's sweet sleeping habits; the way her hand twitched and the way she almost snored. She leaned her body forward until she felt Stella's breath feather against her face and, repeating the word sleep over and over in her brain, she breathed. Her eyes opened wide to inspect Stella, who lay entirely still. Beulah placed a hand against the woman's chest. No pulse. No breath.

Damn.

She woke Stella, confessed it didn't work, and asked if she could try again. To Beulah's relief, Stella agreed. After three more attempts, Beulah almost gave up, but Stella encouraged, "Try one last time."

Beulah paused longer this time, not only visualizing, but feeling Stella's warm body as they snuggled and her rhythmic inhales and exhales. Then she blew against Stella's cheek.

It worked. Stella moved into her almost-snore, a deep, peaceful sleep. Beulah swallowed.

Perhaps I can control it instead of letting it control me.

She curled her body up against Stella's, resting her head against Stella's shoulder and wrapping an arm around her waist. Something new crept into Beulah's chest. Something nonviolent and calming. It wasn't peace. Beulah didn't know if she'd ever live to feel peace. No, it was hope.

After weeping silently into Stella's pajamas for several minutes, Beulah woke her.

"It worked!" Stella's eyes were bright and full of the same hope that permeated through Beulah.

"How do you know?" Beulah ran fingers through Stella's hair.

"I had a dream." Stella sat up, and a grin spread across her face. "It was such a good dream."

"Tell me about it?"

"We were in New York. I was showing you all the sights. Things felt so free between us. Like we were new. Going on dates. Holding hands at a Broadway show." Stella released a giggle, bringing a laugh to Beulah's own lips. The laughing grew raucous, and they didn't stop until a knock startled them.

A solemn Beatrice stood on the other side.

"Sorry to interrupt," she said. "We're home."

***

Beatrice and Gwen sat on opposite sides of the kitchen table, staring at the urn in front of them. It was a beautiful pewter finish with vines wrapped around the entirety, and a picture of Gwen and Ben as children laughing etched onto one side.

Stella sat down beside Beatrice and placed a hand on her back. Beulah's heart warmed at the sight of their friendship, and once again, hope bloomed even in the midst of the grief. Beulah sat down, too, and a glance passed between Gwen and Beatrice. Her granddaughter closed her eyes and placed a hand to her chest, rubbing her palm against her sternum in circles.

"Grandmother." Beatrice's voice came out in a raspy croak, and she cleared her throat. "Would you try?"

Beulah surveyed her granddaughter's face, which had been hollowed out by despair, exhaustion, and pain. This wasn't something Beulah imagined Beatrice would ask of her. Bringing a human being back from the dead seemed counter to her ethics, somehow.

"I..." Beulah felt her throat close. So many things could go wrong. Yes, she had revived animals whose bodies had given in to decay. But did they come back exactly as they were? Arcas seemed to, sure. But would a human being who had been burned to ashes? If he wasn't the same, would they blame her? A larger worry loomed. Beatrice would be so distracted by Ben's presence that she may change her mind about the plan. She may decide to leave the mountain behind and let the Goddess go unpunished, something Beulah could not abide. *Which is worse, denying her request or pretending to try?* "I can try."

Another look passed between Gwen and Beatrice, an eager one tinged with apprehension.

"Let's do it outside," Gwen said and moved with quick strides out the door.

The snow had melted quickly but small drifts still skirted the trees. The afternoon sun warmed the air, and no one needed their coats.

"Are we sure about this?" Beatrice asked Gwen, her breath moving quickly in and out of her chest.

"What does he say?" Gwen pointed to her chest, and Beatrice rubbed her sternum.

"Yes."

"Alright, then." Beulah took the urn and lifted the lid with careful, measured motions. She stared into the urn, questioned how she would feel if this was Stella's body reduced to ash. Her heart clenched and a burn formed behind her eyes. *I should do this for her, but not until after the Goddess is gone.* Beulah shook her head, knowing that the entire point of destroying the Goddess was to rid herself of this "gift."

She looked back at Stella, whose arms were wrapped across her chest. *What if I brought him back to a state of sleep? No, that won't work. Beatrice, how could you ask this of me now?*

Mind made up, Beulah thought of death and ash and fire and blew. Nothing. Good. "I'm sorry."

"Thank you for trying." Beatrice's voice cracked as she took the urn from Beulah, securing the lid once more.

Tears slid down Gwen's cheeks and she sniffed.

"We will have rites for him, Bea," Stella said.

"Not today." Beatrice wiped her face. "I just can't today. Tomorrow."

"Where is everyone else?" Beulah asked.

"We didn't want them to know what we were asking," Gwen confessed.

"I see."

"Let's let them know we're back."

Stella wrapped her arm around Beulah's waist as the grieving women walked up the front porch.

"You didn't try, did you?" Stella's voice lacked accusation.

"It didn't feel quite right." Not a lie.

"I get it."

***

The day passed with continued solemnity, but Beulah and Stella made an attempt at dinner. Afterwards, Beatrice pulled Beulah aside.

"It happens tomorrow. I need you to follow the plan and stay with them."

"Beatrice—"

"Grandmother, even if I thought you could defeat the Goddess, that's not what I want. Maybe She will listen to me, and we can keep our home."

"Okay, Beatrice. I'll stay with the plan." *My plan. And if I have to put you to sleep with the rest, I will.*

Beatrice bobbed her head and drew Beulah into a hug.

***

That night, Beulah snuck into each room, studying each face as they slept so that when the time came, the right power would come.

Chapter 28

Beatrice

Beatrice rose before the sun, splashed water on her face, and put on the one dress she had in her wardrobe. Made of a mint green, flowing cotton with buttons all down the front, the dress was easy to wear. She withdrew a hairbrush from her vanity and worked it through her hair in large strokes from root to tip, then used her fingers to smooth the hair into thick curls. Glancing in the mirror, Beatrice felt like both a beauty and a fraud.

I'm not ready to let you go, Ben.

You're not, silly.

Beatrice smiled.

Is there anything you want?

"Spirit in the Sky." It's a song. Gwen will know it.

Tears jumped into Beatrice's. Yes, Ben's soul continued on and lived in the cavernous space between her ribs, but his body was gone. He would never hold her or dance with her or make love to her again. As if he read her thoughts, Ben spoke.

Touch yourself, Beatrice.

Beatrice glanced into the mirror, her eyes wide.

I'll tell you how.

Her breathing intensified, and tears slid down her cheeks.

First, lock the door.

She had never touched herself that way, even during the time she was separated from Ben.

What if I can't? But even as she thought the words, she locked the door and began fingering the buttons of her dress.

I just want you to feel me again, Beatrice. Know that I'm here.

Once unclothed, Beatrice made her way to the bed, lay down, and followed Ben's instructions. When the climax came, her body shuddered not only with pleasure, but pain, and she released angry sobs into her pillow.

That doesn't have to be the last time, sweetheart.

I miss you so much, Ben.

How can you miss me? I've never been closer to you.

Beatrice placed a hand on her chest, closed her eyes, and tried to feel it—this calm closeness Ben seemed to feel.

What if She makes you leave me?

We will cross that bridge when we get to it. Now, go say good-bye to my mortal remains. Ben chuckled, and Beatrice tried to reflect the laughter, but it wouldn't bubble to the surface. *Go.*

***

Beatrice opened her door to find Beulah on the other side, and she started.

"Sorry. I wanted to see how you were doing."

"Unless the Goddess changes Her mind, it's happening today," Beatrice said. "After the funeral, we should leave the mountain."

"I want them to see who She is," Beulah said. "I want them to see her rage. I know you don't agree, but you aren't right about everything, Beatrice."

Beatrice shook her head, believing in her heart that it was an unnecessary action spurned by her grandmother's hatred of the Goddess. "No," she said with finality.

She moved down the hall to her mother's bedroom to wake her and Gwen, knowing breakfast would come later; she found them already awake and chatting quietly with one another. Gwen rested against Madeline's chest, receiving gentle strokes through her hair.

"You should both get dressed."

"Breakfast first," Gwen said as she rose to her feet.

"No. Funeral first," Beatrice insisted. Gwen and Madeline exchanged glances, but she refused to explain. "I'll wake the others."

She woke Stella, Forest, and Dani, and eventually they were all preparing for the rites. As she waited on the others and for the Goddess, she used her gifts to create flower arrangements. The focused pulling and giving acts of creation drew her into her own world, but movement on the other side of the table interrupted her. Gwen sat down and reached her hand across the table, seemingly unable to speak.

"You're going to be okay, Gwen. Mother is—"

"I'm not worried about the rest of us," Gwen said. "I'm worried about you. What's happening, Beatrice?"

"I'm going to do what I need to do to keep everyone safe." Beatrice swallowed the bitterness down her throat. "Trust me."

"Can we not protect you?" Gwen asked, then pulled at her right earlobe. "Can't your mother and your grandmother and the trees—"

"Gwen." Beatrice swallowed, her mind wandering to Alice and how her decision doomed them all. "I only know the beginning of my journey but, for what it's worth, I don't think I'm going to die."

When Beatrice looked into Gwen's face, she was surprised to see genuine relief in her eyes. "Then maybe it's not forever."

"Maybe not," Beatrice agreed.

"Madeline is in the bathhouse getting ready. Go spend some time with her."

Beatrice stood but paused at the door. "He wants 'Spirit in the Sky.'"

Gwen's lips slid into a smile and her eyes sparkled for a moment. "I'll bring my guitar."

***

Beatrice found her mother dabbing at her blotchy red face with a handkerchief.

"Beatrice," Madeline whispered through her sniffles. "You look lovely."

"Let me do your hair."

Beatrice encouraged Madeline to sit on the bench as she grabbed a brush and worked it through the long white strands.

"My hair went gray early," Madeline said. "Yours may, too."

"Well, it's not exactly gray, Mother. It's like snow and it's beautiful. Haven't you seen the silver in mine? It's definitely started." Beatrice pulled Madeline's hair into sections and began braiding one side of it. "I spoke with Gwen this morning," she said. "I know you're both very worried."

"We don't understand what kind of danger you're in. And it sounds like my mother is more than willing to let you face it—"

"I told you. She doesn't know. I haven't been forthcoming with her either." Beatrice let out a big sigh, stopped braiding, and pressed against the desire to tell Madeline everything. To tell her about the dreams she'd had and the meeting with the trees.

"Stella told me, Beatrice. She told me about my mother breathing on the two of you."

"Yes," Beatrice answered, pulling the other handful of hair toward her. "She did, and it worked."

Beatrice pulled the braids together and began weaving them into one larger braid that she encouraged to lay over her mother's right shoulder. Then she sat down on the bench and squared herself to her mother.

"Grandmother is not our antagonist, Mother."

Beatrice stood again, took a washcloth into her hands, and asked the water of the bathtub to cool, then she dipped it in

271

then dabbed the cold cloth against her Madeline's skin.

"You look so beautiful. Please promise me something."

Madeline's eyes narrowed. "Is it a promise I can keep?"

"When this happens, don't..." Beatrice searched for a simile and found one in Stella's words to her in the past. "Don't throw yourself back and forth against the wall like a pinball in a machine. Gwen...our whole family needs time to heal and time to rest. Don't jump into trying to fix it. Let it be. Alight?"

"Are you going to die?" Madeline blurted, her chin quivering.

"I don't know." Beatrice took a deep inhale and let it out. "But I don't think so."

"I pray every moment to the Goddess that you will be safe."

Beatrice raised an eyebrow. All morning she had worked to keep the image of green shimmer and silver velvet horns out of her mind. She turned quickly from her mother and peeked outside where she found Gwen standing with the urn in her hands while Forest, Dani, Stella, and Beulah chatted with her.

"Let's go," she told Madeline, then took her hand.

The group settled into a circle, all eyes on Forest.

He brought forth a folded piece of paper, closed his eyes, and inhaled deeply. Throughout the entire ceremony, Beatrice couldn't take her eyes off her son. His smile. His dark hair that curled like hers. Her mind replayed his entire life. His first steps. First bite of food. The first time he met Arcas. Once in a while, Forest would catch her eyes, and his smile would soften. If nothing else, Beatrice knew she was leaving him with the awareness that he was loved and respected.

When his words were finished, Gwen sat on a stump and began to strum the guitar and sing. Beatrice and Beulah didn't know the words, but the rest did, and they sang them with resigned faces.

"We should eat," Gwen said after wrapping up the song.

Beatrice held Forest back as the group made their way to the kitchen.

"Forest..."

"Are you alright, Mother?"

"Yes," Beatrice lied. "I just wanted to let you know how much I love you and respect you. You make me so proud. I'm so glad you've found your community and your magic."

Beatrice almost crumbled in Forest's arms as he encircled her in a tight squeeze. She would never love another child like she loved him. The sound of his rumbling stomach told Beatrice it was time to withdraw.

"I, for one, am going to put on more comfortable clothing," she said. "Don't want to get breakfast on this dress."

"Me too," Madeline said, and Gwen followed.

***

Once in her room, Beatrice pulled her satchel toward her and filled it with the wand Forest gave her, her book, and Ida's quilt, though she didn't know if she could ever use it again without feelings of sadness. She tucked in the pouch of mixed herbs meant to bring about a deep sleep. Inhale. Exhale.

Time for breakfast.

The family sat around the kitchen table enjoying the same morning fair they ate every day, and Beatrice wondered what she would eat the next day. She gorged herself on biscuits until she felt sick and then excused herself from the table.

"I need some fresh air," she said.

Beatrice sat down on a rocking chair and peered out at the trees. No chattering entered her head, nor the air. No branches waved. All was still. Beatrice scanned the land around her home—the bathhouse and the outhouse, the smokehouse and the dairy shed. In the kitchen, she could hear them talking, the ones the Goddess would take her from. Beatrice rocked and listened and waited.

The end of the stillness came slowly. A light breeze tickled tree branches, and Beatrice stood as its strength grew. A tightness formed in her bowels, her teeth clenched, and her hands drew into fists. Wailing and crying flowed from the trees and the volume built until everyone had joined Beatrice out on the porch.

"We have to go," Beatrice whispered. Her body trembled like the branches in the wind. She pulled her backpack off the ground, slung it across her back, and looked toward the others, all of whom stood with questions in their eyes. All except Beulah.

"You heard her," Beulah said, and stood alongside Beatrice, squeezing her hand.

"Where are we going?" Forest demanded.

"Wanda's," Beulah said.

"For what?" Forest panted.

"To hide," Beatrice said.

A green shimmer began to whirl around them, and Beatrice's patience ceased.

"She is coming." The words roared from Beatrice and into the wind that whipped around them. "Run!"

Stella took off first, followed closely by Forest and Dani. Gwen and Madeline exchanged glances, then ran. That left Beatrice and her grandmother glancing behind them to see the tornado of green form. The shape of the Goddess grew clearer, more solid. Arms. Torso. Limbs. Neck. Face. And the wicked anger in the face propelled Beatrice faster. Behind them, the trees wailed until the sound of cracking trunks cut off their voices. Beatrice felt the loss of each soul, each voice in her head, and she wondered if they were in pain.

She turned to check on Beulah and found she had fallen. She stopped long enough to pour vines from her hands, wrap Beulah up in a tight ball, then pumped her legs toward the edge of the forest. The rest of her family had made it to the road. Beatrice released her grandmother down the cliff, then slid down the vines herself, unable to imagine the sudden stomach drop she was sure Beulah felt at the bottom of the mountain. The vines peeled themselves away from Beulah, and as she stood, she shook her head to regain her footing.

"We have to keep going," Beatrice said, taking the woman's hand and running across the street with her. The rest had gone on—figures scurrying across the bridge. Beulah's legs slowed down as they turned left down a side street and drew closer to Wanda's house.

"Come on," Beatrice said, leading the group behind Wanda's empty home to her shed.

"Mother, what is going on?" Forest asked. "What is chasing us?"

"We'll explain when this is all over," Beulah said. Beatrice released vines from each palm and entwined around each member of her family. Madeline's eyes glowed red. Gwen fixed her eyes on Beatrice while Stella focused on Beulah. Forest and Dani thrashed in resistance to the green chains. Beulah started with Forest and Dani to stop their incessant thrashing, then Gwen. She paused and stared into her Madeline's flaming eyes.

"Why is the Goddess chasing us?" Madeline finally asked, and Beulah lifted her hand to her cheek, which was flushed with heat.

"Don't worry," Beulah whispered and then blew onto Madeline's cheek.

Finally, Stella. "Are you going to be okay?" Stella asked Beulah. "Beatrice?" Her eyes flickered at Beatrice and back to her lover.

"We're all going to be fine," Beatrice replied.

Beulah kissed Stella on the cheek. "You'll wake up and it will be like nothing happened, alright?"

Stella nodded and returned the kiss. Beulah breathed in. She breathed out. As the woman pressed her forehead against Stella's, Beatrice's vines slithered around her grandmother's legs, and she turned to see vines beginning to crawl up her torso.

"Beatrice, what are you doing?" she cried. "Don't do this. Please. You can't do this alone."

"You're not the only one who can put others to sleep." Beatrice quickly pulled herbs from her pocket and blew them into Beulah's face, and she drifted slowly away.

***

A despondent hopelessness weighed Beatrice's legs and heart

as she climbed the side of the mountain, using her hands and feet instead of her vines. There was no need to hurry now, no desire to run. No clear picture of the future offered itself, no expectations arose to her mind, no cries filled her throat.

Once she reached the top, Gertrude came swooping overhead in large loops that brought her down and around Beatrice in all efforts to keep her from progressing forward. Arcas bounded toward her, his black fur gleaming in the spring sun, and when he came to a stop in front of Beatrice's face, he released the loudest and longest bellow Beatrice had ever heard from him. He pushed at her chest with his nose, but Beatrice pressed his face to the side and kept walking. Behind her, she heard the combined mourning of eagle and bear.

Silence greeted Beatrice as her leaden-footed steps brought her closer to the spot where the trees once stood; the silence, she expected, but the sight of the bones and the smell of death caught the breath in her throat. Where Alice, the oldest tree once stood, a pile of bleached-white bones lay, but dry flesh still wrapped around the youngest trees to fall. At the edge of the circle, two women sat on the ground. One with pure white hair that fell down her back had her hands on the shoulders of the other, whose head boasted silver and black tightly curled strands woven into many braids. Beatrice moved toward them, her feet easing onto the earth without making a sound, and before she circled in front of them, she noted the rise and fall of their chests. These grandmothers were alive.

She took in their eyes first. An agedness folded the skin of the woman to the left, Edith, the one with snowy hair, into deep wrinkles the likes of which Beatrice had never seen. Ola's brown skin gleamed in the sun, but her face held a tired misery Beatrice could relate to. Though they both made eye contact, neither spoke.

Beatrice surveyed the placement of the bones and aligned them with her own mental map. Edith and Ola sat in the spots where they once stood tall, wrapped in bark. The trees, it seemed, had much less power against the Goddess than they thought.

Or perhaps they didn't fight Her at all.

"Let me help you," Beatrice said. She reached out a hand to each woman, still unwilling to use her gift, and hoisted them until they were on their feet. "Come on."

When Beatrice and the women turned to the homestead, they found destruction. All the buildings were leveled, including the smokehouse Papa built. Debris scattered along the ground—jars of Beatrice's herbal creations, pens, pairs of scissors, reading glasses, bottles of oil, all things bought from the town, all things foreign to the mountain.

Turning back to her grandmothers, Beatrice whispered, "We have to go." Even as Beatrice spoke the words "we'll go down the mountain," she knew from that space of all knowing that her path was not the same as her grandmothers'. She would deposit the women with her mother and her grandmother and return once again to face the Goddess.

Edith's watery eyes peered into Beatrice's eyes and asked, "How?"

"I can get you off the mountain. What about the two of you... do you still have your gifts?"

The eldest shook her head, prompting Beatrice to put her hands in front of her, palms up, just to be sure. Green life slithered forth like it always had.

"At least I have mine," she whispered. *Why do I have mine?* "Can you speak?"

A dry clearing of her throat turned into an aggressive cough before Edith tried to speak.

"I'm so sorry," she said, her voice crumbling with each word. "We were tired of her, and tired of being trees. Well, all of us except Imogene." Edith's eyes glanced in Imogene's direction, and Beatrice followed her gaze, thinking of the stories she'd taken from the tree. "We watched as Beulah took her future in her own hands and couldn't believe it when we learned about Gertrude. Most of us realized we wanted something different when Beulah breathed us to sleep." Edith paused and glanced at the ground, then back up at Beatrice. "The two of them—Alice and the Goddess, I mean—had a private conversation we weren't allowed to hear. She was furious at Alice's betrayal."

Beatrice shivered at the words and thought of the nightmare she had had. She rubbed her arms and hugged herself as she listened. Edith explained that the Goddess changed them back to human bodies at the ages they should be, not the youthful age they were when they transitioned.

Beatrice furrowed her brow and stared hard into her great-great-grandmother's face. "Did Alice try to offer her anything?"

"I don't know," Edith replied, shivering in the breeze.

"It's me," Beatrice said. "She offered me up to the Goddess."

"Offered you up for what?" Edith asked.

"I don't know now." Beatrice scratched her forehead. "I thought maybe she wanted another child. Another family. With me, perhaps."

Edith and Ola exchanged glances.

"What?"

Edith's face shifted from quizzical to understanding, as if there was a truth she could share, but it wouldn't be worth the headache it caused. "The Goddess left the mountain, Beatrice, and She took all her energy with Her. If that's what She wanted, it seems She's changed her mind."

But she left me my vines.

"I need to get both of you to town," Beatrice said, surveying the disaster around her. "I'll point you in Grandmother's direction, then I have to find the Goddess."

Ola erupted into a coughing fit that left her doubled over, then she slowly straightened, squared herself to Beatrice, and locked eyes with her. "You should not go to her on your own, Beatrice."

"Mother and Grandmother and Stella and Gwen and Forest and Dani," Beatrice said, swirling her hand in the air with each name as if to emphasize just how many people populated her life now. "They won't understand, and they'll try to interfere."

"Then I guess we have no choice but to go with you," Edith said with a tender smile.

Beatrice looked down at the fragile body of her great-grandmother and her great-great-grandmother.

"Absolutely not. Your gifts are gone, your bodies are old, and—"

"Excuse me. Speak for yourself." Ola's voice held a chastising tone Beatrice had never heard pointed toward herself. "I am certainly not fragile."

"Fine," Beatrice said, her face hot. *Perhaps I should have said yes, ma'am.* "Stay here. I'll gather things."

Beatrice searched the detritus for usable items. Many of Madeline, Gwen, and Stella's things remained on the ground, including suitcases and bags. Beatrice felt emotion rise within her as she moved toward Madeline's property. Clothes were scattered everywhere along with her mother's hairbrush, reading glasses, and the small felt doll of the Goddess. Beatrice bent to pick up the doll in her hot, sweaty palm. She squeezed it tightly to avoid ripping it into tiny shreds, regretting the most cherished thing her mother had ever given her. Taking no more time to wallow, Beatrice found what she was looking for: suitcases. Gwen's. Madeline's. Stella's.

She wasn't expecting to have the time to pack for a trip, but now that she had it, she rolled one toward the place her bedroom once stood and began folding as many items of clothing as she could fit, including Ben's pajamas. She inhaled the flannel. She wore them so often, most of his scent had been washed away.

Are you still there?

Yes, my darling. I'm with you.

Stay with me?

As long as you'll have me.

She sifted through the others' clothes as well and took many of Gwen's to cover Edith's tiny frame and a few of Beulah's for Ola. When she had loaded two suitcases full of clothes, she moved toward the kitchen. She filled another case with jars of canned meats and vegetable soups and spiced peaches and tomatoes and green beans. She layered her small jars of herbs on top of them. Her teas and tinctures. She gathered pots and pans of various sizes, knives, and the one pair of scissors they had in the house.

Though her heart beat forcefully in her chest, Beatrice demanded her body move slowly, for she knew that Edith and Ola would need much care. Papa taught her how to start a fire, how to track, trap, and skin woodland animals of all sizes: deer, rabbit, wild boar, and more. Still, she collected matches and lighters. Wheels of cheese, smoked meats, and nuts littered the ground, and Beatrice gathered them. Laying in what used to be the corner of the smokehouse grounds rested Papa's hunting rifle. She had only held it when he was training her. He taught her to load, aim, and fire.

The man who shot Willow dropped his gun, but Gertrude had seized it and dropped it with him into the river. Even though this one was Papa's, Beatrice could barely stand to touch it. The cold metal felt foreign in her fingers.

And what use was this weapon against the Goddess?

But Beatrice remembered how it felt when the bullets ripped through her flesh and the sight of Forest's blood seeping into the white snow, so she wrapped the gun in her hands and gathered the boxes of ammunition with it.

The late afternoon sun pressed a March warmth against Beatrice's back, gentle enough to remind her that the winter chill was ending but not strong enough to counteract the winds. Her grandmothers, whom she had disregarded, sat watching her as she tied up the last few ends and wrapped all the luggage in vines. She looked down at them.

"Are you hungry?"

"I could eat," Edith answered, her voice dusty again from the lack of use. Edith looked to her daughter, who nodded in agreement.

Beatrice supplied nuts, dried meat, and opened a jar of spiced peaches, which they ate up before their journey.

"I had forgotten how good food was," Edith said with a chuckle, and Ola nodded beside of her. Beatrice wished she could smile at the moment, but even as she searched every corner of her being, she knew joy and hope were gone.

Though Beatrice hadn't know what to expect as she made her way up the mountain, she certainly had not anticipated searching for the Goddess with grandmothers in tow. She thought the Goddess would meet her at the top of the mountain. She looked at the women. Both of them, she was certain, would like a nice bath. Strewn around the footprint of the bathhouse were broken bottles of Beatrice's shampoos, conditioners, and lotions. She salvaged a few toiletries that she hoped would make them all feel more comfortable. Once she had provisioned three bags with food, clothing, and other supplies, she looked into their faces.

"Let's go."

CHAPTER 29

Forest

Forest woke first, his eyes dry and throat even drier. The vines his mother had wrapped around him were brown now, shriveled, and easily loosened as though they were straw. He could have gently wiggled himself free, but both fight and flee instincts had kicked in, and he thrashed his body against the vines while visions of Beulah and Beatrice spurned his violent gestures until the dead plant matter lay brittle and broken at his feet. His eyes widened as they found Beulah also bound.

How am I awake?

He scanned each face, each body, and though they were still warm and breathing, they didn't respond to his squeezing them by their shoulders. But when he gripped Beulah tightly, her eyes flew open.

"Where is my mother?" The words ground through his throat as Forest gave one shake of the woman's shoulders. "Where is my mother, and what did the two of you do?"

Beulah's eyes widened. "She put me to sleep, too. That wasn't part of our plan." She worked her way out of the vines. "I don't know where she is now, Forest. Let's wake the rest of them, and I'll explain what I can."

Forest watched as she moved from person to person, breathing life back into them. Forest pulled Dani into his arms and pressed their body against his. "You're alright," he whispered into their hair. It did not surprise Forest that Beulah saved her daughter for last. Madeline's blue eyes widened, and her arms ripped through the vines.

"Why did you do this?" she asked, bringing herself nose to nose with Beulah. "Tell us. Now."

"The Goddess wanted us off the mountain. If we didn't leave, she would have killed us all," Beulah said, and Madeline jerked back with a scoff.

"All of us? Even Beatrice? I don't believe you."

"Alice didn't want to be with the Goddess anymore, and when she told her, the Goddess said we had to leave the mountain. I planned to go back up. I hoped the trees would stand up against Her, too. I wanted…" Beulah paused and swallowed. "I want to destroy her."

Forest furrowed his brow and lifted his chin, as if scrutinizing the flare of Beulah's nostrils or twitches in her jaw would answer his questions. Perhaps if Madeline had raised him, he would have rejected these words and struck her with the energy of the power he kept hidden. But his mother was Beatrice of the woods, and she taught him to be temperate. Forest's mind, heart, nor gut could digest the story Beulah told of an angry goddess and of the trees and the secrets they hid and the plans they made.

"The Goddess must have defeated them." Beulah sobbed.

"Where is my mother?" Forest asked, his voice calmer now.

"I think she may have told us," Madeline said, pointing down to envelopes resting at each person's feet.

Forest bent to collect a creamy envelope that lay at his feet. He traced the ink of his mother's swooping letters with his finger. He looked up to see the others holding their letters in their hands, somehow unable to open them.

He cleared his throat. "Let's get inside," he said, "and warm up. Wanda's on a trip, but she won't mind."

Spring had temporarily handed March back to winter and a brisk wind wafted icy mist into Wanda's shed, the door of which, Forest assumed, Beatrice had left open. He wasn't used to taking the lead, but on this cold March morning, leadership belonged to him.

He clenched and released his jaw again and again but refused to fight the tears that gathered in his eyes. The others followed as he cried and walked, wrestling with the anger inside of him. Anger that grew into a giant, icy ball that he wanted to hurl at his great-grandmother.

How could she have let this happen?

The icy rooms in Wanda's home begged for a fire.

We can't open the envelopes with icy fingers.

A couch and two recliners provided enough space for all but Forest, Dani, and Stella, who nestled themselves on the floor. Eyes looked toward Madeline, who gathered the wood that rested on the hearth into the center of the fireplace and lengthened her hands out in front of her. Nothing came. No red glow emanated from her hands, and she slowly closed her eyes. Saying nothing, Madeline bent down, grabbed a long match, and struck it. The wood didn't catch.

"Here, Grandmother," Forest interjected, and he crumpled up the newspaper and tucked it underneath the firewood. When the paper caught fire, he moved on to kindling, tucking small pieces in first. Forest looked back at Madeline, whose eyes focused on her hands. She rubbed them. Nothing. Her eyes moved to a vase of wilted flowers Wanda had neglected to throw away before her trip.

"It's all gone," she whispered. "The fire. The healing. I can't move anything. It's gone." Her voice was steady and wrapped within it, Forest thought he heard notes of relief.

"We need to read the letters," Gwen said, and Madeline sat back down.

Forest slid his open gently.

Dear Forest,

Oh, there are so many things I want to say to you, Son. To start, I'm very sorry. I never meant for you to feel strange or less like a child of the Goddess because you are a man. I'm sure you felt frustrated because you didn't have a gift. I know I didn't always provide you with the security that you needed.

Forest paused in his reading. It wasn't her fault. His mother was wrong. They were all wrong about him. He did, in fact, have a gift. A gift he kept to himself because She told him to. Only once had the Goddess spoken to him directly. Her words pulsed through his head, a constant refrain throughout his life.

Tell no one. The time will come when you need to tell others, and you will know when it is. Until then, you have my permission to play.

Growing up, there were nights Forest couldn't sleep. Nights when the secret fried his nerves and he would get up, warm some milk, and pace the grounds outside the house. Other times, he would use his gift to make his mother happy. To bring her a bit of peace.

He continued reading.

I don't know exactly what I'm facing, Forest. First Mother— Alice—told me that the Goddess wants us gone. But I think She wants me. I'm not exactly sure what for. I won't fight her. How could I? I don't think she plans to kill me. Why would she?

Please don't let the others blame Grandmother. She didn't know I was going to put her to sleep. I'm sure she will be angry that I lied to her, but she is like my mother in some ways. Stubborn.

Forest laughed a little through his nose. "Apples do not fall far."

She wanted to climb this mountain with me and try to destroy the Goddess. Even if she could, it's not what I want. Don't let my mother rage. Don't let her race to find me. Even my mother, even my grandmother, with their superior gifts, cannot look into the face of the Goddess and hold their strength against Hers. Even as I write these words, I know that nothing I say will stop you. But give it time and space before you come searching.

Forest glanced around at the others, who were reading their own letters. Beulah's nostrils fumed, and she balled up the paper and threw it into the fire. Everyone's eyes flicked briefly toward her as she stormed out of the house and allowed the door to slam behind her. Stella followed her, her letter in her hand. Forest returned to reading.

I make you this promise, Forest: I will keep breathing until I see you again, though I'm not sure how. Already, the loneliness tears at me.

Lean on them, Forest, and let them lean on you.

I love you,

Mother

Forest folded the letter and tucked it back into the envelope.

"What did yours say?" he asked Dani.

"Take care of each other and work your magic," they said.

"That's it?" he asked, drawing Dani close.

He stared through the window at the rain. He searched the clouds with curiosity, looking for answers, and they came to him as the clouds parted and the sun shined through.

Acknowledgements

Binds and Breath, a novel born of imagination, soul, tears, and tireless work, is out in the world, and my heart is full of gratitude. This project would have been impossible to complete without the support and care of those around me.

Thank you to my beautiful wife who has always encouraged me with my self-publishing journey. To my children for showing respect for the art I create. To my English teacher friends for your kind words and feedback.

Thank you to my line editor Megan Harris and cover designer My Lan. To my students whose creativity, silliness, and devotion to your own writing practices teaches me something new every day.

Thank you to my coven, whose commitment to deep connection with one another and to the earth.

Thank you to butter and salt and flour and buttermilk that bring Madeline's biscuits into my home on an almost weekly basis.

Thank you, my sweet garden. Thank you to those little seeds that germinated into fruiting tomato plants and unwieldy sunflowers. Thank you to the surprise brown-eyed Susans who made a prolific appearance in late spring. To the unfailing chamomile that pops up wherever it wants. And yes, even to the mint that is threatening to take over the entire back garden.

And to my readers, thank you for giving this novel series your time and energy.

ABOUT THE AUTHOR

Sorrel D. Richmond, author of the Goddess of the Trees series, is a West Virginia transplant now living in a small town in central North Carolina with their wife, two kids, two sneaky cats, and willful beagle. Sorrel teaches English and Creative Writing on the high school level and is an avid backyard gardener with a love of okra and a hatred for squash bugs. Their characters often have a passion for nature and a love of love itself.

Coming Soon

Beatrice and Beulah take their final journey toward a shared destination, one that holds imaginable power that could destroy them both.